ROUGH WATERS

Rough Waters

Austin Moon

Rough Waters. Copyright © 2024 by Austin Moon.

Triomphe Press 2024

Cover illustration and design by Austin Moon

ISBN 978-1-958123-10-2

First Edition: July 2024

Printed in the United States of America

10 9 8 7 6 5 4 3 2

To all the queer kids who were told that they had to move to the city in order to find happiness and feel safe. Stay in your small towns, enjoy life, thrive.

ONE

Berk

Sour mouth? *Check.* Headache? *Check.* An empty pit deep in my stomach that reminded me that today was a Monday? *Check.* I struggled to untwist my arm out from under me and opened my eyes, stealing a glance at the sleeping body to my left, covered in dark, rumpled sheets. He was handsome, more handsome than I'd remembered from last night.

Last night...shit.

My whole body tensed as I realized that I couldn't be here right now. Was it possible to perform some matrix-level shenanigans to get out of this room?

I slid one leg over the edge of the bed until my foot touched the cold wooden floor. The sheets slipped off as I pulled myself to a standing position, executing painfully careful movements so I didn't wake him. *What's his name, again?*

Where are my clothes? I searched the parquet flooring for lost pairs. I found my trousers first—though not my underwear—and I slipped them on. I found the silky much-too-expensive black shirt I had been wearing last night and pulled it on, only buttoning as many buttons as strictly necessary. I still hadn't found my underwear, however I did find one sock. I pulled it on gracelessly, almost falling over in the process.

I tore a glance at the figure in the bed—still sleeping. Now where were my fucking shoes? Oh yeah, by the door—he was one of *those* people. Leaving one sock and my underwear behind, I pulled on my shoes, the leather squeaking into place. I patted down my pockets, finding my wallet, my phone, but not my keys.

Did I bring my keys? Shit, that would be the third time I'd lost my keys this year. *Did I lose them in here?* I couldn't leave them in a stranger's apartment.

I tiptoed across the floor towards the bed, my careful steps echoing through the large, though minimal, apartment.

I moved aside clothes and sheets, searching for the familiar shape of my key ring. *Oh, there's the other sock.* I stuffed it in my pocket for later. My eyes darted around the room and eventually onto the bedside table.

There they are. Why were they on the table when everything else was in my pockets? Right, I forgot that I'd used the bottle opener to open our beers last night. There were the two empty bottles on the floor. I scraped the keys against the wood, trying as carefully as possible to pick them up without making noise.

"Are you leaving without saying goodbye?" a sleepy voice asked from the bed.

I laughed, trying to ease the tension. "I'm not exactly a morning person. *Sorry.*"

He smiled and pushed himself into a sitting position. "That's okay, neither am I." He spread his bare legs—his body half covered in the twisted sheets, and put his chin in his hand, trying to look casual. "So...any chance I can get your number?"

I quirked up the corner of my lip apologetically, and shoved my keys into my pocket—the one that didn't have a sock in it. "Sorry, I don't really do that either."

His smile dipped, although he tried to hide it, bouncing back at 110 percent. "That's cool. See you around, I guess?"

I scratched the back of my neck and moved to the other side of the bed. "Yeah, maybe." Maybe meant never, although he didn't have to know that. I gave him a pathetic little wave on my way to the door, only realizing afterwards I'd still left my underwear behind.

Oh well—a souvenir for him to remember me by.

I rushed to get out of the apartment building, taking the stairs since the elevator was broken, checking my phone as I did so. *Shit*, it was dead. I caught the clock on the wall in the lobby as I raced out the door—thirty minutes past the start of the workday. Once outside, I looked to the left and then the right. What part of Boston was I in? Downtown—*good*. I obviously hadn't driven to the stranger's apartment—drunk as I was last night—so I hailed a taxi and asked him to floor it towards the Sandy Brook office building. My hellish place of employment.

Today was the day. The day I finally got fired.

I'd been pushing my luck for months, taking advantage of my parents' recommendation which landed me the job in the first place. Adem Kaplan held a lot of power in Boston. Maybe not enough to keep me employed, though. My parents were going to be *pissed* at me.

I pulled out the second sock and put it on now that I had a moment. My dead phone meant I couldn't tell how many times the office had called me this morning. Once? Twice? Five times?

The taxi pulled over to the curb and I paid. Thank God I at least had my wallet.

"Good luck, buddy," the driver said, making me feel self-conscious. If *he* could tell I was having a bad morning, my boss certainly would.

I passed the security guy, Harvey, in the lobby on the way to the elevators. He was six-two and ex-military. He shook his head and laughed, looking me up and down. "Rough night, Berk?" he asked.

I entered the elevator a short distance away and pushed the button for the correct floor. "Rough life," I replied. With my extra ten seconds of travel time I used the mirrored surface of the elevator to get a good look at myself. My hair was a mess, my eyes were tired, and my collar was rumpled. I patted down my short, dark locks and brushed over my scratchy, unshaved jaw. I tried to wipe the bleariness out of my eyes with little result. The elevator dinged open. I didn't run, I *walked* to my cubicle. Maybe if I didn't look hurried nobody would notice I was late.

Jessie, in the cubicle next to mine, gave me a questioning look, arching her brow. "Trying to win the record for most late days in a row?"

I grinned tightly. "At least I'd be *winning* at something," I retorted, my voice laced with vinegar.

She frowned and ducked her head back down—her fiery red hair still visible over the top. *Sorry Jessie,* that was probably unnecessary, however I *was* about to get fired, and I *really* didn't need a lecture. I turned on my work computer and pulled out some papers to make it look like I had been there the last thirty or forty minutes. That wouldn't trick the boss, though—he had eyes like a hawk.

His upper floor office was visible from my cubicle along the open walkway that ran the perimeter of the space. I managed a glance. The blinds in front of his glass door were drawn, and he was staring directly at me. *Fuck.* His mouth was set in a grim line, his finger curled into a *come here* motion. I pointed at myself in surprise as if I didn't see this coming. He nodded somberly.

"Good luck, dickhead," Jessie said over the dividing wall. The employees of Sandy Brook had sharp eyes and ears, with nothing better to do than gossip to release tension from their high-stress positions.

I grabbed a photograph and a couple knickknacks off my desk and shoved them into my pocket—in case I wasn't allowed to come back for them later. I scanned the room, though I didn't spot security anywhere. Would Harvey escort me out?

I jumped up from my chair and peeked my head over the partition. "How do I look?" I asked.

Jessie spared me a glance. "Like shit."

"*Thanks.*" I attempted to smooth my hair one more time and made my way to the metal staircase that led to the second floor. I took slow and deliberate steps, trying to plan what I was going to say that would convince him not to fire me. Could I play the powerful dad card? *No*, I'd played that one already. The powerful mom card? *No*, definitely already played. I was out of cards.

I stopped in front of his office door and took one final deep breath, trying to calm my nerves. I put my hand out to knock, only, the door swung open before I could. Mr. Schwimmer pulled his lips into a semblance of a smile, his eyes hollow. "Slow morning?" he asked. He had a balding head and a fat belly that stretched his white dress shirt.

"Um, I'm really sorry, Mr. Schwimmer. There were unforeseen circumstances that stopped me from getting here on time," I bluffed, hoping he wouldn't ask *what* unforeseen circumstances.

"What unforeseen circumstances?" he asked. *Crap.* Now I had to pull something out of my ass. "My dog...threw up on my suit right before I was about to leave, that's why I'm wearing these old rags," I said, gesturing to my outfit. "He's *super* sick. I had to take him to the emergency vet before I could come here."

Is he buying this? I didn't have a dog, although hopefully he didn't know enough about me to call me out on it.

"I did wonder why you were dressed like crap," he said flatly. "Sorry about your dog. But, I hate to remind you how many times you've been late, Mr. Kaplan. *Unforeseen circumstances* included."

I laughed nervously. "Yes, I guess you could say that, however I'm willing to make it up to you anyway that I can, Mr. Schwimmer."

He smiled again, and this time it did reach his eyes, only not in a friendly way. "Good, that's what I like to hear from my employees. Why don't you sit down?"

He moved to the other side of his massive dark maple desk and sat in the plush, leather chair. I set myself in the simple metal seat in front. It seemed a million miles away from his throne.

"So you're willing to do anything to make it up to me, huh?" he asked, a cruel glint in his eyes.

"Yes." *Crap, what did he want me to do?*

"You remember that we're expanding our resort properties, don't you? Or did you miss that meeting?" he asked with an arched brow.

"Yes, of course I remember," I lied.

"*Good.* There's a certain project that the boys have been cooking up that I think you would be perfect for."

"A project?" I asked. That was my punishment?

"Yes, a little island out by Cape Cod. One of the lesser known ones. Cheap," he stressed. "They're willing to sell us some land for a new development project, however we need someone on the ground."

"On the ground, sir?"

He pulled out a toothpick and began rolling it between his teeth with his tongue, as if cleaning his teeth was more important to him than this meeting. "Yes, you'd need to leave straight away. Today if possible. The mayor there is being a little wishy-washy. We need you to solidify the details, sign some contracts, take some photos, and build a marketing plan. Make sure it's going to be profitable for us when they do say yes."

"You...want me on location?" Usually I was simply a pencil pusher, manning my desk and looking over paperwork for the higher-ups.

"That is why we hired you, isn't it? To work on the marketing team? Unless you think you can find employment elsewhere?"

"Yes...I mean, *no.* I mean, *yes*, I can do this assignment, sir."

He grinned, his lips pulling over his artificially white teeth. "*Perfect.* I'll have the boys hand over all the paperwork you'll need. Better get packed. The mayor is expecting you tomorrow morning."

He'd known I couldn't say no, the bastard. He'd *already* planned everything.

"Yes, thank you, sir, for this opportunity. I won't let you down." I forced a smile with as much as I could give and shook his hand.

He gestured towards the door "All right, get to it, then."

"Yes, sir." I rose from the chair and left his office. Once out on the walkway, I stood there for a moment, staring down at the maze of cubicles. I caught Jessie's eye. She held one thumb up and one thumb down, trying to gauge my reaction. I put my thumb up and then flipped her off. She smirked and flipped it right back to me. *What a great work environment.* After slowing my anxious heartbeat to somewhere near normal I went back to my cubicle and started gathering my station.

"So, not fired, huh?" Jessie said with surprise.

"Nope, special assignment actually." I put all my energy into the words, trying to make them seem important.

"*Really?*" She was stunned, her eyes wide.

"Yep, big resort deal out on Cape Cod the boss wants me to finalize." I left out the part about the island being small and unknown— she didn't need to know the details.

"Wow, maybe *I* should come in late tomorrow. Nothing like failing upwards, huh? Must be nice to have such important parents."

I pressed my lips together for half a second, and then I grinned. "Yes, *you're right*. It is nice." It wasn't nice, in fact it sucked a lot, however the lie was worth seeing the reaction on her face. "Have fun doing..." I gestured at her station, "whatever it is you do."

She narrowed her eyes and opened her mouth to no doubt retort, but I was already gone. I'd grabbed my papers and laptop—shoved them into an empty bag from under my desk—and started walking towards the planning department.

Jim was in his office—he was always in his office. Some say his ass was superglued to the seat. He looked up right as I knocked on the door frame. "*Ah*, Kaplan, just in time. I have those documents ready for you." He swiveled in his office chair and sifted through a large heavy filing cabinet until he found what he needed. The folder was slim, much slimmer than I was expecting for a fleshed out land development deal.

"So, how much work is left on this gig?" I asked, already dreading the answer.

Jim laughed through his nose as if he knew something I didn't. "Well, there's an architect who's been looped in, and I believe the land has been surveyed already, however those reports are probably old and will need to be redone. The mayor is on the fence. It's your job to convince him of something great." He handed me the file.

I opened it to the first page which was a rough sketch of a resort. No blueprints, no anything really. "And how long do I have to complete this task?" I asked, trying to stay as professional as possible under the circumstances. Not that Jim gave a shit.

He shrugged. "About two weeks, give or take? Any longer than that and Mr. Schwimmer might decide it's not worth it."

He said *it's*, however I knew he meant *you're*. "Okay, I hear you loud and clear. So how do I get to this island—what was it called again?"

"Ruby Island, just south-east of Cape Cod. It's not that popular because there's no direct ferries that go there. We'd have to change that of course. *If* the deal goes through."

"And...how am I getting there?"

Jim tapped the folder in my hand. "My secretary has already planned everything for you: train fare, boat times, and lodging. I believe the last train leaves midday—better pack fast."

The information was all too much, although I didn't exactly have a choice. It was either *this* or go to my parents and tell them I'd been fired from the job that they'd fought so hard for me to get. I'd stick with option one.

"Okay, thanks. I guess I better get going, then." I slipped the folder into my bag and waved Jim goodbye as I went out the door. I checked my phone for the time—forgetting that it was still dead—and then glanced at the clock on the wall. It was almost noon. How long did I have to pack and call my parents to tell them I'd be gone? *Not enough.*

I rode the elevator down to the lobby and said goodbye to Harvey.

"Not fired?" he asked when he noticed I didn't have a cardboard box of my stuff—or security trailing behind me.

Why was everyone so surprised that I hadn't gotten fired? "Nope, *promotion* actually," I lied. Why not? I was probably going to fail this assignment and nobody cared anyway.

"No shit?"

"Yep." I waved and ran out the revolving door to the street. I grabbed a taxi and directed him to my apartment on the northside of downtown. When I arrived I was exhausted, and the day had only just begun.

I was opening my front door—thanking myself for having found my keys—when a wave of something putrid hit me. I flipped on the light and turned towards the kitchen. Takeout from Wednesday was sitting on the counter. It was Monday.

I went first to the large windows that made up one wall of the much-too-expensive apartment and pulled open the gauzy curtains to let in some light. It looked like a bear had trampled my living room.

My cleaning lady had quit last month when she'd found me passed out drunk on the carpet with vomit covering two walls. I didn't know if I'd scared her because she'd thought I was dead, or if I'd simply grossed her out to the point where *even a cleaner* couldn't handle it anymore. Either way, my apartment smelled and looked like shit.

I plugged in my phone by the kitchen counter only to find I had many missed calls stacking up: two from my mom, one from my dad, and one from my younger sister Ada. I clicked on her contact, knowing she didn't have any classes today.

She answered on the second ring. "What's up, *abi*? Where the hell were you yesterday? Both Ma and Dad called me. I didn't know what to tell them, so I made up a story about an art event. You know...if they ask."

"Thanks, Ada. I was occupied."

She laughed. "Oh, I see. *Occupied.*"

Ada knew I was gay, and she also knew I didn't like playing by our parents' rules. I never lied to her.

"What were they calling for?" I asked.

"*Hmm*, I'm not sure, but it probably has something to do with Ma's friend being in town. She has a younger daughter named Alyssa. I think she wanted you to meet her."

"*Seriously?* Can I catch a break today?"

"Why, what happened?" she asked.

I ran a hand through my already messy hair, not knowing where to begin. I put the phone on speaker and with a sour expression I threw away the take out containers into the trash. "I got a big assignment today at work."

I noticed as she tried to hide her shock. *"Are you serious?"* She cleared her throat. "What's the assignment?"

I tied off the garbage bag and pulled it from the bin, setting it on the floor. "I have to go to some island and sign some contracts. It might take a while."

"How long?" she asked.

"I'm not sure, possibly two weeks?"

"Two weeks? So this is a big deal, then?" she asked.

"Yeah, I guess. I have to leave straight away."

Ada sighed. "Ma and Dad are not gonna like that. Are you going to see them before you go?"

I shrugged even though she couldn't see me do it. "No time." It was true that I didn't have the time, but I also just didn't want to see them. I'd been avoiding them for the last week and I was sure they were stockpiling lectures for me.

I found the broom in the corner and began sweeping up all the gross shit that was on the floor. *I don't have time for this.* I dropped the broom and picked up my phone. "Sorry, Ada, I'm gonna have to run. I still have to pack my bags and rush to make this train. Smooth things over with Ma and Dad for me?" I asked.

She blew out a breath. "I'll do what I can, though you know they're gonna call you, right?"

"Of course, but by then I'll be on the train already," I argued. "This *is* a work trip. They can't exactly be mad at me for that, can they?"

"Oh, they can try."

I smiled despite myself. "I better go, love you, sis."

"Love you too, *abi*. Text me or call me when you get there. And I'll see what I can do about Ma and Dad. Don't get your hopes up, though."

"Oh don't worry, I never do," I said under my breath, hoping she wouldn't catch it, but of course *she did*.

"*Berk.*"

"Love you, *bye*." I ended the call and ran to my bedroom to start packing. I pulled my ancient suitcase out of the closet and unzipped it, unleashing a wave of dust. It had been a long time since I'd left the city. The last time had probably been when the whole family traveled to Turkey after I graduated college to visit my relatives. They'd been so damn proud of me. And I'd been disappointing them ever since.

TWO

Will

"Get the gate, won't you, dear?" Aunt Caroline asked, hobbling on one leg and leaning against me for support.

It was awkward to reach down to the small white picket fence and unlatch the gate while also keeping Aunt Caroline upright—I barely managed. We shuffled to the front porch of the inn. Her new black medical boot whacked into the last step; she would have fallen if I hadn't been holding her up.

"Careful."

She smiled warmly. "Thanks. I don't know what I would do if I didn't have you to help me out."

Aunt Caroline and I didn't have anyone except for my cousin Rory who had stayed on the island. Everyone else had either passed or moved to the mainland. He was the one who had dropped us off in his old rust-colored truck from the hospital. However he couldn't help out all the time. He had his own shop to run and a pregnant wife due any week. Their little apartment above the shop was too cramped for an older lady with a broken ankle.

"Well you *do* have me, so don't worry about it." I already worked and lived at the inn. It wasn't an imposition at all to help out my only family.

I unlocked the front door and got her inside, setting her down in a rocking chair in the small sitting room off to the right. The large bay window brought in lots of light and looked out at the rocky bluffs and crystal blue ocean beyond.

"I'm gonna go check the mail really quick. Do you need anything right now?" I asked, getting her an extra pillow from the sofa for her back and making sure she was situated comfortably.

"You're a darling, Willy. I'm okay, thank you."

I hated that nickname, although I would never tell Aunt Caroline. It's what she'd called me since I was a toddler—always Willy, never

William or Will. It made me sound both like an old-world sailor and a certain euphemism that would make a nun blush.

"Okay, sit tight."

She laughed. "Don't worry, I'm not going anywhere."

I chuckled along with her. All things considered, she was taking the broken ankle like a champ in her usual fashion. Nothing ever got Aunt Caroline feeling down. I might have been helping her out, though *she* was the rock that *I* depended on.

I walked out again to the front porch, observing the bushes that desperately needed trimmed and the flower boxes that were blooming from the spring warmth. I added them to my mental list of things to get done that week. The list was long and rapidly growing. Running The Ruby Inn had been one thing when it was the two of us, however with Aunt Caroline out of commission it fell to me to keep things going.

I retraced my steps down the stone walkway to our mailbox which was shaped like a big bass—its mouth being the opening for the box. I pulled down the ruby red lips and checked inside. Many letters had stacked up over our weekend in the hospital. Ruby Island *did* have a hospital...of a sort. It was both the local hospital and the local vet. If you didn't want to catch Magnus' ferry to the mainland it was your only option. Doctor Brenner was an octogenarian with criminal handwriting, though he could still do math faster than a calculator and get to the root of the problem better than WebMD. Even if he did sometimes start checking you for fleas before remembering who you were.

I grabbed the stack of letters and walked back to the porch, fingering through the lot: an electric bill, a gas bill, and wouldn't you know it, a mortgage bill. The Ruby Inn had been fully paid off back when my grandparents built it at the turn of the century. However, when my parents had fallen on hard times they'd had to take out a mortgage to keep the inn afloat. Tourism wasn't what it once was with more popular islands along Cape Cod like Martha's Vineyard or Nantucket.

I slipped the bills into my inner jacket pocket and stacked the rest to give to Aunt Caroline. She had many pen pals and liked to do all her correspondence by hand rather than email or social media. She said it reminded her of her youth when letters were the only way off the island, when landlines telephones only worked during certain hours of the day and pesky neighbors could still eavesdrop on your call.

Yeah, Ruby island was what you might call *slow to progress*. We had internet now and cell service of course, though neither worked especially well. Watching a movie was damn near impossible without lagging every few minutes and that was only if the satellite dish was working that day.

I walked in through the small lobby towards the sitting room to give Aunt Caroline her mail.

"Oh, thank you, dear." She sifted through the stack and looked up at me with narrowed, quizzical eyes. "No bills?"

I shook my head. "Not yet, must be running late this month."

"*Hmm.*" She didn't look like she quite believed me, but she let it go, opening one of her many letters in need of a response.

"I'll go open up shop."

"Good idea, we have a reservation in the books."

"*We do?*" I asked, surprised. It had been a *slow* month.

She glanced up from her letter. "Oh, did I forget to tell you? I must have. There was a reservation made for a two-week stay in the Randolph suite starting tomorrow. I took the call right before...you know. I was trying to clean upstairs and get the room all prepared so you didn't have to do it later."

"Oh." A pang of guilt punched me in the gut. Aunt Caroline had broken her ankle coming down the stairs with a basket of dirty linens. I should have known it was because she was trying to be helpful and lessen my workload. So it was *my* fault she was in pain. "I'll go make sure that's ready, then."

"Okay. Can you grab the stationary kit from my room on your way back?"

I forced a smile on my face. "Of course, Aunt Caroline. Be back in the shake of a dog's tail."

I turned towards the lobby, my smile melting away. Aunt Caroline worked too damn hard. She wasn't old, although she was older than my parents would be if they were still around. She was my dad's older sister, a decade his senior. She shouldn't have to be running up and down rickety stairs and desperately cleaning rooms for tourists. I could do more. I *wanted* to do more. The Ruby Inn could be restored to its heyday, like how I remembered from my childhood—the lobby full of customers, all the rooms booked out for weeks. This old place could be something special again.

I ran up the wooden stairs to the upper floors. The middle floor was for paying lodgers with ten normal rooms and two suites with oceanside views. The upper floor was our home. When I was young we'd lived in a small house down the lane, however when my parents decided to mortgage the inn they didn't see the point of trying to pay two at once, so we'd moved in upstairs. What was at one time storage and attic space was refinished by my parents and my uncle Nick into a small three-bedroom apartment—our own belongings displaced by the numerous supplies for the inn.

I entered the Randolph suite and opened the windows to let in some fresh air. The room hadn't seen any in a long time. The sheets were already stripped—thanks to Aunt Caroline—so I went about my usual tasks, having grabbed the cleaning cart from the supply closet. I wiped down all the surfaces of dust and grime and straightened everything into a clean, orderly fashion. New sheets were laid down with military corners, and pillows were fluffed and primped. The Randolph suite was all cream and ocean blue with dark wood furnishings original from when the inn was built. It was more cozy and lived in than a simple hotel room. If you wanted a simple hotel or motel you could easily find one for cheap on the mainland.

I sat in the chair in the corner of the room, readjusting the navy pillow behind my back. I used to play in this room as a child. I remembered the painting on the wall fondly. It depicted an 18th century cargo ship, *the HMS Conqueror*, coming into port during a raging storm, the sky dark and vengeful. I remembered the faded carpet underneath the foot of the bed, its complicated lines and patterns acting as roads and railways for my toys to explore. Even *this* room had so much personal history—the whole inn did.

I had to keep it alive. I couldn't let a room full of stuffy businessmen tell me what was possible, what was *fiscally responsible*.

I finished cleaning the suite and grabbed Aunt Caroline's stationary from her room for her to write her letters. When I reached the lobby I caught her gazing wistfully out the bay window with glassy eyes.

"*Aunt Caroline?*" She wasn't usually one to get maudlin.

She quickly brushed her cheek with her sleeve and smiled. "Oh good, you found it." She accepted the pile and placed it on the small side table to her right. "Willy? I meant to ask if you could run to Rory and Maria's shop today and get me a couple postcards. I'm running low."

I fiddled with my fingers in my trouser pockets. "Of course, Aunt Caroline. Do you...want anything else?" A shot of brandy perhaps? *I could use one.*

"No, no, that will be fine. Say hi to Maria and the baby for me, won't you?"

"Sure."

She smiled and turned back to her stationary. "Thanks, Willy."

I paused a few seconds, staring at her back, before forcing myself into action. I grabbed Aunt Caroline's emergency cell phone from behind the front desk and set it down on the table beside her. "Just in case," I said, knowing how much she hated the thing. I'd found it in the strangest of places before, almost as if she was ditching it on purpose: in the laundry basket, in the desk drawer behind the front counter, in her basket of knitting needles and yarn, and under a cushion of the cream-colored sofa.

"Thanks. What would I do without you?"

I laughed. "That's the second time today you've said that. You're a pretty strong lady, Aunt Caroline. Something tells me you'd be just fine."

She blew out a breath and batted the air with her hand. "Nonsense."

"If you say so. See you in a minute."

"Bye, dear."

I left her in the sitting room and went out the front door to the street. The Ruby Inn wasn't on a main road, it sat on a corner lot along a small lane that dead-ended at a small bluff overlooking the ocean. The road was dirt and gravel. Most of the roads on the island were unpaved, except for the main downtown area where there was cobblestone. It didn't matter much since there weren't many cars on the island. Most locals biked, walked, or owned a golf cart like our neighbors.

The walk would be quick, though it was even quicker by bike, so I grabbed the old cherry red ten-speed from the shed around back and rode into town.

Main Street was vibrant in the summer. All the shops and businesses were dressed in ribbons and string lights, flags and bunting. It was straight out of a postcard, in fact it *was* on a postcard. Maria made her own with her amazing photography skills.

I stopped outside Rory and Maria's shop aptly named The Merry Marauders. Tourists loved it. I set my bike against the wall and walked in, a bell jingling above my head.

The very pregnant Maria looked up from the front desk and smiled from ear to ear. "Will, we weren't expecting you today. How's Caroline doing?"

"She's a trooper, for sure."

She raised one brow. "Refusing pain meds?"

I chuckled. "Of course."

She nodded knowingly. "Of course." She pushed her long dark curls over her shoulder and stood from her chair. "So, what's up?"

"Aunt Caroline said she needed some more postcards and asked me to run over and grab some."

"Really?" She frowned. "We could have brought some over."

I waved my hand. "I have a heavy suspicion that she just wanted to be alone for a while. I'm sure she has a whole drawer full of postcards." I stopped at one of the racks of prints and spun it on its base, admiring Maria's artful compositions. One that caught my eye was of a sailboat out at sea, it's sail a flurry of rainbow colors against the bright blue summer sky. "So how's the pregnancy going?" I asked as Maria placed her hands on her back to find some relief.

"Like a bitch, actually."

I laughed. "*Oh, no.* Is she still kicking you in the bladder?"

"Only every thirty seconds, so in hindsight, an improvement on last month."

"*She?*" a deep voice called from above. Rory, my one and only cousin, stalked down the stairs at the back of the shop from their apartment. He stood over six foot with an Irish-red beard and a messy head of blond curls—our hair being the only thing we had in common. "Are you talking about my athletic son again?" He walked over to Maria and placed a hand on her swollen belly.

"Hey, don't be sexist," I scolded. "Your daughter is going to be the next forward for one of the top soccer teams in the country."

He smirked. "I don't think the baby's a boy because he's a strong kicker, I think he's a boy because we have a male curse in the Kirkpatrick family." He was sort of correct about that. The Kirkpatrick line had given birth to only sons for the last four generations—Aunt Caroline being the one and only exception. All the other women of the family had married in.

"You never know," Maria said. "She could be lucky, like your aunt. I have three sisters. That's got to count for something," she argued.

"*Maybe*," Rory said, but he didn't sound convinced.

"Either way it's going to be the most spoiled baby on the island," I added.

Rory smiled at the idea, then his mouth dipped down. "He might be the *only* baby on the island if things keep going the way they're going."

"*Hey!* Things change; anything can happen," I reminded him. "And I have a feeling this summer is going to be our best summer yet."

Maria grinned. "Exactly. So stop being such a realist, Rory. Our daughter will have many friends to play with and hopefully many siblings. Ruby Island isn't going anywhere."

Rory laughed. "Okay, point taken. I'll zip my trap." He mimed zipping his mouth closed and throwing away an invisible key.

Rory sobered, looking out the large window behind me. "Oh shit."

"What?" I turned to catch what he was staring at—a woman in a denim jacket and a pale yellow sundress was walking down the opposite side of the street, her short brown bob tucked under a pale blue baseball cap. "*Crap.*"

I instinctively ducked behind the display of postcards, hiding my tall frame. "Did she see me?" I asked in a panic.

"Who are we looking at?" Maria asked in confusion. "The cute brunette with the cap?"

"That was Alicia, Will's ex from high school," Rory explained.

Maria's mouth dropped open. "Oh."

"What the hell is she doing on the island?" I stage whispered.

Rory snickered. "Why are you whispering? She can't hear you."

"Is she gone?" I asked, unable to look for myself.

"Uh, no. Actually...I think she's coming this way," Rory said.

"*What?*"

The telltale sound of the bell rang as the front door opened.

I peered out from my hiding spot, catching a glimpse of her. Alicia hadn't changed much; she'd chopped her hair and started wearing lipstick, though overall she looked exactly like how I remembered her.

"Hi," she greeted.

"Welcome in," Maria said. "Looking for anything in particular?"

"Oh, well I just noticed that bike outside—the red one? I think it belongs to someone I used to know." She turned to Rory who was a mere foot away from me. If she came any closer she'd spot me around the corner. "Oh wait, *Rory*? Will's cousin, right? I almost didn't recognize you with that beard."

Rory grinned. "Yeah, I couldn't grow *squat* in high school."

She smiled. "So is he here?"

Rory played dumb, scrunching his brow. "Is *who* here?"

"Will? That is his bike, right?"

Rory put his hands in his pockets—his tell—though she didn't know that. "No, that's *my* bike. He gave it to me years ago."

Her expression fell slightly. "*Oh.* Does he still live on the island?"

"*Uh...*" He stalled, glancing down at me for confirmation.

I shook my head vehemently.

"Yeah, he does. But he's on the mainland...doing some errands."

I could kill him. I peeked through the gaps in the cards to catch her expression.

Her brows pinched together. "Oh, will he be back later, do you think?"

"It's hard to say." He waffled, his lie falling apart. "He might be gone for a few days."

Great one, thanks Rory.

"Okay, thanks anyway." She deflated. "I'm sure I'll catch him later."

"Yep." Rory waved. "*Bye.*"

The bell rang as the door opened and closed.

"Is she gone?" I asked.

28

Rory nodded. "Yeah, she's gone."

I stood from my crouched position, shaking out my tense limbs. God, that was so dumb, hiding from a girl like I was nine years old.

I punched Rory in the arm. "*Dumbass*, what the hell kinda lie was that?"

He raised his hands in surrender. "Sorry, I panicked. At least she won't be going to the inn looking for you."

"Yeah, *today* maybe. Did you know she was back?" I asked.

He shook his head, biting his lip. "No way, man. I would have told you that."

"I'm guessing it didn't end well if you're hiding behind postcards?" Maria asked, intrigued.

We never talked about my dating life. Not that I had one. Dating on a small island of under a thousand people was difficult. Especially when I'd gone to school with most everyone in my age group, so the pool was the same as it had been a decade ago. Sometimes I resorted to dates or one-night stands with tourists—which was fun, but never satisfying. Watching them leave on the last ferry for the summer, back to their real lives, hurt.

"No, *it did not*."

Maria waited for me to say more and when I didn't she frowned. "That bad, huh? That you can't laugh about it years later?"

I sighed, distracting myself by looking through the postcards again. "It was high school. No need to get into it."

"Nothing else ever happens on this island, are you actually going to rob your pregnant sister-in-law of some juicy gossip?" She pouted her lips, one hand massaging her pregnant belly.

I rolled my eyes. "As dramatic as Rory is making it sound, it's not that exciting of a story." I rubbed the back of my neck, ignoring the heat rising to my ears. "We dated for two years and when we graduated I thought she was going to stick around, however she decided to go to college on the mainland. Enough said."

I left out the part about her dumping me only a month after my parents died. I couldn't be mad at her for wanting to see a world outside of Ruby Island, however I *could* be mad at her for how she went about it.

Maria prodded for more. "And you didn't want to chase after her?"

"I couldn't. I had to help keep the inn open." *My parents' inn.*

"Right."

There was a drawn out silent pause.

"This is the first time she's been back since she left. I wonder why she's here?" Rory asked. "Does her family still live here?"

I shook my head. "No, not anymore. They left a couple years after she did for the mainland. She's got no reason to be here."

Maria laughed through her nose, her lips pulling into a smile. "It's a free country, isn't it? Why are you being so serious if it's not a big deal?"

30

she asked, trying to dissect my lies. Maria was too smart for her own good.

I forced myself to smile, pinched my brows together, and blew out a breath. "I'm not, you're just bored and making it sound exciting. She's probably here for a couple weeks like the rest of the tourists. Whatever."

She narrowed her eyes, still analyzing me. "*Sure.*"

I picked a couple random postcards from the display rack and moved to the front counter. "Can you ring these up for me?"

Rory chuckled. "What are you doing, man? You know they're on the house."

I pulled out my wallet, then grabbed a couple bills. "But the house doesn't pay for itself," I argued.

Maria grabbed the money and stuffed it in the tip jar sitting on the counter. "There, problem solved. Now I can buy a cup of coffee and a donut."

I laughed. "I could have bought you a cup of coffee."

She patted my hand on the counter. "But doesn't this feel so much better? You're supporting the arts *and* we all get our way."

Rory shook his head with a grin. "My wife, always the peacekeeper."

I slipped the postcards into my jacket pocket. "Enjoy that donut. Get two since I know you have to split it with the soccer champion."

She laughed and pushed her dark locks behind her shoulder. "Will do. Say hi to Caroline for us. We hope she heals fast. I know how she hates sitting around when there's work to be done."

I shook my head. "There's *always* work to be done."

"Exactly."

"Thanks guys. See you later." I waved them off and exited the shop. I couldn't lie, I definitely looked both ways before crossing the threshold, just in case Alicia was still hanging around. I didn't see her, though. She must have slipped into one of the other businesses.

I didn't dare tempt fate. I hopped on my bike and booked it out of town center and back to the south side of the island—back home. I didn't know why Alicia was on the island and I really didn't want to be forced to find out.

Hopefully the universe listened to my silent prayer.

THREE

Berk

One train ride and one ferry ride later I was waiting at the docks for yet another boat to pick me up and take me to this *Ruby Island*. I'd read about the island as much as I could while on the train. It didn't seem like there was much there—prime for redevelopment. It was small and out of the way. That would be perfect for the rich clientele who wanted to stay on their own *private* island. There was a huge market for that.

The docks were currently empty. I seemed to be the only one waiting for this godforsaken ferry. There were *no* signs. You wouldn't even know this was where you were meant to wait unless you'd taken it before. I had to ask for directions twice, once from a man busking with his guitar, and another from a man in a suit walking his overly-manicured dog. There was also nowhere to sit, no bench or seat, so I stood at the edge of the ancient pier—waiting. My shoes were killing me. I should have changed them before I left, however I'd been in such a hurry I hadn't bothered. The stupid six hundred dollar Italian leather loafers were pinching my toes. I shifted my weight to try and find some relief.

The sun was high in the sky and I was feeling the afternoon heat. I'd already shed my coat and rolled my sleeves to my elbows.

There—a boat was coming across the distance. *No.* That couldn't be the ferry, it was too small. It looked more like a fishing boat than one that carried passengers. I stared down at the page of instructions left for me by Jim's secretary. Was I absolutely sure I was in the right place?

The vessel whistled as it arrived, careening to a stop at the end of the pier. An older guy with a shaggy white beard waved a hand. "Coming to Ruby Island?" he asked, his voice hoarse, probably from years of smoking.

"*Yes?*"

He barked out a hearty laugh. "Is that a question? Are you or aren't you, son?" He lowered an actual *wooden plank* to the ground as an on-ramp.

I breathed out a deep sigh and debated my shrinking number of choices. "I guess so." I *walked the plank*, pulling my suitcase behind me.

34

The man offered me a calloused hand when I almost stumbled to the deck. "How far is it to Ruby Island?" I asked. I'd looked at a map earlier, but it had been pretty hard to tell.

He smiled, his white beard bobbing along with his mouth. "It's about a twenty-minute boat ride, not long at all." He gestured to a row of metal folding chairs set along the back of the boat. "Have a seat."

I sat down, never letting go of the suitcase in my hand. With this tiny little boat, one big wave and we'd be dumped into the Atlantic Ocean.

The man seemed to wait for a few more minutes, maybe expecting others to magically arrive. "Do you get many tourists on Ruby Island?" I asked out of curiosity. Surely this man was the guy to talk to if he was the only way on and off the island.

"*Hmm*, yep. Mostly in the summer of course. The season is just starting, so it's a bit slow at the moment."

"Fair enough."

Seeing that nobody else was running down the dock, desperate to board, the boatman roared the engine to life and pulled away from the pier. As we increased speed bile crept up my throat. I was *not* good with boats. The ferry earlier had been okay because it was so big you could hardly feel the waves. Not now. I could feel *every single bump* and wave as we rocked and swayed over the water. It was such a nice spring day with full sun and a seemingly calm sea. I couldn't imagine being in this boat on any other day.

I brought my hand to my mouth and closed my eyes, willing myself to calm down. I was *not* going to debase myself by being sick on this boat. I just wasn't. Another wave lurched us to the left. I jumped out of my chair and ran to the railing where I threw up the meager lunch I'd had on the train into the bright blue water.

"You okay there, son?" the boatman called out over the whipping wind.

I groaned and wiped my lips with the back of my hand. "*Absolutely peachy,*" I replied.

He laughed and maybe for my benefit slowed the boat's speed a little bit. I raised my head—nauseated as all hell—and caught sight of the island in the distance. It was small—minuscule, really. Maybe it was only the angle that made it seem smaller. The plans Jim had given me were for a five-story resort. I supposed if you built *up* instead of *out*...maybe. I lowered my chin to my chest, still clutching the railing for dear life.

When I was finally able to stand once again I peered down and realized I'd soiled my expensive Italian silk shirt. *Why did I not change earlier?* I dabbed at the offensive stain with a stray napkin from my pocket with little result. Silk didn't agree with greasy train food.

I never sat again as we got nearer to land. Small shops and houses came into view as well as a small marina. A few yachts and sailboats littered the water, however the vast majority of the slips were empty, cementing the idea that the tourist destination was unpopular. Maybe there had been lots of boats at one point in time—the marina had the infrastructure for it—but not anymore.

The boatman, whose name I learned was Magnus, docked his little trawler by the pier and helped me out of the boat, depositing my suitcase on the dock for me with a sympathetic smile. "Sorry about the rough waters there," he said, even though I knew he was exaggerating the circumstances for my benefit. If I had known I was going to be riding in a dinghy I would have taken some drugs or something.

"It's fine." I paid the man in cash—seeing as there were no official tickets available—and rolled my suitcase along the pier towards a steep, cobblestone street lined with matching stone retaining walls on either side.

I didn't want to show up at the hotel covered in vomit, so I entered the first touristy shop along the main stretch. The woman behind the counter wore a friendly smile and waved me in. I crossed my arms over my body to try and hide the gross stain and smiled tightly. She helped me pick a heathered blue t-shirt with *I love Ruby Island, established 1789* written on the front in bold font. The saint of a shop owner let me use her changing room to grab some new trousers from my suitcase and change out of the murderous leather loafers, replacing them with my gym sneakers. I examined myself in the changing room's full-length mirror. I'd gone from Italian businessman to suburban dad real fast. I pulled a hand through my hair trying to tame it from its wind tossed state with little success.

"*Whatever*," I mumbled under my breath. I paid for the new shirt and the shop owner kindly drew me a map on a scrap of paper for how to find The Ruby Inn. Of course it was on the *other* side of the island. I thanked her and rolled my suitcase down the cobblestone street, passing other shops and restaurants. This area *was* charming. The colorful bunting and string lights were fun, and the quirky businesses were interesting to window-shop as I passed by. I was about to maybe find a taxi when I realized that I hadn't seen a single car since I'd arrived on the island. I supposed it was so small there was no need for quick travel. Everything was slow here.

The main road curved to the right and sloped down, the cobblestone melting into compacted dirt. The cliffside to my left was covered in new green grasses and wildflowers—limestone plunging into the water below. There was also a rickety looking staircase that led downwards. That would have to be changed. I wasn't sure it was even structurally sound—a lawsuit waiting to happen.

The single-lane dirt road was lined with small houses from the early 1900s on either side, spaced out by flower gardens and grassy hills. I swept my gaze left to right searching for this inn. The road grew steeper and I slowed, my shoes digging into the dirt as I climbed the hill. There, on the top of the rise was a sign for the inn. It was hanging from a wooden post, its white paint chipping off. In red and gold letters it read, *The Ruby Inn, established 1916*. Wow, that old, huh? I was not looking forward to this. I prayed they at least had working electricity and plenty of hot water. I needed to wash the train and the sick off of me.

The structure itself was three stories, painted in the same chipping white paint with red flashing and trim. Rose bushes and hedges grew unyielding on either side with an overgrown lawn of grass in-between. The wraparound porch was quaint with twin rocking chairs on one side and a porch swing on the other. The views from the back of the hotel must have been incredible. I unlatched the gate and climbed the front steps, my suitcase thumping against each rise. The front door was inlaid with a large stained glass window—a geometric red rose blossoming in the center.

Am I supposed to knock? I'd never been to an inn before, only large chain hotels where the rules were clear. I decided to enter instead. I pushed open the door, and it squeaked on its ancient hinges. Inside was a small lobby area with a long front counter. Everything in sight was covered in white beadboard with pops of navy blue and red littering the space. The dark wooden floors seemed freshly shined and buffed. At least the inside was better kept than the outside.

I rolled my suitcase to the front desk and inspected the room. There wasn't a bell to ring, only a small handwritten card that read, *back in a jiffy*, with a smiley face. *Back in a jiffy?* Were we stuck in the 1950s?

"Hello there," a voice called to my right. An older woman sitting in a rocking chair smiled at me. I left my suitcase and walked towards her, examining the room she was sitting in. The large windows looked out over the water with a spectacular view of the cliffs. There was a door in the corner that presumably led out to the wraparound porch.

"Hello. Do you...work here?" I asked, unsure.

She laughed. "*Usually.*" She tapped the large, clunky medical boot I hadn't noticed. "I'm tragically out of commission. My nephew should be back to check you in any second. He's out grabbing some milk." She had long graying blonde hair up in a loose bun and pale eyes.

"Okay."

"Sit down while you wait." She gestured to the plush cream sofa beside her below one of the large bay windows.

She didn't have to ask me twice. What I truly wanted was to curl up in bed and never wake again, however the sofa was a nice second best. I sunk into the cushions, releasing a heavy breath.

"Long journey?" the woman asked, seeming to read my mind.

"How did you know?"

She smiled warmly, lines creasing around her eyes and mouth. "You have the look."

"*The look?*"

"I've been running this hotel with my family since I was a little girl, so I recognize the look of exhaustion that comes from traveling all day. Relax, you've made it."

I laughed through my nose. "Thanks, uh..."

"Caroline Kirkpatrick, although you can call me Caroline. And you are...Mr. Kaplan?" she asked.

I crossed my legs and shifted my weight, relieving my muscles. "No, that's my father. My name is Berk."

"*Berk,*" she said the name slowly as if rolling it over her tongue. "I like that. It's different."

I chuckled. "Tell that to all my cousins in Turkey with the same name."

She laughed, smile lines and crow's-feet wrinkling. "Oh, really? I guess every group has their own overused names. I know too many Fionas and Liams."

"*Hmm,* must be." I didn't get a chance to talk to many older women anymore. When I was a kid my mother's friends were always around like aunties, gabbing on the phone or bringing us covered trays of rich Turkish food. When I got older though, they all began bringing their daughters around with them, and the treats suddenly seemed more like bribes. I missed talking to people my parents' age. The only conversation you ever really got in night clubs was: what does your body look like, what are you into, and do you workout?

"So, I remember a woman called to make your reservation for you—your girlfriend?" she asked, a twinkle in her eye.

I laughed. "Uh no, definitely not. That was my co-worker's secretary. I'm not sure we've even actually spoken face to face before."

She nodded. "Oh, so you're here for...*work*?"

I pulled my lips into a smile, not wanting to give too much away about why I was on the island. That would make my job harder than it needed to be. "Something like that. I'm going to take some photographs and explore the area." That was all *technically* true.

"A photographer?" She beamed and pointed to the large framed print that was hanging on the wall behind her. "My nephew's wife Maria took that one. She's a photographer too." It showed the island—a different area I hadn't seen yet—with the sun dipping to the horizon in the background, casting the cliffs in a golden haze of orange and pink.

"It's beautiful."

"You should go talk to her if you want to get some insight about the island. Her and my nephew own The Merry Marauders on Main Street."

"Cool, I might just do that." She could give me some tips about how I should plan a marketing package for this place, like what the best features were.

The front door swung open in the lobby. "Aunt Caroline? I'm back," a deep voice called out across the space.

"We have company," she shouted.

A tall guy with curly blond hair hidden under a cherry red knit cap walked into the room carrying five enormous glass bottles of milk. He looked from his aunt to me. "Uh, hi. I'd shake your hand, but..."

I laughed. "I'm not offended." I rose from the sofa and hurried over, taking one of the milk bottles from the top of the stack. "I can give you a hand."

"*Oh.*" He grinned. "Thanks, that would be helpful. Let me show you to the kitchen."

I grabbed a second bottle and followed him across the lobby— through a wooden swinging door that I hadn't noticed before because it blended in with the rest of the wall—and into a small galley-style kitchen.

"You can set it there." He gestured to a long butcher block countertop, worn with age and use.

I set the bottles down, careful not to clink them together and cause a huge disaster. "So, what's with all the milk? Are you having a dairy party or something? Is this an island thing us city folk aren't aware of?"

He laughed and placed his own bottles on the counter. "Nope, that sounds like it would be quite the party, though." He opened the massive restaurant-style fridge and placed the bottles inside. "We have to stock up on most things we buy because it all comes from the mainland. You have to get it while you can or you don't get it at all."

"Huh, most people don't shop on the mainland?"

He shrugged. "Some do, though it's a long journey for coffee creamer, you know?" He placed the last bottle inside, closed the fridge, and turned to face me. "You must be our new lodger." He stuck out a large hand. "I'm Will."

I returned the gesture. "Berk. And yes, I'm going to be here for at least a week, maybe longer."

He smiled with his teeth, the soft sunlight coming in through the windows making his pale blue eyes glimmer. He was definitely attractive. Probably straight, though. He gave off local-fisherman-who-modeled-on-the-side vibes.

"Awesome, thanks for helping me with those bottles. I should have brought a crate or something, however I'm stubborn. Let's go get you checked in."

I bobbed my head. "*Yes, please.*"

He chuckled. "Long day?"

Apparently everyone could see it on me. "Yeah, let's just say that boats don't agree with me."

A light glinted in his eyes. "*Ah,* I understand."

I followed him through the kitchen back to the lobby where my suitcase was still waiting. Will went around the other side of the counter and turned on an absolutely prehistoric computer sitting on the desk—something I hadn't seen since the nineties.

"Berk Kaplan, here for seven days, staying in the Randolph suite," he said as he typed something out.

"The Randolph suite, huh?"

He grinned. "Yes, it's one of our rooms that looks out over the water."

"Amazing."

He pulled a heavy leather-bound book from behind the desk and placed it atop the counter. "If you could sign here you'll be set to go and I can show you to your room."

"I have to sign?" How outdated.

He shrugged. "It's a tradition."

"Okay." I took the pen from his outstretched hand and signed my name on the dotted line. From the looks of all the empty spaces on the page it didn't seem like they'd had many customers lately—or lodgers, as he'd called them.

I held out the pen to return it, and our fingers brushed for a brief moment.

"Uh, great, let's go see that room," he said with an awkward smile.

Huh, maybe not straight.

I went to grab my suitcase, however he beat me to it, lifting it with ease. "No, let me."

"I can carry my own bag," I argued.

"I'm sure you can. This is part of the experience."

I laughed through my nose and smiled. "Are you the bellboy?"

"I'm the...everything boy." He chuckled. "The bellhop, the front desk concierge, the cleaner, and the cook."

"You cook?" I imagined his strong hands grasping a meaty steak and hacking at it with a sharp cleaver. Why was that so hot?

"Yep, let me know if you want anything. We don't exactly provide formal meals, though if there's anything you want I can probably make it happen." He lifted the suitcase onto his shoulder like a fireman and started up the steep stairs. The view was *not bad*. Maybe this trip wasn't going to be so terrible after all.

I quickened my pace to follow him up the stairs and down the hall to the last room. He opened the door with a flourish and ushered me inside ahead of him. The room was nice, in a quaint vintage-y kinda way. The bed was full-sized and looked incredibly soft. That was all that truly mattered.

Will set the suitcase down at the foot of the bed and pulled aside the blinds covering the large-pane windows. The view from downstairs was nice, however this was even better. Seagulls flew in circles around a stack of ragged rocks out in the water; they were covered in barnacles and other sea life. I'd never been much of a beach person—maybe because of the whole seasickness thing—however this was beautiful and cozy.

"Thanks." I pulled out my wallet to find a few bills, but he put up his hand to stop me. "No tip—everything is included."

I hesitantly put the bills back in my wallet. "Are you sure?" It seemed like they could use the money if I was being honest with myself.

"*Completely.* I hope you enjoy your stay." He walked backward towards the door. "I'm always around, so if you need something, just holler."

I smiled. "Will do." I wanted another excuse to touch him, so I put out my hand for another shake—in lieu of a tip. "Thanks for everything."

If he thought it was odd he didn't say anything, merely took my hand in his. I held on for a second too long, to gauge his reaction, staring into his sea-blue eyes. The tips of his ears grew decidedly pink. "I'll, uh, let you settle in, then."

I dropped my hand. "Yes, that would be good. See you around."

He waved his hand as he crossed the threshold, looking back one final time before closing the door behind him.

Hmm. This trip *was* going to be interesting.

FOUR

Will

I closed the door and stood outside in the hallway for a few seconds. Was he...flirting with me? It had been so long I wasn't a good judge anymore. Maybe he was just the friendly sort? An unbidden smile formed on my lips as I walked downstairs to the lobby. Berk *was* incredibly good looking. He had this messy dark hair that looked pretty fun to play with and ears that stuck out just enough to be endearing. I wondered what was underneath that silly Ruby Island t-shirt?

No, he was a paying lodger, it would be inappropriate to try and start anything with him, even if he *had* been flirting. Which he probably hadn't been.

* * *

The rest of the day was quiet and Berk didn't come downstairs. "Probably sleeping after his long journey," Aunt Caroline suggested when she noticed I was staring at the stairs from the sofa like a puppy waiting for his owner to come home.

"You're probably right." I poured Aunt Caroline another cup of tea, set it down on the side table, and flipped to the next page of the book I wasn't really absorbing.

The sun was starting to set, the sky growing into a hazy purple. He *had* to be hungry. He probably hadn't eaten most of the day if he'd been traveling. Also he said he'd been sick on the boat.

I turned another page. "I should make him something to eat," I said into the silence.

Aunt Caroline looked up from her knitting, the yarn trailing down to the floor in a messy pile. "If you think that's best, dear. He might be sleeping, though."

"*Hmm.*" I hadn't thought of that. "I'll knock quietly, and if he doesn't answer I'll leave it outside on a tray. He can't *not* eat."

She smiled. "You're so kind, Willy."

A blush crept up the back of my neck. "It's just good hospitality. Word of mouth is the best marketing strategy."

"If you say so." She turned back to her work with a grin.

"*Hmm*," I mumbled under my breath, rising from the sofa. I'd make him a simple sandwich. That was good for an upset stomach, right? I entered the kitchen from the lobby and rummaged through the fridge for what we had on hand. The problem was, I didn't know what he liked or what he could eat. I decided to keep it simple with a turkey and cheese sandwich with mustard. If he was gluten free or dairy free he was shit out of luck, however I covered kosher and mayo hating just in case.

I placed the plain sandwich on a tray and covered it with a metal cloche to keep it protected. I went upstairs and stopped in front of the room, hand poised to knock. Was this too pushy? What if he didn't want to be disturbed? Or what if he *was* sleeping? I took a breath and gently knocked on the old wood, as soft as I could manage.

"Come in," a voice mumbled from the other side.

Oh good, he's awake. I cracked open the door and searched for him. He was sitting at the desk behind an open laptop with a pile of papers spread out on the desk's surface. He shuffled the papers together and put them away in a folder.

I smiled awkwardly. "Hi."

He turned in the chair. "Hi?" He'd clearly taken a shower recently; his hair was wet and he'd changed clothes, now in a charcoal t-shirt and dark sweatpants.

"I thought you might be hungry...so I made you a sandwich."

He pinched his eyebrows together and then broke out into a smile. *"You did?"*

"Uh, yeah. I figured you probably hadn't eaten all day since you were traveling, plus you were sick earlier." I stepped closer and set the tray down on the edge of the desk farthest away from him.

"Thanks, that's super nice of you." He stood up and patted down his locks, the gesture causing his shirt to lift above his stomach—dark hair trailed downwards. He walked around the chair to where I stood. "What do we got?"

I shrugged. "Just something simple, I didn't know what you liked or anything." After a self-conscious beat I lifted the cloche revealing the sandwich. God, this man had me acting like a nervous wreck. It was just a freakin' sandwich. "It's turkey and cheddar."

He grinned. "Awesome. I love turkey. How'd you know?"

My ribcage released its grip on my lungs, allowing me to breathe. "I guessed." I rubbed the back of my neck. I was *never* this awkward. *What in the world is happening to me?*

"Thanks, what do I owe you?" he said slowly, staring into my eyes with a hint of a mischievous grin.

I took a step back. "Um...nothing. Free of charge, remember?" I laughed, trying to ease the tension. "I'll let you get back to whatever you were doing, just wanted to make sure you didn't starve."

"Yeah, I was doing some work," he said, gesturing to the desk. "I always get distracted when I'm stuck in a project."

I arched a brow. "Working on vacation?" *Curious.*

He shrugged. "I suppose so."

I took another few steps back towards the door. "Okay, well let me know if you liked the sandwich. And you can just leave the tray outside your door when you're finished and I'll grab it later."

He was staring at me so intently. "Thanks again."

"Bye." I waved awkwardly, and left the room. Ten steps down the hall I realized I'd forgotten to close the door, so I ran back and closed it, not looking inside again. *Jesus*, I really needed to get laid if this totally normal human interaction had me so flustered and tripping over my words.

When I returned to the sitting room and picked up my book again Aunt Caroline looked over. "*Better?*" she asked.

I nodded. "Yep, better."

* * *

I didn't see Berk the next morning, although the tray was out in the hallway, empty. I took it back to the kitchen and joined Aunt Caroline in the sitting room. "Did Berk leave? I didn't hear the front door."

She nodded. "Yes, early this morning. I was about to put the kettle on when I caught him going out. He was wearing a nice suit too. I wonder what he was doing?"

I wondered that too. What did a photographer need a suit for? Maybe he was taking some self portraits or something like that? "*Huh.*"

About thirty minutes flew by before Aunt Caroline decided that lunch was needed. "Can you go pick up some soup and bread from Sal's?"

I sighed. "You don't want anything we already have at the house?"

She shook her head. "*No,* I think for the healing of my ankle I need some good clam chowder."

I gave her a look and then broke out into a grin. "I'm glad you're not above leveraging your injury to get what you want."

"Whatever do you mean, dear?" She gave me a coy smile.

I relented. "All right, I'll get the damn soup." I stood to find my khaki-colored jacket and my hat; it was still cool outside in the mornings for late spring. I waved Aunt Caroline goodbye and started off down the road. My bike didn't have a basket so carrying it while walking would be easier—although it would take longer. *Cold* soup from Sal's was better than *no* soup from Sal's.

Seagulls squawked overhead, circling the island, dropping clams and other goodies to crack open on the rocks. The wind pushed against me as I marched down the hill; I wrapped my coat closer around me.

I turned off the lane and away from the cliffs towards Main Street. Sal's was directly across from The Merry Marauders, Maria and Rory's shop. I stepped up to the sidewalk and ducked under a falling string of bunting.

To my right, through the window of the local restaurant Pierre's, I caught a glimpse of a familiar head of dark hair—Berk. He didn't see me, but I saw him. I would have gone in and said hi, however then I saw who was sitting on the other side of the table—Mayor Lancaster. Why would Berk be having lunch with the mayor? He'd made it seem like this was his first time on Ruby Island. What were the odds that they'd simply bumped into each other and decided to join tables? One in a thousand? One in a million?

I walked another few feet forward, pretending to check my phone in order to take a longer look at them from a better angle. They weren't eating; papers and folders were laid out on the crisp, white tablecloth. Berk was pointing down at a document for emphasis. The mayor seemed entranced. Something was definitely going on here. Their meeting was *not* about photography.

I turned before anyone could spot me staring and continued down the street. What could they possibly be doing? It didn't make sense. I passed Sal's and stopped. I knew the one and only person who could answer my questions. I changed direction and quickened my pace, passing by Pierre's again and walking to the end of the street. I turned left and caught sight of the familiar building of the mayor's office. Everything in town was built next to each other with such little land to work with. The office was a white colonial-style building with dark green shutters, repurposed from the man who used to own Ruby Island—Captain Reginald Ruby. His house had been the first structure built in the center of the island.

I entered through the heavy front door and hiked up the curved staircase to the second-floor landing where I found Marjorie at her desk, reading a naughty romance book with a salacious cover. "Hi, Marjorie."

She peered up from her book, although she didn't put it down. "Oh hi, Will. Did you have a meeting with the mayor?"

"No, no, nothing like that." I knew I couldn't just outright *ask* what I wanted to know because Marjorie had *some* tact. But, she *was* also the biggest gossip in town. "I saw the strangest thing a minute ago."

She lowered her book an inch, no doubt deciding if she should take the bait. "Oh?"

"Yeah at Pierre's. Mayor Lancaster was sitting with this strange man. It seemed pretty intense." I upped the dramatics, really going in on it. "It looked like they were arguing over something."

She put down her book, saving her place with her thumb. "*No way!* They were fighting?"

I widened my eyes. "*Yeah*, and the other guy didn't look familiar, not a townie."

She leaned forward, looking left and right as if someone could be watching us. "You know, I probably shouldn't be telling you this—it's very hush-hush—but that guy is from a development group, Sandy Brook. They're trying to strike a deal with the mayor to buy some land on the island for a new resort project. Though it doesn't seem like it's going well if they're fighting. Did you hear any words?"

My brain shuttered. Development group? New resort project? "Uh...what?"

"I asked if you overheard anything good. What did Mayor Lancaster say?"

I shook my head. "I only saw them through the window," I answered quickly. "Hey, if the mayor is planning on selling some land to developers isn't that something we'd have to vote on? I don't remember getting that letter."

She waved her hand. "Only if the deal goes through first. I think the developers aren't sure yet, though it would bring the island a lot of needed money and tourism."

"Uh-huh." So Berk was a liar. He wasn't a photographer, he was a devil in a suit. "Thanks, Marjorie. I'm sure it was nothing, no need to ask Mayor Lancaster about it later. It might embarrass him, you know how men can be."

She nodded slowly. "You're *so* right, Will. We have to be careful around these tough subjects."

"Yep, men are pretty sensitive." I pointed behind me. "I'll let you get back to work, I gotta go run an errand for my aunt."

She pulled her purple-stained lips into a grin. "Tell Caroline I said hello and that I hope she heals fast."

"Thanks." I turned to go back down the stairs, each footfall getting heavier and angrier as I went. That little handsome shit wanted to buy part of Ruby Island? And put in a major resort? What was Mayor Lancaster thinking? That would destroy the island. People came here for a relaxed and out of the way feeling. You couldn't get that at a towering resort with hundreds of identical rooms. He wanted to give money to a big conglomerate instead of small businesses? What would be next, selling off shops on Main Street and replacing them with fast-food restaurants and chain stores?

I left the mayor's office and stormed off down the road, kicking up dust in my wake. When I got back to the inn I shut the door harder than needed.

"Willy?"

"Uh...yeah." I entered the sitting room and took off my coat.

She stared at my empty hands. "What happened to the soup?"

"Oh." Crap, I knew I'd forgotten something. "Uh, they were out," I lied.

She raised an eyebrow. "*Of soup?*"

"Yep. Sorry, Aunt Caroline. I'll heat some canned chowder. It's almost as good if you doctor it up a little bit."

She gave me a funny look. I probably appeared crazed. "All right, dear."

Should I tell her about Berk's devious intentions? I didn't want to upset her. She didn't need any more worries this month. The leg, the bills piling up, and now this? It was so unfair.

I went into the kitchen and hunted through the back of the pantry for the old cans of soup.

What was I going to say to Berk? *Should I give him a piece of my mind? Or act like I believe his lies?* Why was he lying at all? It was so duplicitous it made my blood boil.

I poured the can of soup into a pot and turned on the gas. Damn the soup. Damn Berk. I *was* going to tell him what I thought of him. No way was I going to let him stay in this inn—my family's legacy that he could be destroying—and stay quiet on the subject.

I stewed in my anger while the soup heated through. I grabbed for the saucepan, not realizing the handle was already hot, and burned my finger. "*God damnit.*" I rushed to place the finger under the cold tap to soothe the burn.

What were we going to do if the resort deal went through? The inn would close. Everything I had would be gone. My parents' legacy would be gone—just like them.

FIVE

Berk

The meeting with Mayor Lancaster that morning ran long, and I truly meant *long*. He wanted to know every single minute detail about the project—most of which I didn't *actually* know. I was bullshitting *a lot*. All I had was an idea and a couple sketches from an architect. Plus, a few statistics about how similar projects worked on by Sandy Brook had panned out financially—how much money had been brought to the local economy, etc. Some of those figures went over my head, however I understood the gist of it. Building a space for rich clients to summer meant more customers at local businesses. It was a perfect win-win for the little island.

"And you're sure that Sandy Brook is firm on these numbers?" he asked, tugging at his starched white collar. Was he nervous? Why? This seemed like a no-brainer from where I was sitting.

I gave him my corporate smile. "As sure as I can be. I can get you in contact with our financial department if that would put your mind at ease," I offered. I took a sip of the black coffee sitting beside me. When the mayor had planned this meeting I'd imagined it would be somewhere a *little* more quiet, like an office. I wasn't quite sure why we were meeting at this restaurant, Pierre's. It was nice by all accounts, though neither of us were eating. This was business—it didn't mix with marinara sauce.

"That would be great." He sighed. "I just want to be sure that this is the best option to bring to the people of Ruby Island. I still have to get their approval, you see."

"It sounds like that should be easy," I argued. "It's a great deal. Stimulating the local economy is *always* a great deal."

"Yes, you're probably correct about that." He fiddled with his watch. "So what steps need to happen next? Mr. Schwimmer made it seem like you would be here for a couple weeks overseeing some of the details in order to get the ball rolling."

"Yes, he certainly *did* say that, didn't he?" I cleared my throat. "I'll be working primarily on building a new marketing package for the island that we can employ once the resort starts getting underway. Ruby Island is beautiful, so that shouldn't be hard to accomplish."

He seemed to grow an inch from the praise, straightening his frame. "Yes it is, isn't it? We have a lot of history here. We might be able to win over the townsfolk if we can stress the importance in preserving the story and culture of our little island."

I hadn't realized when Mr. Schwimmer gave me this job that I'd have to win over the mayor *and* the people who already lived here. Hopefully I'd made a good impression so far.

I rose from the table and put out my hand for a shake. "We've done some good work today. I'll get started on my end and you can work on yours. Then we can meet again, say, in a week?" I asked. I'd already been at this restaurant for an hour longer than I'd planned.

He stood, scraping his chair against the floor. "Yes, that would be fine. I'll have my secretary call you. You're staying at the Ruby Inn, yes?"

"That's right. I do have a cell phone, though," I reminded him, because this wasn't the nineties anymore.

He chuckled. "Yes, that's true. I'm so used to everyone being easily accessible here on the island; I didn't even think about it. Okay, she'll call your cell and plan a meeting." He shook my hand.

"See you in a week." I waved goodbye and left the restaurant, taking off my suit jacket as soon as I reached the sidewalk. It was getting warmer, the sun coming out to greet me. I was used to air conditioning in every building. No one had it here. The oscillating fan inside the restaurant did little to cool me down. I probably had sweat stains on my nice dress shirt. Not the silk one covered in vomit—that one would have to be sacrificed to the trash.

I walked back to the inn after having grabbed a couple of bagels at the local bakery. I carried the little paper bag up the hill, my suit jacket slung over my shoulder. I was regretting the stupid leather loafers again, but I'd only brought one nice pair of shoes and even though this island was a little bit homespun, I couldn't arrive at a business meeting in sneakers.

There was the inn. I didn't imagine I'd be so glad to see it, but I was. I climbed the steps to the porch and went inside. Will was sitting behind the front desk with a book in his hands. He didn't look up as I crossed the lobby. "Good morning," I said. He didn't respond. "Nice day, isn't it?"

Nothing. Huh, what was happening here?

"*Okay.*" I walked up to the counter and placed the paper bag down in front of him. "Do you want a bagel? I got two by mistake." It hadn't been a mistake, though he didn't need to know that. "I guess it's probably kind of late for breakfast, but..."

He placed a bookmark in the book to keep his place, set it down, and finally looked up to match my gaze. "Good morning, Mr. Kaplan. Good business meeting?" he asked dryly, his face stony.

"I-uh, *yes?*"

He examined the pastry bag. "I don't eat bagels from liars who want to destroy my town."

"Whoa." That was so intense. How did he even find out about my meeting? "How did you—"

"I saw you this morning when I went into town."

"Okay. And this changes your opinion of me because..."

He dropped his jaw. "*Because?* Because this deal you're making could destroy Ruby Island—and more importantly—*my family's legacy,*" he said that last part in a stage whisper. He turned towards the sitting room.

I followed his gaze. His aunt was sitting in her rocking chair, knitting something with a ball of blue yarn.

So he hadn't told her about my meeting. *Interesting.*

I cleared my throat. "First of all, this isn't *my* deal. This is *my firm's* deal. I have no control of it whatsoever, so jumping down my throat isn't gonna help you. Haven't you ever heard of the phrase, *don't shoot the messenger?*"

"Messengers don't have important meetings with mayors," he replied, narrowing his pale blue eyes.

God, why did he have to be so hot when he was angry? There was an uncomfortable tightness in my trousers I was all too familiar with.

"I don't understand why you're being so dramatic," I stressed. "This deal could actually be great for the island—your economy is dwindling. You need rich tourists, and right now you don't have that. This resort deal could bring in lots of money."

He shook his head. "Of course you'd think the money was the most important part."

I laughed through my nose. "Money *does* make the world go round. In more ways than one."

He scowled. "Don't you see what this means for my family? We already struggle booking lodgers. How are we supposed to compete with a huge new resort?"

How to spin this? "Haven't you heard of trickle down economics? What's good for one is good for all," I argued. "Sure, most of the new tourists are going to want to stay at the resort; it's comfortable; it's safe. However if we bring in fifty percent more tourists, at least a handful of those are going to want to stay somewhere small and out of the way. You'll still have new *lodgers*, as you call them. More than you've got now."

He scoffed. "If you think that's actually true you're more of an idiot than I thought."

I put up my hands. Why was him insulting me *also* hot? "Hey now, let's put our guns away and stay civil, huh? You're not *actually* mad at *me*. You're mad because your inn isn't doing as well as you'd like."

His face flushed, which told me I was probably correct. Either that, or he was so enraged he was changing colors. "Hey, how about this? I can help you refresh your image and formulate a plan to draw in new customers; that's what I'm good at. What do you say?"

Surely he wasn't going to refuse such a generous offer of free advice?

"*Screw you.*"

He'd said it calmly enough, though I could tell we weren't going to get anywhere this way.

I took a step back. "Okay then. I can see you're still a little bit heated. We can have this conversation when you've cooled down." I took the paper bag and pulled out one of the bagels. "Your bagel is still up for grabs if you want it."

"Fuck the bagel." His fists were grinding into the wooden counter top like he wanted to punch through it with sheer willpower.

"All right, then." I backed up some more. "We'll talk later." I sauntered to the stairs and slowly climbed them to my room, making sure he knew I wasn't intimidated by his dramatics. Did he think this was the first time someone had cussed me out?

If anything it kind of made me like him more. The whole angry fisherman thing was strangely working for me.

I closed the door and checked my phone to find a text from my sister. I'd forgotten to call her last night. I'd been so tired from the train ride and the stupid boat.

A: You made it, right? You're not dead in a ditch somewhere, right?

I snapped a photo of the view from the corner window—the sun shone across the blue expanse, and the waves created fluffy white foam against the rocks.

B: Not dead physically, only mentally. Sorry.

She called me and I answered on the second ring. "Hi, Ada."

"Wow, that's pretty. I thought you were working?"

I laughed. "This *is* the job, actually."

"Sign me up, *abi*."

"I wish I could. How are classes going?"

She sighed over the line. "Kicking my ass, but it's fine. I have a study group tonight."

"*Ah*," I said knowingly. "The same study group that has Mr. Hot-stuff in it?"

She laughed. "Maybe."

"I'm sure you'll be getting a lot of work done—ogling strange men over textbooks and wine."

"I don't ogle!" she cried. "He's just nice to look at. Is that a crime?"

"In some places, probably. Women aren't allowed to lust, remember?"

She gasped. "*Berk!* I'm not lusting after anyone. He simply makes studying a little more fun. Sue me."

66

I laughed through my nose. "Come on, sis, you know I'm only giving you a hard time. Sleep with whoever you want. *I* do."

"Oh, *I know*." She paused. "Meet anyone interesting on this little island getaway?"

I smirked. "Maybe. He's kinda mad at me right now, though." I took off the horrid pinching leather shoes and laid down on the bed, crossing my legs and stretching my free arm out over my head.

"That tracks."

"Hey!"

"*What?* You *can* be kind of a dick sometimes, *abi*."

"Yeah, but you're supposed to be on *my* side."

"I am. I'm always on your side. Just don't expect that to help with your relationship woes."

"Yeah, well, thanks." A moment of silence passed between us.

"Have Ma and Dad called yet?" she asked.

I let out a deep breath. "Only a dozen times. I sent them a text saying that I'd be out of town for a while. I guess it upset them."

Ada laughed through her nose. "Yeah, that's one way of putting it. I tried to tell them that you weren't avoiding them, that you were busy with work."

"And?"

"Yeah, that didn't work. Ma said something like, *how can he be too busy for a five-minute phone call?* Then Dad said something like, *when I was his age I still made time for my family responsibilities.*"

"Nice."

"So, how *is* the job going?" she asked. "Had your toes in the sand recently?"

I chuckled. "*No.* Actually, I haven't been to the beach at all yet. Maybe tomorrow. I had a horrendous meeting with this little town's mayor today. It's like drawing blood out of a stone with these people. I'm afraid this might take longer than I had hoped."

"*Tsk*, I'm sure Ma and Dad will be happy to hear that. I'll be missing you, though."

I unbuttoned the too-tight dress shirt, releasing my chest and stomach. "No, no. You have much younger and more interesting friends than me to talk to, sis. Don't flatter me."

"You are not old." I could imagine her rolling her eyes as she said it. "And you're plenty interesting. Remember the white elephant story? That one always makes my friends go wild."

I let out a quick breath. "You're telling your friends *that* story? My most embarrassing moment? How could you?"

She snickered. "I mean, it is the best story I've ever heard. Accidentally wrapping the wrong box and giving a group of wide-eyed college freshmen a vibrating dildo for white elephant is pretty freaking great."

I groaned, burying my face in the crook of my arm in shame. "It was an accident! How was I supposed to know they would come in the same sized box?"

"That's why you open the box and check!" She pulled away from the phone to laugh until she could calm herself down. "It doesn't matter. It was great."

"How much of a mess I am, you mean?"

"You're not a mess, Berk. It's that you're still cooking. We're all just slow cookers and we finish at different times; some are brisket; some are pork chops."

I smiled warmly. "What a beautifully poetic description about how we're all simply pieces of meat waiting to be eaten."

"You know what I meant." She laughed. "Are you really okay? You sound tired."

I sighed. "I'm always tired, Ada. At least I have a little pet project that can happily pass the time."

"You mean the guy who's mad at you?"

"How'd you know?"

"Because I know how your brain works. Just don't strain your flirting muscles too hard. You'll make all the Boston men who never got a call back super sad."

"Yeah, yeah. I better let you go study or whatever collegiate thing you get up to with Mr. Hot-stuff."

She laughed. "Okay. Love you, *abi*."

"Love you, sis. Bye." I ended the call and stretched out, pulling off the shirt so I didn't rip it. Damn these sheets were soft, I had to give them that.

I stared at the crown molding on the ceiling and imagined Will simmering downstairs. How long would he be mad at me? Why was he so much hotter when he furrowed his brow and pouted? I'd thought we might have had something going yesterday. He'd passed the handshake test *and* he'd made me dinner like some country gentleman. He was giving off a certain vibe that was hard to confuse.

And now he was pissed with me. Over something that, honestly, wasn't really my fault. However, if I fucked up this project somehow, I *would* be out of a job, and I couldn't afford to do that. Mr. Schwimmer wouldn't hesitate to blackball me from other firms if I pissed him off— he had that kind of sway in the industry.

So I had to figure out how to keep this deal going *and* win everyone over, including Will, who was acting like he had a stick up his ass. *Damn*, and what a nice ass it was, though. His pretty eyes didn't hurt either.

So I'd have to convince him I was a good guy. I *was* a good guy, sort of. It shouldn't be too hard to persuade him of that.

I got off the bed and rummaged through my suitcase, looking for the perfect outfit. What did small town guys want? I pulled out a soft gray t-shirt that was a size too small and a pair of dark jeans that hugged my thighs just right. *Casual hometown vibes.* I threw the stupid loafers across the room and replaced them with a pair of dark blue boat shoes I knew I would need somehow. I messed with my hair in the bathroom's mirror before realizing he probably didn't like guys who were too done up. I pulled my fingers through my dark locks and shook them into unruly waves.

I grabbed my laptop from the desk and took it with me downstairs. I avoided Will—who was still standing behind the front desk—and beelined it to the sitting room where Caroline was still knitting.

"Hello, Berk. Lovely day today, isn't it?" she asked.

"You're so right, Caroline, it is beautiful. A perfect day to edit some photos I took this morning."

She raised an eyebrow *"Oh?* I wondered what you were up to so early in the morning in that suit."

Technically *I had* taken some photos this morning before my meeting—a couple of the hotel and the surrounding cliffside. I needed to start on my marketing package for this resort deal, however I'd also told Will that I would help him with the inn's image problem. If I wanted to earn back his trust and get closer to him, I'd have to stay true to my word.

"Oh yeah. Sometimes a nice suit can help motivate me to get more work done. Not that capturing this beautiful island feels like work, but you know what I mean."

"*Hmm.* Can I peek at some of the photos when you're done?" she asked.

I smiled warmly. "Of course you can. I took some of the hotel too."

She grinned. "*Lovely.*"

I went about editing those photos from earlier. They were from my phone's camera. I hadn't thought to bring an actual camera, figuring I would hire a real professional to help when the time came. Even still, the photos came out pretty great.

I only looked up from my computer once, in Will's direction. He was looking straight at me. When he realized he'd been caught, he cut his eyes back to his book.

Yep, I've got him right where I want him.

SIX

Will

Berk was acting like our little fight hadn't happened at all. Every time he caught my eye he smiled—the little shit. How could he be so casual about everything? I understood that he was only one man—a cog in a machine of powerful people—however that didn't stop him from being one of the most important pieces. I still couldn't believe that the mayor was even courting the idea. It was insane to prioritize profit over people. Even if we *had* endured a couple slow tourist years—the pandemic hadn't helped either.

Something Berk had said stuck with me, though. He could design a new marketing package for the inn and save our image. It seemed so simple, though I'd never thought about changing the inn or marketing online to get more lodgers. I didn't need *him* for that, though. I could do it myself; I was a capable adult. I ran the inn my way—in a controlled and orderly fashion like the captain of a ship. I could create *my own* plan.

The next day, Berk stayed in the sitting room with Aunt Caroline all morning. It pissed me off, however I didn't want to tell Aunt Caroline about his lies. There was no reason to upset her when she was trying to rest and heal. I stayed out in the lobby most of the time, not wanting to share his air space. Every so often one of them would laugh and I'd look over. Why was he so jolly? And how did he make Aunt Caroline laugh so freely? Like they were old friends?

I got out a pad of notebook paper and a pen to start writing down a plan for the inn. Step one: *clean up the yards*. The front yard was a disaster of overgrown shrubbery and weedy planter boxes. Step two: *clear out the side garden*. We used to host events down on the lawn when I was a kid, but soon after my parents died it went to ruin. The grass sloped down from the side of the inn to the shoreline. The old boathouse sat at the edge of the gardens above the water on salt-bleached wooden posts. We hadn't used the boathouse in over a decade aside from pulling the boat out every once in a while. It could potentially become a prime entertaining space if I cleaned it up nicely. The Ruby Inn was the perfect spot for a destination wedding or big party of some kind. We needed to draw in that kind of attention—the kind that booked rooms.

Berk's story about trickle down economics infuriated me. Did he actually believe his own bullshit? The new resort would presumably have *hundreds* of rooms; the Ruby Inn had twelve. We couldn't compete with their services or their prices. Even if some folks did choose us over the big guy, there was no way we could compete. Not to mention that with a new luxury resort all our taxes would skyrocket since the land would be valued higher now that it was more *profitable*.

When is the mayor going to let the townspeople know about this little deal of his? I had a hard time believing local businesses would be okay with it. Unless they were manipulated by Mr. Tight-pants, who was currently sitting in my living room, schmoozing my aunt.

Step three: *create a local event hosted by the inn*. It was something I'd been debating for a while. We used to host things all the time when my parents were still around. Something as simple as a book club or a cheese and wine night. Something to bring the community together and keep The Ruby Inn on everyone's minds.

I spent the next hour writing down ideas of how we could improve the inn. *See*, I didn't need his stupid marketing package. I was capable of doing everything myself. I scrolled through the booking spreadsheet on the computer screen. We didn't have any bookings until next month, other than Berk. It was dirty taking his money—or rather his company's money. The same company that wanted to gentrify the island.

I willed the phone to ring. I checked our business email. Nothing. Nobody wanted to come to Ruby Island in May. Spring break was over and summer had yet to begin.

"I'm going outside, Aunt Caroline," I yelled into the sitting room.

"All right, dear."

"I can answer the phone if anyone calls," Berk offered, looking up from his laptop.

"*No*, that will not be necessary—"

"Oh that's so nice of you, dear. Thank you," Aunt Caroline said at the same time as me.

Berk quirked up the corner of his lip, his stupid eyes twinkling in the early afternoon light.

"*Sure*, thanks." I smiled tightly and went out the front door. I needed to whip this front lawn into shape. I found all the old gardening tools in the small woodshed out back and got to work. I trimmed the hedges on either side of the lawn and used the old push mower to cut the grass—it took hours. Sweat began to drip down my back, so I took my shirt off to stay cool. My pale Irish skin would no doubt burn. When I was about halfway done weeding the planter boxes the front door squeaked open.

Berk walked out in his outfit of the day: thigh length pale blue shorts, boat shoes, and a navy polo. He was holding a sweating glass of lemonade in his hand. "You've been out here for a long time. I thought you could use a drink." He held out the glass, and when I didn't grab it he placed it on the porch and sat down on the front steps. "It looks great out here. You've done an awesome job." His eyes trailed my body and I had the urge to put my shirt back on. *Not because I was self-conscious*, but because he didn't *deserve* to see what I had going on.

I took off the thick gardening gloves and grabbed the lemonade. I wasn't relenting to him in any way, however *I was* incredibly thirsty, and there was no sense passing out over a feud.

I went back to weeding the planter beds in silence. He didn't leave. "Did you need something?" I asked.

He shrugged and then leaned back on his hands. "Nope, just keeping you company."

"I don't *need* any company," I stressed.

"How long do you see yourself being mad for?" he asked, which threw me off guard. He didn't ask as if he was begging for forgiveness, he asked as if I was behaving like a child and he was chastising me.

"*As long as I damn well please,*" I replied, my voice measured and cool.

"Okay. Let me know." He rose from the steps.

I scoffed. "Why do you care? Because you certainly don't care about this town, so why do you keep trying to talk to me?"

He frowned and slipped his hands in his front pockets. "Because I like you."

Huh?

"And I like your aunt Caroline. I like this inn. I can't do anything about Sandy Brook building this resort, though I *can* help you guys out... if you let me."

I shook my head. "Not gonna happen. We've always been fine on our own."

He raised an eyebrow. "Has anyone ever told you that you're incredibly stubborn?"

I let out a quick breath through my gritted teeth. "Every damn day."

"Good. At least I'm not the only one." He examined the outside one more time. "It really does look nice. I'll have to take some updated photos now that it's all cleaned up."

I put my hand on my hip. "Why do you keep telling my aunt that you're editing photos of the inn? What are you getting at?"

He pinched his brows together. "I'm not *getting at* anything. I *was* editing some photos I took of the inn. It's a beautiful building, with an even more beautiful view." He waved and slipped through the open front door. "See you."

Was he playing with me? What was his angle?

I gulped the rest of the lemonade and slammed the glass down with a hard *thump*. "Liar," I mumbled underneath my breath.

I got back to work. I finished the rest of the planters and found a broom to sweep the porch and porch swing. I collapsed down into it and let my momentum sway me back and forth. *Step one complete.* I didn't need his help or his phony *plan*. I could save the inn all on my own. I'd make my parents proud.

* * *

When I finally came in it was way past lunch. Aunt Caroline had fed herself, so I went to the kitchen and ate some leftovers straight out of the fridge. Afterward, I went upstairs and took a shower to clean off all the sweat and dirt that covered my body. I left the upstairs bathroom in a haze of steam—a navy blue towel wrapped around my hips.

"Oh." A figure walked out of Aunt Caroline's room to my left and bumped into me. I grabbed the edge of the towel so that it didn't fall off. "What the—"

"Sorry." It was Berk, clutching something in his hands.

Why was he loitering on the upper floor? It was for family only. "Lodgers aren't permitted on the third floor," I reminded him.

He rushed to explain. "Your aunt asked me to grab a book off her nightstand." He raised the thick volume.

He'd changed clothes. Now he was wearing a pair of black trousers and a tight, sheer black t-shirt that left nothing to the imagination. He was also wearing those silly loafers he'd been wearing when I first met him. "Going somewhere?" I asked, not curious *at all*.

"Yeah, I was about to go get dinner at a bar." He held up the book again. "She asked me on my way out."

I held out my hand. "I can give it to her."

He grinned and looked down my length with a raised eyebrow. "You're *clearly* busy. I can do it, it's on my way."

I gripped the towel tighter, forgetting in my annoyance that I was naked. "Right, okay then."

He took a few steps towards the stairs and then stopped to look back at me. He grinned mischievously. "You keep it tight, Will. *Looking good.*"

Heat rose up my neck, burning my ears, as I opened my mouth to respond. He was already down the stairs before I could form a cutting reply. *Damn him.*

I dashed to my room and got dressed, slamming my dresser drawer a little harder than necessary. When I went back downstairs to check on Aunt Caroline I rearranged my features so it looked like nothing was bothering me.

"That Berk kid sure is interesting, isn't he?" she said as I walked into the room.

"He sure is," I agreed, although probably not for the same reasons as her.

"Pretty cute too."

I pinched my brow and dropped my jaw. "*Aunt Caroline.*"

"What?" She set down her book. "I have eyes, don't I?"

"Don't you think he's a little young for you?" I asked, collapsing into the sofa, and making sure to sit on the opposite side that Berk had been sitting on before.

She let out a hearty laugh. "Not for me, obviously. I was talking about for you."

"*Me?*" I was about to list off all the reasons why Berk was the last man I'd ever want to date, however I stopped myself. If I did, I'd have to disclose that half of those reasons were secrets I'd been keeping from her.

"Yeah, *you.* When's the last time you went out on a date? That girl from Portland last year?"

I gave her a deer-in-the-headlights look. "You knew about that?"

She grinned and clucked her tongue. "Of course I knew about that. Did you think I wouldn't notice you sneaking her in and out of your room? Did you think you were being quiet?"

I cringed, my face flushing crimson. "I don't want to know any more."

"Come here." She gestured with her hand.

"What?"

"Just come *here.*"

I reluctantly left the safety of the sofa and knelt down beside Aunt Caroline's chair. She pinched my cheek and smiled. "You don't have to hide things from me, Willy. You know that, right?"

Was she talking about the truth about Berk? Or my relationships? "Yeah," I said weakly, not knowing what exactly I was agreeing with.

"Good." She released my face. "So go take that boy out on a date. I can tell he's wild about you."

I scoffed and returned to the sofa. "You can't know that. *I* don't even know that."

She waved her hand. "I can tell these things; I'm intuitive."

I leaned back and released a heavy breath. "Did you ask him to bring me that lemonade this afternoon?" It was something I'd been wondering all day.

She raised an eyebrow. "No. I told him we had some when he asked about drinks earlier, why?"

I shook my head. "No reason." So he'd brought the drink on his own, *big deal*. It could still all be a ploy to get me to...what exactly? Stand up for him against the town counsel, maybe. It *would* be a smart plan to have one of the oldest businesses on the island in favor of his new development project.

That was probably it. No way he liked me for real.

* * *

Later after dinner, I was sitting behind the front counter of the lobby in my pajamas. It was past two in the morning and Berk still hadn't come home. It wasn't that I was *worried* exactly. I didn't care enough about him personally to be worried. I was just...*concerned* for him, as a lodger, as a customer of the inn. He'd said he was going out for dinner at a bar. There were only a couple bars in town and I had the urge to pick up the phone and call. I also had the urge to go wait on the front porch with a flashlight, although I stopped myself.

He was probably doing this on purpose too. Another trick to weaken my defenses. I wouldn't put it past him since I already knew he was duplicitous in other ways.

Aunt Caroline had gone to bed hours ago after a late night cup of herbal tea. Neither of us had been sleeping lately with all the pressure to maintain the inn during the off-season and now with her broken ankle. I was glad she was asleep; she needed the rest. *I* needed the rest.

I crossed my arms over my middle and practiced my sternest expression. I wanted to look him straight in the eye when he came in, dragging his tail between his legs for making me *worry* about him.

That did not happen. Two o'clock turned into three o'clock, which was quite literally witching hour. Nothing good could be happening during witching hour.

The door hinges squeaked. My eyes fluttered, and I shook myself awake. *There he is.* The door cracked open. I was expecting a very repentant Berk, however who entered was a different man entirely—blond with tattoos. He was carrying Berk with an arm around his shoulder.

"What the hell happened?" I asked. Berk's eyes were barely open, and he didn't seem to register where he was.

The blond guy smirked. "He's just had too much to drink. We're gonna go sleep it off upstairs. Which room is his?"

I frowned. "*You're what?*"

The guy stared at me like *I* was the idiot and said even slower than before. "*Which room is his?*"

I stood from the desk and walked around to the front of the lobby. "If you don't know already, you don't deserve to know. He's fucking blackout drunk. What do you mean, *going upstairs to sleep.*" I put the last phrase in quotation marks.

"Uh."

I took the burden of Berk's full weight from the stranger and hiked him up until he was almost standing. I caught his gaze, although he still didn't seem conscious enough to recognize me.

"You can leave now," I said firmly.

The blond frowned and knit his brows together. "Says who, man. Who the fuck are you?"

"I'm the fucking owner of this inn, *creep*. Now get the fuck out before I call the sheriff on your ass."

"*Whatever.*" He backed down and left out the front door. I locked it behind him for good measure.

"Berk, are you all right?" I asked. I got a severely different answer than I'd anticipated. He unleashed his stomach in front of me. Most of it hit the floor, however some of it splattered my sweatpants. Great. I didn't have the heart to be mad at him in that moment, so I rubbed his upper back and got him into an upright position again. "Come on, let's get you to bed before you drop."

"*Will?*" he mumbled.

"Yeah, that would be me. You're back at the inn."

He turned his head as if looking around, though his eyes were almost fully closed. "What happened with...that guy?"

"I sent him home."

He scoffed in a drunken way that sounded wet and full of mucus. "The fuck? *Why?*"

"Because you can't even stand, genius. The night is over." I angled him towards the stairs even though he was dragging his feet.

"Screw you, ruining my fun. You're no fun, Will."

"Yeah, I'm sure it would have been *super* fun to get assaulted," I mumbled under my breath.

"What?"

"Nothing. Come on, walk. Let's go." We went up the stairs, painfully slow. It might have been easier to carry him fireman style, though I didn't want a repeat of the floor show, so I bit my tongue and bided my time. I got him to his room and flopped him face first onto the bed. I took off his shoes and convinced him to turn onto his side. "If you throw up on this vintage quilt I will end your life, do you hear me?" I said sternly, though I didn't receive a response.

I left him on his own for a minute to get a glass of water and two Aspirin. I placed them on the nightstand and forced Berk to sit up.

"*No*, I don't want to."

I scoffed. "I haven't even said anything yet." I picked up the pills and placed them in his hand. "Here, take the Aspirin. You'll thank me tomorrow."

"I don't want to."

Wow, he turned into a real bratty baby when he was drunk. "I'm obviously not gonna force you, but you're going to regret it in the morning if you don't."

He scowled at me, holding the pills in his hand. After a minute, he threw them into his mouth and swallowed them dry.

"And the water." I gestured to the glass.

He groaned. "I hate you."

"Likewise. Drink the water."

He did as I asked, managing to drink about half the glass before giving up.

"*Good job.*" I whispered in a high pitched voice like he was a child or a dog.

"Fuck you."

I didn't bother trying to undress him at all. He hadn't gotten any of the puke on himself—lucky him—so I wasn't worried that he'd be soiling himself any further. Plus that would be crossing a boundary. Something that blond fuckwad didn't seem to understand.

"*Sleep tight.*" I said in a sing-song voice.

Berk mumbled something I couldn't make out. He was back home —safe—that was all that mattered.

SEVEN

Berk

Fuck. I cracked open one eye, breaking the seal of sleep dust gluing my lid down. My throat was so dry. I tried to clear it only to feel pain.

What happened last night? I opened the other eye and thanked the universe that the blinds were fully closed, only a crack of sunlight had snuck through. I peered down at myself. I was still wearing all my clothes from last night. My belt was digging into the skin of my waist. "*Ow.*" I moved my head too fast, and the blood rushed, making me woozy. I pushed myself into a sitting position and ripped off the belt, finding some relief.

Memories from last night slowly trickled back to me. The bar. The blond. Will managing to get me up the stairs in one piece. "Oh shit." I'd probably behaved badly last night. That was not going to win me any brownie points with him.

I glanced over at the nightstand and found two glasses—one full of water, the other full of orange juice. There was a note beside it.

Drink this. Eat this.

Two pills sat on top of the note—Aspirin. Oh, yeah. He'd gotten me to drink some water and take some Aspirin last night. That was probably why my head was only mildly throbbing instead of full out waging war against me. The glass of juice was still cold. He must have *just* left it there. I downed the whole glass like a mad man, taking the two pills along with it.

I was surprised that Will had cared at all. He'd been so mad at me when he found out who I worked for. I took a second look at the note, at his looping scrawl. *Huh.*

I pulled off all my wrinkled, dirty clothes and took a long, hot shower. When I got out I dressed in a comfortable and casual outfit, then dared to open the blinds. It wasn't as bad as I'd imagined. Only a *slight* stabbing pain.

I checked my phone—many texts from my parents and a couple from Ada. *Oh, no.* An email from Mr. Schwimmer. He *never* emailed me directly. It was always his assistant or one of his handlers.

I sat down at the edge of the bed and after a moment of hesitation opened the message. I skimmed it quickly, *He'd received a positive phone call from Mayor Lancaster.* I let out a sigh of relief. Mr. Schwimmer had also sent an overnight package to the hotel containing an expensive camera; he wanted me to take some professional photos of the entire radius of the island so the architects could start working on layouts for the resort. They had to choose which parcel of land they were going to invest in. I hadn't realized there was more than one area up for discussion. Mayor Lancaster must be softening to the idea.

"Well, okay then." I grabbed the empty glasses and carried them with me downstairs. Will was sitting behind the front desk as usual. It was odd that over the last couple days I'd been the only one staying here. They really *did* need some help.

"Good morning."

He raised his head and nodded at me, impartial.

I set the glasses down on the counter. "Thanks for, you know...last night."

He frowned and leaned forward to look into the sitting room. I followed his gaze; Caroline was sitting in her rocking chair with a stack of letters.

"*Uh.*" Was it something I said?

"It's not a problem," he answered, crouching down behind the counter. "You have a package."

"Yes, I was going to ask about that."

He placed the cardboard box on the counter.

"Thanks."

He evaded my eye. "*Sure.*"

I used my key to cut open the tape. In the box was a small plastic case. I pulled it out and opened it up. An expensive looking professional camera was wedged inside a protective foam cutout. I picked it up, turned it on, and began messing with the settings. I'd taken photography on the side during college figuring it would help with my degree. My parents had thought it was wasteful—since they were paying for it—however they finally gave in when they realized its practicality in the marketing industry.

"Nice camera," Will said, looking over the edge of his book.

"Yep." I aimed the lens at him and took a sneaky photo.

He scowled. "*Delete that.*"

I grinned. "It was only a test shot, to make sure the settings are correct."

"Delete it anyway."

"Fine," I mumbled, pretending to delete the picture from the memory card. I walked into the front room and said good morning to Caroline. I snapped a couple pictures of the view from the window.

"Oh, how lovely. Where'd you get that?" she asked, dropping a stack of letters into her lap.

"It came from Boston," I answered—which again, was not a lie, *technically*.

"Now you can take some real photos, *huh*? It's such a beautiful day outside."

"Yes, it is." I practiced with the zoom lens, focusing on a faraway island of rock sitting out in the distant ocean. "I'd like to get some views of the island from the water. I could probably get some of the inn too. That would really sell it nicely, don't you think?"

Caroline grinned. "That's a wonderful idea." She turned her head towards the lobby and called, "Willy!"

Willy? That's what she called him? I couldn't help but smile at the pet name.

Will walked into the sitting room from the lobby. "Yes?"

"Berk needs to go out on the water today to take some photos. Can you take him out on our boat?"

He frowned, then caught himself, moving to a more neutral expression. He cleared his throat. "*Our* boat?"

She set down her letters and started playing with the many rings on her fingers. "Yes, when was the last time we used it? It's due for a trip and a cleaning, wouldn't you say?"

He looked between me and his aunt. "I don't know about that, Aunt Caroline. I don't like the idea of leaving you here alone for such a long time, unable to get back in an emergency."

She waved her hand. "*Pshaw*, nonsense. I can always call Rory or Maria if something happens—which it won't, you worry wort."

He chuckled, although it seemed strained. "We haven't used that boat in a *long* time. It might not be safe." He turned to me. "Wouldn't you rather someone from the marina show you around? Maybe Magnus?"

The memories of throwing up on myself flooded my brain. I turned to Caroline. "I wouldn't want to impose, if he doesn't want to, that's okay."

Caroline turned to face him. "That's not it, right?"

Will smiled tightly, his arms locked rigidly at his sides. "Of course not, if *you're* okay with it then *I'm* okay with it."

I grinned. "Great. I'll get my hat." I rose from the sofa. "Better put on some sunscreen, you're so pale."

He frowned.

* * *

So...his aunt's definition of a boat was apparently a loose one—it was more of a dinghy or a rowboat. The vessel was small with chipping white paint—a lot like the inn itself. Two red stripes ran down its length with the words *The Ruby Traveler* written on the side in fading gold font.

"Is she...seaworthy?" I asked, examining the craft.

Will glanced over his shoulder at me. "Of course it is. But if you're too scared we can go back inside. We don't have to—"

"I'm *not* scared. I was just admiring your maintenance skills—she looks *great*." I bit my tongue. I wasn't supposed to be acting cheeky, I was supposed to be likable.

"*Ha, ha.*" He ran his hand down the side, a layer of dust and mildew flying into the air. "Help me get her into the water." The boat was resting on two wooden supports. Will ducked his head underneath—so he was standing inside the boat—and waited until I did the same. "Lift on three, okay? *One, two, three.*" We pushed up until the boat was lifted off its dry dock and into the air.

"Damn, this is heavy," I grunted out. I hadn't been hitting the gym lately, *clearly*.

He chuckled. "There's no other way to get it to the water."

"It's fine." I followed his lead out of the weathered boathouse and over to the dock. The water was at high tide.

He cleared his throat. "I'm going to come to your side so we can flip it over."

"Okay." Could he tell I'd never been to summer camp?

He walked his hands forwards, tipping the boat back until one end hit the dock. "*Lift.*" He was standing only a few inches from me, pushing my side of the boat into the air. "Ready to flip?"

"Uh, as ready as you are."

If I wasn't mistaken he cracked a smile. He could probably tell how out of my element I was.

He turned around and took hold of the lip of the boat, standing next to me. "On three we go left. *One, two, three.*"

I hoisted my side high and he cradled the boat so it barely made a sound as it flipped over onto the dock.

Now I was a boat flipper. I could flip a boat.

He returned to his side and we lifted the vessel to the edge of the water.

I'd made sure to take some seasickness medication this time around. If the goal was to win Will over, throwing up on him, *again*, was not the move.

"All right. Let's do this thing, I guess." He grabbed the boat's propeller and attached it to the back. I climbed inside and made myself comfortable. As comfortable as I could be in a moldering and dusty wooden dinghy.

He pulled the cord on the engine and after a couple false starts it roared to life. Not quite as romantic or quiet as a sailboat, however it would have to do. I cradled the camera in my hands, the strap around my neck so I didn't drop the object worth double my paycheck into the water.

Will pushed off the rocky shoreline with his boot, moving us into deeper waters. "Where to, *sir*?" Will asked with a smirk, controlling the rudder with a practiced hand.

"Uh, how about out that way?" I pointed to my right. "So we can get a good shot of the inn."

He didn't respond, he merely moved the rudder and shot us forwards. The Ruby Inn sat on a short bluff of tan cliffs that dropped down into the water. The back windows of the inn stared down at us. I pulled the lens cap off the camera and snapped a few photos. Will slowed the engine until we were merely drifting. The light caught on the inn perfectly.

I glanced down at the screen to make sure it was capturing what I was seeing. Yes. We drifted far enough that I was able to snap a few shots of the side of the inn, half obscured by the growing trees on the edges of the lot.

"How far are we going, exactly?" Will asked.

"All the way around the island if possible. I need to take some photos of the most eastern and western points."

He nodded and revved the engine, tearing us across the Atlantic so fast I had to grip the sides to steady myself. Clearly, I was wasting his morning. I needed some way to turn the tide between us. He couldn't stay mad forever. Or maybe he could, I didn't really know him well enough to say.

The inn disappeared around the bend as more of the island came into view. Houses dotted the cliffside between groves of small trees. Not many people lived here, that was clear enough. I took some more pictures, as best I could. It seemed Will didn't want to slow down for me anymore. Luckily, the camera was doing most of the hard work.

"I didn't see that coming in," I said, pointing to the red and white lighthouse sitting out on a lone rock in the water. It didn't appear to be active.

Will nodded. "That's Ruby Lighthouse, built in 1824. It used to be one of the most important lighthouses on this side of Cape Cod to keep sailors safe from the rocks."

But it was out of commission, dormant, much like the island itself.

Even though Ruby Island was small it still took the better part of an hour to get all the way around, only stopping now and again to take pictures. The wind was whipping through my hair, destroying whatever work I'd put into it. *Whatever.* The sun was high in the sky beating down on our backs and it was nearing lunch time.

I could just about see the red trim of the inn on the curve of the horizon. We were almost back home—or what passed as home. If I was going to do something stupid and impulsive, it needed to be soon.

Without Will noticing I placed the camera back in its protective case and tucked it under my seat to keep it safe. Mr. Schwimmer would definitely fire me if I destroyed the camera. Even if he *could* replace it tenfold. I also took off my hat and shoved it deep in my pocket so I didn't lose it.

How to go about this. I placed my hand on either side of the boat and then lurched my weight to one side, pretending we'd hit a large wave or something. Before Will had time to react I was overboard, hitting the ice-cold water. We'd been going only a few miles an hour so I wasn't truly in danger, however *he* didn't know that. I flailed my arms and watched as the boat surged by for a few seconds before Will cut the engine.

"*Berk!*"

I flapped my limbs, imitating what I could remember from movies about people who were drowning. I took in a mouthful of disgustingly salty seawater and spit it out with a breath to make it look like I was choking. I *was* choking. Shit that was a bad move. The salt burned, traveling down my esophagus as I fought for a good breath. Stupid lungs. The cold water made it harder to move my limbs. I hadn't expected it to be so cold in May.

Will didn't hesitate before jumping out of the boat—clothes and all —after me. He hit the water like a diver, barely making a splash and swam in my direction.

I dunked my head under the surface to complete the effect, though I was also starting to get tired from flailing and kinda *scared* that I was getting tired.

Did I actually need him to save me now?

Will cut through the water quickly and reached me in mere seconds. He put his strong arm around my waist and lifted me up to find some air. "Are you okay?" he asked.

Kinda. I nodded, coughing on the remaining salt and grime in my airway. I let him drag me along as he paddled with one arm.

I wasn't a total dick; I helped paddle. If he realized I'd learned to swim in the last two minutes, he didn't show it. We reached the boat and he threw me forwards, my stomach landing on the edge. It tipped slightly as I pulled my heavy, drenched body into the dinghy. I turned around and offered out an arm to Will, who looked more tired than I'd expected after his impressive rescue dive. He climbed in, water dripping from his hair and shirt.

"Thanks," I got out through a breath. I *really was* out of breath— no need to fake that.

"What happened?" he asked after composing himself, his eyebrows pinched together with worry.

I shrugged. "I don't know, we must have hit a choppy wave or something. Sorry."

He shook his head. "Don't be sorry. I should have grabbed life vests before we left. *I'm* sorry."

Oh, I hadn't even thought of that. But I wasn't angling for him to feel guilty; this was supposed to be sexy. I put my hand on his chest—his musculature visible through his soaked shirt—and laughed. "Your heart is beating like crazy."

His brow was furrowed in a serious expression, but then he let out a quick chuckle. "Yeah, you scared the shit out of me."

"I'm okay," I promised.

He skimmed his hand across his face to wipe away some of the water and let out a deep breath. "You don't know how to swim?" he asked.

I shrugged. "Never needed to learn, living in the city." *Of course* I knew how to swim. When I was a kid I'd gone with my father to the Turkish baths and swam laps while he sat in the steam room with his buddies every Friday.

He pulled his fingers through his wet curls. "We need to go get dry and warm. Even though it's sunny outside, the cold water can still make you sick."

"Yes." I rubbed my hands up and down my arms, the chill starting to seep into my bones.

Will restarted the engine that had died and steered us back to the inn's dock. When we made it to shore Will tied a rope from the boat to a wooden post at the end of the dock in a figure eight fashion I'd never seen before. "The boat can stay there," he explained.

"I agree." There was no way I was lifting that thing soaked with twenty extra pounds of water. I grabbed the camera case from under my seat and followed Will up the hill back to the inn.

"It's lucky you put your camera away before you fell in," Will said. "That could have been terrible."

I nodded. "I know. Thank God, right?"

We climbed the front steps to the porch. Will had already taken off his flannel and begun ringing it dry. "I'll go grab us some towels."

We went inside and he raced off to some hidden room and came back with a stack of fluffy white towels.

"Willy?" Caroline called from the sitting room. Two others walked out—one shouldering Caroline so she could hobble into the lobby.

I held up a hand and waved. "Hi."

Caroline's mouth was downturned, her brows scrunched with concern. "What happened?"

"Only a little run in with the ocean," I said, hoping to lighten the mood now that the *danger* was gone.

One of the strangers—who resembled Will, but with a ginger beard —stepped forward, a smaller Latina woman following him.

"Hey, Rory," Will greeted, drying off his hair with the towel.

"Are you okay?" Caroline asked, looking us up and down.

"We're fine," Will assured her. "Just a little wet, that's all."

It was awkward standing there dripping wet in front of strangers.

"Oh, Berk, this is Rory and his wife Maria. Rory is my other nephew, Will's cousin." Caroline filled in.

I crossed my arms. "Oh yeah. Caroline mentioned you."

Maria laughed. "But not Will, I bet?"

Will blew out a puff of air. "I mention you guys all the time."

Rory smirked. "*Okay.*"

A fluffy golden retriever walked through the maze of legs and stopped in front of me. I dropped to my knees. "And who is this?" I scratched him behind the ears and he wagged his tongue. Golden retrievers were never afraid of strangers—they just loved love.

"That's Barnabas."

I raised an eyebrow. "Barnabas, huh? A fancy name, must be a fancy dog."

Will laughed. "Nah, it's an old seafarer name, right, Rory?"

Rory knelt down to the floor—which was currently being soaked with sea water—and scratched Barnabas on the top of his head. "He's an old sea dog, only now he's retired, so I guess you could say he's a little spoiled."

"And incredibly cute," I added.

"We should probably let you dry off," Caroline said, leaning against the front counter for support. "We'll put on a pot of tea to warm you both."

"Thanks, yeah that would probably be good," I said. I was wet in places I didn't enjoy being wet in.

I waved at Will's family and then followed him up the stairs. Once in my room, I chucked all the wet clothes into the tub to deal with later and put on a dry t-shirt and sweatpants. I was running out of clothes quicker than I'd anticipated. I wondered if they'd let me do laundry.

Will was coming down the stairs as I left through the doorway. I was still cold, rubbing my arms with my hands. He stopped in front of me and frowned. "Did you not bring a sweater?"

"In May?" I asked. "*No*, I didn't imagine I'd be falling into the ocean, so I didn't exactly prepare for that."

He rolled his eyes and motioned for me to follow him. "Come on." He marched up the stairs and I trailed close behind. He stopped at what must have been his own room and after a second of hesitation opened the door. I paused at the threshold and leaned against the doorframe. His room was similar to the Randolph suite with navy sheets and curtains. His bed was pushed up against the wall, unmade.

Will rummaged through a dresser drawer and pulled out a cream cable-knit sweater that was easily two sizes too big for me. "Here." He tossed me the sweater.

"Are you sure?" I asked, feeling the soft wool in my hands.

"I wouldn't have given it to you if I wasn't."

I slipped it on over my head, the sleeves dropping over my hands. He wasn't *that* much larger than me; someone had clearly made the sweater for a giant. The soft material pooled around my frame like a cozy hug, and it smelled like him too—like citrus and sandalwood. "Thanks."

We went back downstairs where everyone had convened in the sitting room. Caroline noticed the sweater straight away. "Oh, you got the Aran out."

"The Aaron?" I asked. Did the sweater once belong to someone named Aaron? Was he the giant?

She pulled her lips into a smile. "It's an old Irish fisherman thing—an Aran sweater. The name comes from the Aran islands in Ireland. Every family has their own pattern of cables and stitches, so if your fisherman's ship sinks and the dead wash up on shore you can identify your kin."

That's morbid.

"This is the Kirkpatrick design, which was passed down from my great-grandmother. You never wear that old thing, Willy," she said. "It looks good on you, Berk. I haven't seen that sweater since it was on my needles, years ago."

I peered down at the sweater. "You *made* this?" Suddenly I was worried about ruining the soft cream wool.

"Yep, when Willy graduated high school, I believe. It's kind of a gift for a man's rite of passage, at least in our family."

"Wow, I'll take care of it, then."

Rory, who was sitting over on the sofa with his wife, laughed. "Don't look so scared. We have about a dozen of those old things."

I sat down in one of the plush chairs across the room, and Will joined me in the matching chair, a slight blush on his cheeks. Was he embarrassed that I was borrowing his clothing? Or was it that everybody had noticed immediately?

"Tea?" Maria asked, holding out a delicate white cup to me.

"Thanks." I accepted the cup and took a sip of the bitter, warm drink.

Barnabas was lying on the sun-faded rug by the sofa, his eyes fluttering closed. Will got his cup of tea and relaxed into his chair. It had been a while since I'd been in a room full of people—much less a family.

"So, Caroline was telling us that you came to Ruby island to take photos? Are you a photographer?" Maria asked.

"Uh, yep," Might as well keep up the lie. I *had* been taking photos, and that made me a photographer of sorts, didn't it? "We were out taking photos when the accident happened."

"You two are okay though, yes?" Caroline asked, looking between me and Will.

"Yes, Aunt Caroline," Will said, taking a sip of his tea. "We're feeling better already, right Berk?" He asked me, urging me to agree.

"Absolutely. Great tea by the way; we Turkish are pretty particular about our tea."

Caroline smiled, creasing her eyes. "Lovely."

Eventually, Rory began talking. He asked me a few questions about myself, although he mostly just told stories about their life on the island.

I was curious what Will was like as a kid, and Rory was more than happy to spill.

Will furrowed his brow. "Don't tell that one, Rory. You promised on the curse of death that you wouldn't."

Rory smiled mischievously and then clamped his mouth shut.

I Frowned. "No, I *need* to hear this. He did *what* to the principal's car?"

Rory's impressive ginger beard bobbed with his giddy laughter, however he stayed quiet.

"I didn't realize that living on a small island was so eventful."

Rory gave me a mischievous smile. "What, did you think we all sat at home tying sailor's knots and singing sea shanties?"

I laughed and waved my hand through the air. "Something like that."

They stayed past lunch—the teapot empty—though eventually they had to get back to re-open their shop.

"You can only be gone on lunch for so long, even in the off-season," Maria remarked while pulling on her coat.

I raised one brow. "Yeah, I heard the tourism here isn't doing well."

They took the bait. "Yeah, hasn't been for the last couple years at least," Maria said. "They closed the ferry line that used to travel directly here because of covid. It never reopened."

"*Huh*, seems like someone needs to get on that."

"Rory rolled his eyes. "We've been trying for a long time. The bastards won't budge."

Maria sighed, her hands on her bulging belly. "Hopefully things will start to change pretty soon."

"Hopefully," I agreed.

I turned to Will, his expression hardened. He knew I was referencing Sandy Brook, though the others didn't. They left after saying their goodbyes, taking the sleepy-eyed Barnabas with them.

"Well, that was fun," I exclaimed. "Your family is super interesting."

Will raised an eyebrow, while Caroline only grinned. "They are, aren't they? Love them to death." She stood from her chair and grabbed my hand. "And I'm sorry about the boating accident. I feel terrible about it."

"*No, don't.* Things happen. We're all okay." I gestured down at the cream sweater. "No need to identify me by my *Aran*."

Caroline laughed through her nose. "No, you're right. I'm overprotective of my lodgers, is all. They become like one of my own."

Oh. Her words warmed my heart, however the muscles at the bottom of my abdomen tightened around my organs. Would she be as mad as Will when she found out what I was actually here for?

EIGHT

Will

Berk had spent the rest of last night in his room editing his photos. Probably to send to his corporate overlords. It was hard staying mad at him seeing how he interacted with my family. He was *so damn charming* when he wanted to be. And I was still guilty that I hadn't made him wear a life vest yesterday. Why hadn't he said he wasn't a strong swimmer? He'd scared the shit out of me. My protective instincts switched to overdrive, forcing me to dive into the cold water. I was glad that everything had worked out.

I glanced down at my notebook and checked off another step from my to-do list: *Host a small gathering of local business owners*. I'd spent last night sending out texts and making phone calls. It was pretty last minute, however with everything going on I wanted to act on my best ideas as soon as I had them. There was no one staying at the inn other than Berk, so right now was the perfect time for action.

I'd explained my plan to Aunt Caroline and she'd been delighted to help me decide on a menu so we could order from the local market to come from the mainland the following morning. I'd ordered *lots* of oysters, however when I went down to the marina to pick them up, I realized they'd sent me *unopened* oysters. "*These were supposed to be pre-shucked*," I'd told Magnus. He'd only shrugged. "*What do you want me to do about it?*"

So I loaded all the groceries in Rory's truck and drove them back to the inn. I explained the situation to Aunt Caroline. How I now had *hundreds* of oysters that needed opening.

"Oh, Berk, dear?" Aunt Caroline called as Berk was walking down the stairs to the lobby.

He stopped in his tracks, pulling a hand through his dark locks. "Yes?"

"Do you have some time to spare? We're in a bit of a pickle."

"*Aunt Caroline.*" That was *not* the kind of help I was looking for.

"Do you know how to shuck oysters?" I asked begrudgingly.

He shook his head. "Nope."

"I turned to Aunt Caroline. "*See*, he doesn't know how—he can't help." *Problem solved.*

"Oh, he can learn if you show him. It's not that hard. Right, Berk?" she asked.

He shrugged. "I don't see why not. I have hands." He held up his hands like I needed proof or something. *Idiot.*

"I can see that."

He grinned. "Just show me what to do, *boss*."

I sighed internally, regretting this immediately. "Okay, follow me." I led him into the kitchen and stopped in front of the sink. "Usually you have to soak oysters for a while to soften the shells. These have been soaking since I got home this morning." I showed him the large stock pot that was filled to the brim with oysters and salt water.

He leaned over to look inside. "Whoa, are you feeding an army or something?"

"Just a small gathering of townspeople tonight."

He snapped his fingers and beamed at me. "Smart, hosting an event like that. I would have suggested something similar if you'd listened to me."

I resisted the urge to roll my eyes. "Which was clearly not necessary, but thanks for the praise. Let's get to shucking." I handed him a pair of gloves and a small shucking knife. "You want to catch the blade underneath the lip of the shell and pry it open that way. If it doesn't come easy, throw it back in the pot and let it soak some more."

"Sounds simple enough."

"*Yeah.*" I opened the first oyster and put it in a wide bowl that was lined with ice to keep them cool. There was nothing worse than off seafood.

Berk attempted his first shucking, wedging the knife in like I'd shown him. He tried for about two minutes with no luck.

"Try another one," I suggested.

He grabbed a fresh oyster and pried at it again with no success. "*I can do it,*" he said sternly, staring down at the oyster.

I smiled and turned down my brows. "I didn't say that you couldn't. It just takes practice. Keep trying." I went back to opening my own oysters—staring at him probably wasn't helping the issue. I placed a couple more down on the ice, keeping my expression neutral.

"Can you...Can you show me again?" he asked quietly.

"Sure." I grabbed a new oyster and wedged my knife in. "You kinda have to wiggle it a little bit sometimes." I showed how I shimmied the knife until the shell popped open.

"Okay." He attempted it again with a fresh oyster, getting his knife in and really wiggling. After about a minute it popped open. He raised his head and grinned like a small child. "*I did it.*"

"*Yep*, now you only have to do it a hundred more times." I clapped him on the shoulder. We worked together in silence for most of it. It was hard to resent Berk when he was helping me achieve my goals. We were standing so close in the small galley-style kitchen, our shoulders brushing every time he grabbed a new oyster. His cologne was sharp and dark—like licorice and spices. He'd done his hair today with some kind of shiny product and whatever else he used. It took everything in me not to run my fingers through it and mess up its perfection.

When all the oysters were open I placed them in the fridge. Berk stood by, waiting for more instructions.

"Thanks for the help," I said as way of a dismissal.

He raised an eyebrow. "Surely you're not just serving raw oysters?"

I shook my head. "Of course not."

"Then...I'll keep helping."

I looked him up and down appraisingly. "Do you even know how to cook?"

He grinned. "That's never stopped me before. Come on, you know it'll go faster with two people."

He was right about that. Everything was so last minute, and I had a lot to get ready before the party. "*Fine,*" I relented. "You can help, but you're gonna need something."

"What?"

I rummaged through the back closet and found what I was looking for. I looped it over Berk's neck and moved behind him to tie it at his waist.

Berk looked down at himself. "Oh my God."

I turned him around to see, proud of myself. It was an apron with oil-slicked abs printed on its front with the words *kiss the cook* in a fun font at the top.

"It was a gag gift from Rory, for some Christmas a long time ago."

"And this is a requirement to cook in this kitchen?" he asked, looking down at himself.

"Oh, *definitely.*"

He laughed through his nose and put his hands on his hips. "Okay then, let's get started. What's first?"

I showed him my menu: a soup course, the oysters, fresh bread and cheeses, a fruit salad, and lobster rolls as the main entrée.

"That's a lot."

I handed him a clean knife and cutting board. "You can make the fruit salad. It's pretty hard to fuck that up."

He laughed. "Thanks for the vote of confidence."

I smirked down at him. "*Oh,* I have *every* confidence in you. If you can cook half as good as you can deceive and lie you'll be fine."

He rolled his eyes. "*Ha, ha.* Are we still on that topic?"

"Of course."

He began cutting the fruit while I started the base for the soup—combining my mirepoix in a large pot over the stove.

Berk had apparently been holding it in over the last thirty minutes while we shucked oysters, because what I had hoped would be more quiet contemplation, became a yak fest. He *wouldn't stop* talking. First he asked a million questions about where I'd learned to cook (my dad), and how I planned the menu for tonight (everyone's favorites, obviously). Then he moved on to asking about my childhood and growing up on the island. I'd thought we'd covered enough of that yesterday with Rory and Maria. I supposed he was still curious. But was he being genuine?

And I was curious about Berk too—I was. However, I was trying hard to keep my feelings about him separate. I wanted to focus solely on the cooking, on the party, so that I didn't have to worry about my waning resolve against his charm. He was here on Ruby Island to ruin this town, whether he saw it that way or not. I couldn't let someone like that get too close; I couldn't let him in.

"My parents never taught me how to cook," Berk explained. "They tried a few times when I was a kid, though they always gave up. Whenever I didn't succeed immediately they would take over and say I was wasting time or I was screwing it up."

I stirred the soup pot. "*Harsh.*"

"Yeah. The only good thing about the situation is that my sister, Ada, sucks at cooking. She burns water, she's so bad."

I smiled against my better judgment. "Why is that a good thing?"

He shrugged. "Well, like in a lot of patriarchal cultures Turkish women are supposed to be great cooks so that they can prove themselves to their future husbands. However, it's the only thing Ada is truly terrible at. It brings us an odd sense of joy, I guess. Defying our parents' expectations."

"And, you said your sister is in law school to become a lawyer?" *Agh, why am I asking him questions? That only promotes talking more.*

He nodded. "Yep, if she couldn't be an amazing housewife, being an amazing lawyer was the next best thing in my parents' eyes."

"So they have two overachiever children, huh?"

He scoffed. "Try *one*. I'm my parents' biggest failure."

I turned around, brandishing a wooden spoon. "*What?*"

He pressed his lips together into a tight smile, looking down at the cutting board where he was cleaning off the discarded fruit skins. "Yeah, I know you see me as some criminal mastermind or whatever, but I'm actually on my last chance at Sandy Brook. If I don't finish this project with a gold star I'm out of a job. No biggie."

Huh. I'd imagined Berk was some big shot money man at the front of the pack. Maybe Ruby Island was considered small potatoes to these people. " I *do* find that hard to believe." In a bizarre way I was impressed by him. Not because he'd tricked me and Aunt Caroline, but because he'd been so smooth and professional about it. Maybe that was what pissed me off so much. I should have seen it coming, however he was simply a *normal guy*, with wants and needs like everyone else. *Not* a monster in a Gucci suit. Which made this doubly hard.

"I-I'm not much of a success either." I didn't know what possessed me to say it, and yet, it slipped past my lips.

His mouth turned down into a frown. "What do you mean? From what I've seen this week you work extremely hard."

I laughed through my nose. "And what do I have to show for it? Haven't you noticed that you're the only lodger staying here this week?"

He gazed at the counter, which informed me that *he had* noticed. "I thought that was because the season hadn't quite started yet?"

"Yeah." I bit back a bitter laugh. "That's what I tell myself. That's what I tell my aunt Caroline. Truthfully? The inn has been suffering since my parents died a decade ago. We never fully recovered." *In more ways than one.*

"I'm sorry." He turned his head to face me again. "I know you really care about this place. It shows."

I mentally shook my brain and slapped it around. *Get back on track.* "Well that's what tonight is all about. Reminding local business owners in the community that we're here, and we're not going *anywhere*," I said the last bit a little forcefully, though Berk didn't seem to notice.

We cooked the bulk of the morning and into the afternoon—prepping everything we could in advance. It took half the time thanks to my assistant. "Thank you, Berk. You didn't have to help me out like that."

He shrugged, taking off his *kiss the cook* apron. "It's no problem. I said I wanted to help you guys out, and I meant it."

But, did he mean it because he was trying to assuage some of his guilt? Knowing his big deal was screwing us over? I studied him with an analytical eye, trying to find a break in his cheery facade. Who was the *real* Berk Kaplan? Was he truly sweet, or a cutthroat businessman?

"So...am I invited to this shindig?" he asked as we left the kitchen.

"Um, sure. You did half the work, it's only fair."

Is that a good idea? To have a wolf in the henhouse while I was trying to convince all the local business owners to reject the mayor's plan with Sandy Brook?

As if he could tell what I was thinking he said, "Don't worry, Will. I'll be myself tonight, not a land developer or a marketing strategist." He plucked at his shirt and smirked. "Just little old photographer me."

I grinned. "You know, I've yet to see any of these *photographs*. You might be shit at it," I pointed out.

He scoffed and placed his hand on his chest like he'd been affronted. "I'll have you know I'm an excellent photographer. I've been featured in many of my alma mater's issues of The Cawing Blue Jay Gazette."

"Wow, an outstanding accolade at that—*The Cawing Blue Jay Gazette*."

He slapped my arm. "*Shut up*, it's a big deal."

117

"I'm sure."

I leaned against the front counter and caught myself staring at Berk. The light coming in from the stained glass front door washed him in a red glow that suited him. "I should probably get to work, you know, cleaning and stuff like that."

He nodded. "Okay, I'll let you go do that. I'll be upstairs." He pointed up. "What time is this starting?"

I waved my hand through the air. "Around eight. Don't worry, you won't miss it. The acoustics in this old place will let you know when everyone arrives; us island folk are a rowdy bunch."

"Oh totally. From what your cousin Rory told me about you guys, I could be convinced into believing just about anything."

I grinned, thinking back to our conversation. "Yeah, that's true. I guess I'll see you later."

"See you." He climbed the steps to his room leaving me standing on my own. Damn, why did he have to look so good walking away? I shook myself out of my haze and got back to work. The sitting room wasn't going to transform itself.

* * *

Around eight, people began filling in. I greeted them at the door, some old friends, some acquaintances from the community I wanted to get to know better. I'd tried for as wide of a reach as I could.

Aunt Caroline had changed into an old summer dress I remembered from my childhood, her black boot sticking out from underneath. She'd had a good long week of quiet recovery, however she was one of the most extroverted people I'd ever met. Seeing all our neighbors rushing in made her smile with an unbridled joy I hadn't witnessed in a while.

I'd turned the front counter into a bar since the formal dining room was a little small for everyone to gather *and* eat. Wine was uncorked, spirits were opened, and glasses were filled.

Maybe ten or so of our neighbors had arrived by the time Berk came down the stairs, dressed in a crisp black suit. Why he'd brought that with him on a business trip was anyone's guess, however it looked good on him— it was fitted in all the right places. I grabbed a glass of wine off the bar and held it out to him. "You look nice."

He accepted the glass and took a small sip. "Thanks, so do you."

I'd thrown on a more casual outfit comprised of a fitted blue button up and dark wash jeans. This passed for fancy on Ruby Island. Berk on the other hand, would *definitely* stand out. Whether that was good or bad, I was unsure.

"Quite a turnout," Berk said as more people arrived through the front door. Some headed for the sitting room while others streamed into the dining room to grab some food.

"Yeah, it's great." I ran my hand through my messy blond curls. "I honestly hadn't expected it."

Aunt Caroline greeted a new couple; a girl about six or seven hid behind her parents' legs. I waved and she smiled shyly.

Rory and Maria showed up late, which was understandable—Maria looked like she was about to pop. "Dog sitter was late," she said.

I smiled and shrugged to show that I understood completely.

Once everyone was gathered I moved to the center of the sitting room with my glass of wine and turned down the music. I'd brought out grandpa's old turntable and a couple of his favorite jazz records. Classy as ever, that man. I tapped the side of my glass to get everyone's attention. I wasn't great at public speaking—or speaking to a large group of people in general—however I pushed through, understanding how important tonight was.

"Hello, everybody. I'm so glad that you all could make it. I know some of you fairly well. I've lived on Ruby Island my whole life, right upstairs in this inn. Others I'd like to get to know a little bit better. If you couldn't tell from who is standing around you, you're all local business owners on Ruby Island—whether on Main Street or elsewhere. I'd like this to become a regular occurrence throughout the year."

I tugged at my tight collar, feeling the eyes on me. "A night where we can come together and talk about how things are going. How we can improve our profits and work together to create a community that we all want to live and work in. The Ruby Inn has been one of the most important businesses on the island since its construction at the turn of the century by my great-great grandfather James Kirkpatrick. I'm sure some of you know the story, the history of the island, even better than me. We need to preserve that history, and tonight, coming together, is the first step."

Everyone clapped, which I wasn't expecting. It wasn't that kind of a speech, although I was glad anyway. Smiles followed me as I wandered across the room. Aunt Caroline put her arms around me and gave me a tight squeeze. "That was *beautiful*, Willy."

"Thanks." I lowered my voice to a whisper. "Can you maybe not call me Willy in front of our neighbors?"

She raised an eyebrow. "Why?"

"It's not a very respectable title."

Berk, who was standing close by with his glass of wine, grinned. "*I like it.* It's charming."

I narrowed my eyes at him.

"See?" Aunt Caroline said. "Berk thinks it's charming."

"*Well if Berk thinks so.*" I smiled tightly, pulling my lips against my teeth. "Then it *must* be true."

Aunt Caroline slapped my upper arm. "Oh, *hush*. We have guests to entertain. Be nice to Berk."

"I wouldn't dream of not being nice to Berk."

Aunt Caroline left me to hobble over to the couch to talk to Rory and Maria. Maria was fanning her face with her hand. Yeah, the old inn was warming to an uncomfortable temperature with all the bodies pressed together. I squeezed past a group of people and cracked open a window, letting in the fresh ocean breeze.

The night went off without a hitch. I got to talk with lots of people, many of whom had great ideas I wanted to remember to write down. It didn't feel so scary when we were all together. They could tell me about their struggles and I could relate. Dwindling tourism had been hard on everyone, not just the inn. It was an underlying problem on Ruby Island that no one had wanted to talk about—at least not with each other.

I was also hoping that we'd be able to form some partnerships. I had my eye on a deal with the local bakery, Comfort by the Slice. They could recommend the inn to new tourists, and we could stock their baked goods for our morning breakfast bar.

"Your party seems to be a success," Berk said over my shoulder. I'd barely seen him all night; he'd been keeping to himself.

I turned to face him. "Oh yeah? What do land developers consider a success? None of these people have given me any money yet."

He rolled his eyes at the jab. "Most of marketing is about being seen, being present. You did that tonight. Money is always the last step in the process."

"Really?" I'd assumed money was their first priority. Berk's usual almond skin was flushed and his lips were stained red from the wine.

"Oh yeah." He waved his hand through the air—thankfully not the one holding the half-full wineglass.

"How many glasses have you had?" I asked.

He took a sip of wine, then smiled absentmindedly. "I promise I won't throw up on you again. I'm *barely* tipsy."

I couldn't exactly judge him, I'd had a few glasses myself. Something about being in a room packed with people made me anxious.

Aunt Caroline came up from behind me. "Willy dear, can you bring out the second cheese platter from the fridge? We're about to run out."

I grinned. "Of course."

"I'll help," Berk insisted.

He followed me through the hidden swinging door to the kitchen. I hadn't even made it to the fridge before there was a tug on my wrist. Berk pulled me backwards and then pushed me up against the counter, causing an empty bowl to clatter to the ground. "What are you doing?" I asked in surprise.

The kitchen was dark without any lights on. The pale moonlight coming in through the window was only enough to make out the contours of his face.

"This," he said, and pressed his lips against mine.

Is this happening? I was going to push him away, however my body did the opposite—my arms went slack and my mouth opened, inviting him in. He tasted like wine and sage, his lips pillowy soft. His weight pressed against my body, pushing me against the counter. He came up for air, panting warm breath against my cheek.

Fuck it. I threaded my arms around his waist and pulled him in closer, crushing his lips against mine. He was so warm and solid. My hands snaked underneath his suit jacket, feeling the contours of his chest and shoulder blades.

"Willy, are you coming back?" The light flicked on, illuminating our rather precarious position. Aunt Caroline blushed. "Oh, hello. Well, I'll just be outside, don't mind me," she said as she slipped out the door.

My heart hammered in my ribcage, thrumming blood throughout my body. I released Berk and straightened a fraction, pulling at my collar and clearing my throat. "Um, better get back to my guests, it would be rude to hide from them."

Berk's expression was hard to read, with his eyes wide and his mouth slightly open. He shook his head and took a step back. "Of course. You're right. Wouldn't want to be rude."

I paused, staring into his eyes for a second too long before escaping towards the lobby.

What just happened?

NINE

Berk

Well that happened.

I hadn't planned on it, exactly. Alcohol *may* have played a role, though I hadn't been lying when I'd said I was only tipsy, so I couldn't exactly *blame* the wine. Getting caught was certainly *an experience*. It kinda reminded me of when I was sixteen and I got caught making out with a guy I liked by my sister—she was *not* supposed to be home yet.

Did Will regret it? He'd left so quickly afterward. Maybe he was merely embarrassed to be caught by Caroline. His cheeks had been *so* red; I'd been afraid he was going to burst into flames or something.

Something about hearing Will's speech and seeing how proud he was of himself made him so hot. I *had* to kiss him.

I waited a few seconds in the kitchen and then went back to the party to continue mingling like nothing had happened.

Will was busy—or made himself busy—having conversations and entertaining his neighbors. Every time I found him in the crowd and caught his eye he looked away just as fast, the tips of his ears still red. It was fun to know I had such a strong effect on him.

When the night finally came to a close Will and Caroline stood by the front door and said their goodbyes as people left. The inn was a little messy, though overall, no more worse for wear.

Once it was only the three of us the awkward tension was back. "I can help Caroline upstairs if you want to put the food away," I offered.

Will jumped at the opportunity. "Sure, that sounds good." He started backing away slowly. "Thanks."

Picking my battles wisely, Caroline had seemed like the easier adversary —even though I would rather be in a dark kitchen with Will again.

I took her arm and we hobbled up the many flights of stairs. As we climbed—getting further away from Will's prying ears—Caroline's smile grew. "So...what are your intentions with my nephew?" she asked.

"*Intentions?*" I hadn't realized I'd be answering twenty questions when I chose this option. I should have picked the dark kitchen.

"Yes. You know, Will is more fragile than he looks. I know he's tall and sturdy, but he has a heart easily broken."

"Oh?" I was intrigued. "How so?" She was right, he *didn't* seem fragile at all to me—that emotional wall of a man.

"Well, it's not really my place to tell people his business. Let's just say he's been through a lot of heartache in his adult years and he carries that heavy burden. I wouldn't want you punching holes in the wall of a house with a crumbling foundation."

I smiled. "I promise I won't punch any holes in the wall. I'm not sure I *could* punch a hole in the wall...metaphorically speaking."

I usually didn't stick around long enough to even admire the walls, much less destroy them.

"Good, that's good." We reached the third floor landing and walked to Caroline's bedroom door. She turned around at the threshold. "I know you're leaving in a week and going back to Boston, but Will really likes you."

I scrunched my brow, hoping I seemed nonchalant. "He does? How can you tell?"

She grinned and patted my cheek. "I've known that boy his entire life. I know when he's pretending and when he's not."

"*Hmm*, okay."

Her smile dropped a fraction. "On that note, I can also tell when *you're* pretending. Will thinks I don't know why you're *really* on Ruby

Island, like it's a well-guarded secret." She shrugged. "It was pretty obvious to me."

My mouth dropped open. "You've known this entire time? Why didn't you say anything?"

She shook her head and laughed. "Will gets these ideas into his head that he's protecting me in some way by keeping things from me. However I knew right off the bat. When the woman who booked your room called to make the reservation the caller ID said Sandy Brook. I'd never heard the name before, though it wasn't hard to search for it on the computer."

I raised an eyebrow. "You asked me about the woman who'd booked the reservations when I first checked in, didn't you?"

She smiled mischievously. "I was testing you of course."

I was baffled. "But...why?

She waved her hand through the air. "There's not much else to do when you have to sit down all day with a boot on your foot. It was driving me crazy. I only wanted to play along and have some fun. Even though— bless his heart—Will is a *terrible* actor."

I laughed through my nose. "He really is."

"And I was surprised when I saw some of your photographs. You're quite talented.

I grinned. "Thanks. I wasn't lying about that, at least."

"Yes, so now that we're on the same page..." She poked at my chest. "Don't break my nephew's heart."

"I'll do my best, Caroline."

She narrowed her eyes and grinned. *"You better."* She turned and slipped into her room—as easily as one can when they're hobbling with a broken ankle.

Huh, that was interesting. Apparently we'd all been playacting with each other the last few days for no reason. Did everyone on the island know I was from Sandy Brook? Surely not, otherwise tonight would have gone pretty differently.

I slowly retraced my steps and stopped at the second floor landing. *Should I go see if he needs more help?* Or did he want to be left alone? The jury was still out on whether the kiss was being forgotten about or not. He *had* kissed me back, that was a fact. Did he want to do it again, though?

I decided to escape to my room and give him some space. If his heart was truly as fragile as Caroline thought it was I didn't need to add pressure to the organ.

I took a quick selfie of me on the bed and sent it to my sister before I crashed.

B: Consider this party boy officially pooped.

* * *

The next day I found Caroline in the sitting room knitting with that same blue wool. It seemed to be progressing quickly—whatever it was. "Good morning," I greeted as I sat down on the sofa. These last few days had been fairly leisurely compared to most. Mr. Schwimmer was happy with my progress—as happy as that man could be—and the mayor was doing everything he needed to do on his end. I had a meeting scheduled with him tomorrow to see where we were with the progression of the project. I needed to start campaigning. True to my word, I'd been completely unbiased at last night's little soirée. I hadn't mentioned the economy or the possible new development *at all*—which I was pretty proud of. Now however, I had to speed up my timeline to make sure I stayed on target. I'd been *a little* too distracted lately.

"Morning, dear. Did you have an eventful night?"she asked with one eyebrow raised.

If I had been drinking something it would have sputtered out onto the floor. "What do you mean?" I asked innocently, trying to hide the horror from my face. I hadn't seen Will at all since deciding to give him some breathing room.

She pivoted, probably realizing I wasn't going to tell her anything salacious. "At the party, dear. It's not often we get everyone together like that. Wasn't it nice?"

"Oh yes, the *party* was pretty fun. Usually at those kinds of mixers I have to do a lot of elbow rubbing, so it was nice to relax and be myself." I leaned forward and lowered my volume to a whisper. "On that note, are we continuing this little charade with Will, or..."

She waved her hand like it was inconsequential. "Oh, might as well. It's not often something dramatic like this happens on Ruby Island. You're livening the place up, honestly. And if it makes him feel better imagining he's protecting me from some big bad evil, then I say let him."

I laughed through my nose. "Okay, if you say so, Caroline."

As if on cue, Will entered the room through the lobby. He'd clearly been cleaning all morning before I got up. The sitting room was back to its immaculate state after last night's rambunctious crowd, and the lobby looked like it had been spit shined.

"Oh." He stopped at the threshold. "Morning."

I grinned, hoping to convey my charm. "Good morning yourself. How goes it?"

"*Uh*, fine." He took a couple small steps, awkwardly loitering between rooms.

Caroline continued to look down at her knitting, although I caught a smirk at the corner of her lips she was trying her best to hide.

I crossed my legs and leaned back, hoping to look casual. "I was going to explore the town today. I've seen it by sea, but I haven't gotten to walk around on foot. Do you want to join me?" I asked, trying to sound unbothered either way he answered.

"Oh, uh, I don't have time for that." He crossed his arms over his chest. "I have a lot to do around here."

Caroline covered a snort with her hand. "We have no lodgers and you've been cleaning for hours, what other excuses can you come up with?"

"That's not—"

"Exactly, so go have fun." She batted her hand in the air. "Everything will still be here when you get back."

He put his hand on his hip and rocked on his heels.

Is he nervous?

"Uh, okay. I guess so."

"Great." I stood from the sofa. "Let me just grab my coat. It's windy out there."

"Okay."

When I went upstairs to get my coat my phone buzzed—it was Ada. I answered and quickly said, "I might be on a date, so I'll have to call you back later."

She laughed. "Okay, have fun *heartbreaker.*"

I chuckled and ended the call. *Am I actually a heartbreaker?* I didn't think any of the guys I'd dated would say their hearts were *broken* over me. I'd never really dated anyone long enough to find out. I'd be gone in a week if everything went as planned. Surely that wasn't long enough to break someone's heart?

I jogged down the stairs to the lobby. Will had found his own coat— a denim jacket—and put on his hat, covering his dirty blond curls. He hadn't shaved since I'd arrived and a short beard was growing in, not red like his cousins, but dark blond.

"Ready?" he asked, though he seemed unsure himself.

"Yep, lead the way." I was glad I wore my chinos and boat shoes and not something restricting.

He opened the door, said goodbye to Caroline, and ventured down the steps to the road.

I cleared my throat. "I've been meaning to ask, how come Ruby Island doesn't have a taxi service? That seems like a big hindrance for you guys."

Will cringed. "Yeah, we used to have one, of a sort. A guy called Larry would pick people up from the marina for us and drive them to the inn. He moved away after the pandemic hit so he could be closer to his family, and I guess nothing ever filled his place."

"You should probably add that to your list," I suggested.

He raised an eyebrow. "My list?"

I laughed through my nose and slapped his shoulder. "You think I haven't noticed you always scribbling in that notebook of yours? It's not hard to guess its contents; I assume it's your big marketing plan for the inn?"

He rubbed the back of his neck. "Uh, yeah. I suppose you could call it that. I have a lot of ideas."

"That's good." And I meant it. Just because the resort was going in, didn't mean I wanted his family's generations-old business to fail. It would be hard work, but I truly believed both could thrive.

"So what exactly did you want to see?" he asked. The dusty road sloped down towards the middle of town.

"I don't know." I shrugged. "You tell me. What are your favorite places on Ruby Island?"

He put his hands in his coat pockets. "Um, I'm not sure."

I scoffed. "Oh, come on. You have to have a favorite, you've lived here your whole life."

His lips pulled into a wide smile. "Okay, okay. I have *something*, although it's better as a surprise."

I narrowed my eyes at him. "I *hate* surprises."

He grinned, laugh lines creasing around his mouth. "*Good*, even better, then."

"*Jerk.*"

"*Capitalist schmuck.*"

I smiled against my better judgment and sighed. "*Fine*, whatever. Take me to your surprise."

The corner of his mouth lifted as he turned back towards the road. "We have to stop in town first, that's part of the deal."

"Okay." We walked along the dusty dirt path, straight down the middle, because why not? There were no cars to hit us, after all.

Along Main Street lights were lit and colorful banners were hung. Only a few people were wandering around the cobblestone walkway.

Will stopped us in front of a small shop with a pink wooden sign hanging from the awning, *Supernova Sweets*.

"Pastries?" I asked, intrigued. That was part of his master plan?

"Of course."

We entered the space. The brick was painted a galaxy purple, and a plaster spaceship hung from the wall next to a neon sign of their logo—an exploding golden star.

"What are you getting?" he asked. Clearly he knew his order already.

"Uh, I don't know. I haven't had a donut since I was a kid."

He raised an eyebrow "Really? That's a long time to go without a donut."

"Yeah, I'm not a huge sugar person." I peered inside the glass case displaying my options. There was the classic pink frosting with sprinkles, there was the maple bar, the apple fritter, and the bear claw. All sensible options.

"Hey, Mac," Will called out to the man behind the counter. "Let me get the *Super Cosmo five thousand*."

I laughed. "What is *that*?"

Mac slid open the glass case and grabbed a donut that was in the shape of what I guessed was supposed to resemble a rocket, with a slender shuttle and fat rocket thruster at the end. It kinda resembled another thing entirely, if I was being honest, however I didn't say that in front of what was probably the shop's owner.

Will turned to me and explained, "It's a vanilla donut in the front, chocolate in the back, cream filled on one side, stuffed with peanut butter cereal on the other, covered in frosting, more chocolate, and of course...sprinkles." He took the bag with the donut inside. "I've been getting this one since I was in high school."

For some reason I didn't peg Will as a *Super Cosmo five thousand* kinda guy. He seemed more down-home-small-country maple bar...or bear claw if he was *really* getting wild. This was a side of Will I hadn't seen before.

"Decide what you're getting?" he asked.

"Uh, do you have something savory?" I asked, examining the display case once more.

"Yeah, I've got just the thing for you," Mac said with a grin, pointing at the card in the case. "Cheddar and Jalapeño donut with a chive frosting."

"Okay then, I guess I'll try that." I wouldn't say that I was *super* daring when it came to food. Maybe with other aspects of my life, however food was *not* one of them. A savory cheddar donut could be a disaster.

Will insisted he pay for the donuts even though *I* had invited *him* on my day out—the stubborn bastard. We got our donuts to go and walked back through Main Street.

"So, it's not in town, then?" I was trying to pry clues from Will, however his face was impassive; he gave me nothing to work with.

"Nope."

Downtown faded behind us as we walked further East. I'd seen this area on the boat tour, of course, though it looked pretty different from up here. We were practically on the same lot that Sandy Brook was looking to buy—an open field of tall grass that was starting to dry out from the late spring sun. Wildflowers dotted the landscape along with short twisting trees that stood in clusters, providing some needed shade.

"Where are we going?" We seemed to be walking towards nowhere.

"*Hush*, you'll see."

I snorted. "You don't have to be *rude* about it."

He turned around abruptly, and I almost slammed into his chest. He grinned, then put his finger over his mouth.

"*Fine*," I mumbled under my breath.

The tall grasses trailed off as the dirt transformed into rocky cliffs. I couldn't tell what we were supposed to be doing here until we reached a certain angle and I caught the wooden steps built into the craggy cliffside. I'd forgotten I'd seen those earlier in the week.

"Nope." I shook my head. "I don't want to die today. I'd rather get back on a boat without a life vest."

Will had the audacity to laugh. "It's perfectly safe, I *promise*."

I scoffed. "Oh, well if you *promise*, I guess it's okay, then."

We reached the edge where the first tread began. There wasn't even a railing. This monstrosity would definitely be taken out when Sandy Brook took over, it was going to kill somebody.

"Here." Will held out his hand for me.

Oh. I could be persuaded into that. I took his hand—it was warm, and softer than you'd think for someone who worked so hard. And to his credit, it wasn't clammy at all. He wasn't worried about falling to his death, apparently.

"Where does this thing lead, exactly?" I leaned over to get a better look and the queasy angle made me step back.

"You'll see. *Trust me.*"

Do I trust him? He *had* saved my life once already. I supposed I could trust him with it one more time—though I didn't like it. "Screw it, I guess. One second." I pulled out my phone and sent a picture of the stairs to Ada.

B: If I die, this is why.

Will gave me a funny look.

"Oh, just saying a quick goodbye to my family," I explained.

He rolled his eyes. "And you call *me* dramatic."

"*Ha, ha.*"

"Are you ready?" he asked, seemingly content to let me take my time.

"I suppose." I met him on the first step. I decided I wasn't going to look down, since that would be unwise. I'd let Will be my guide dog, leading me down the steps. To where exactly?

What was probably a fairly quick trip normally took us almost ten minutes to get down. It wasn't that I was *afraid* of heights. I just didn't like the idea of falling to my death. That seemed like a rather avoidable and silly way to go. Will didn't seem to mind. He went as slow as I needed, never complaining or begrudging me.

"*Ta-da.*" We must have made it to the bottom. I swept my eyes across the area. The stairs ended at a small semi-secluded beach. Waves crashed up the sand to the rocks that fed into the cliff. It was beautiful, *maybe* worth the arduous journey.

"This is your secret spot?" I asked.

He shrugged. "It's not exactly a secret, I guess. Rory and I spent a lot of time down here in high school. There wasn't much else to do if you could believe it."

I smirked. "I can."

We walked across the sand, leaving the stairs behind. I couldn't help but notice that Will hadn't dropped my hand even though I no longer needed a guide. His fingers were warm and strong, tight around my own.

"Here we are." Two weather-faded lawn chairs sat in the sand, their legs getting eaten by the churning of the tide.

"How long have these been here?" I asked, wiping off the sand from one of their seats.

"Oh, uh, longer than I've been around. It honestly amazes me that they haven't been pulled out to sea during storms or destroyed somehow." He let go of my hand and sat down in the second chair, pulling the donut bag into his lap.

I sat down beside him. The view was spectacular. The sea was calm at the moment, a glacial expanse out in front of us. There were no other dots of land to spot on this side of the island.

"Donut?" He reached into the bag and offered me my strange savory confection.

"I guess so." I grabbed the donut and took a small bite, afraid I was going to hate it. I chewed for a minute while Will waited for my reaction. "It's actually...pretty damn good." I was surprised. *Who knew, huh? Savory donuts. Supernova Sweets would do well with the new tourists.*

Will grinned and then bit into his own monstrosity. The cream oozed from the side and he rushed to lap it up. Something about it was both disgusting and slightly erotic at the same time. I laughed at the sight.

"*What?*" he asked, unaware of the chocolate that dotted his chin.

"Nothing."

We sat and ate our donuts looking out at the ocean and eventually got to talking. It was easy. Will didn't seem mad at me anymore—at least not in any *real* way. I told him more about my sister and he told me about growing up living at the inn.

"That must have been strange," I said. "I'm imagining a Suite Life of Zach and Cody situation, or maybe Eloise."

He laughed. "It wasn't *that* fancy. We were all pretty cramped on the third floor. I loved it, though. I liked helping out my parents and Aunt Caroline. I liked talking to the lodgers and playing with their kids outside on the lawn. Some might have thought it was a strange childhood, but it worked."

I knew his parents were a delicate subject, so I treaded carefully. "And you kept living there, even after..."

He turned to me. "My parents died? *Yeah*, I did. It was...hard, I couldn't simply leave all that behind."

"Can I ask how your parents...you know, passed?" *Is that an inappropriate question?*

He stared out at the sea, his blue eyes reflecting the bright water. "It's no secret. They got into a car crash on the mainland. They were driving back from a business conference for inn and B & B owners. My mom had called me from the car, she'd been so excited, brimming with ideas to improve the inn. It hurts that they never got to see it through."

"I'm sorry." I didn't know what else to say except the lame thing everyone always said.

He met my eye. "Don't be sorry. I'm glad that I was able to talk to her and tell her I loved her. Not everyone gets that chance."

So they'd been trying to make improvements on the inn for over a decade? I couldn't imagine how hard that was to lose both your parents on the same day. I would crumble.

"We should probably head back," he said, taking a look at the time on his phone. "I don't want to leave my aunt alone for too long."

"Yeah, okay." Our donuts were gone and my butt was numb from sitting in that chair for so long. I checked my own phone. I hadn't realized how much time had passed—we'd been talking for a couple hours.

He stood and offered his hand. I didn't want to tell him that I probably had no problem *going up*, it had only been *down* that worried me. I took his hand anyway, finding comfort in his tight grasp. We climbed the stairs in about half the time it took to descend them and made our way back across the island to the inn. He let go of my hand when we reached the porch.

Caroline raised her head as we walked into the lobby. "Good exploring?" she asked.

I nodded. "Yep, perfect."

"Take any good pictures?" she asked with a mischievous smile.

"Oh, uh, no." Right, we were still acting like I was a photographer. "I forgot to take my camera with me. It's all good, though. Plenty of time to take more photos."

Will grinned. "*You know*, I never got to see any of those photos," he reminded me.

"That's right, you haven't."

We waved Caroline goodbye and went up the stairs to my room. "My laptop is on the desk," I explained. I'd already edited a bunch of editorial snapshots for the inn and a few of the island just in case Sandy Brook wanted to use any of them, however they would probably hire someone else to take more pictures once the project was finalized.

The tension while we climbed the stairs was palpable. We'd been alone for hours this morning, though it had still been *almost* public. Anyone could have found us if they tried. Here at the inn, we were truly alone. I opened the door to my room and Will trailed in behind me. Then, I warmed up my computer, sitting down in front of the desk.

"Obviously you can use any photos that you want," I said. "I don't know if you guys have a website or social media, but you should."

He laughed through his nose. "No on both. I'll add it to my list."

No website in this day and age? They really *did* need help.

I opened my files and scrolled through the photos I'd previously edited. I'd only tweaked the lighting and the colors a little bit, nothing extreme—the beauty of the inn and the island did all the real work.

"Wow." Will leaned in, hovering over my shoulder. I could feel his warm breath against my neck. "These are great."

"Thanks." I turned to catch his gaze and found his lips instead. His hand snaked along my jaw as he deepened the kiss. My neck was straining, so I stood to meet him halfway. I locked my arms around his neck and trailed kisses down his jawline, his scruffy facial hair scratching my cheek.

We broke apart. "So, I guess...last night wasn't a fluke?" I asked, taking a second to catch my breath. I'd been worried that I'd scared him off, being so bold. But I couldn't have helped myself, his lopsided smile and kind nature had pulled me in.

I could feel as he grinned against the side of my face. "Apparently not." His hands wound around my waist and under my t-shirt, skimming the muscles of my back.

I leaned in to kiss him again.

"Willy?" a voice shouted from downstairs.

I bit back a laugh. "That woman's timing is impeccable," I whispered against his neck.

He laughed through his nose. "I uh-I better go see what she needs."

I unlatched myself from him. "Okay."

His face was a warm shade of pink, his neck, and what was visible of his chest, flushed. "Rain check?" he asked.

I crossed my arms. "I'll hold you to that."

He grinned. "*Promise*." He slipped out of the room leaving me alone.

Damn, all pent up and nowhere to go.

TEN

Will

I could never be mad at Aunt Caroline, however her timing *did* leave something to be desired. It turned out she'd needed someone to grab her glasses from the other room.

I was *going* to march back up those stairs, straight through Berk's door...but I didn't. I couldn't have Caroline wondering what we were doing upstairs for so long. Not after learning she knew about all my previous one-night stands. Slipping into a lodger's room was *not* a great idea.

When I finally did climb the stairs I passed his room for the next floor. I needed to stay away. Whenever I was around Berk it was easy to forget all the reasons I was meant to be mad at him. He had this magnetism that drew me in against all my better judgment. Between the stupid hair and the eyes—I was outmatched.

I went to bed unsatisfied, although with the knowledge that I'd probably done the right thing. Exploring the island had been fun, though. I'd never brought anyone who wasn't family to my special spot. It's not that it was all that secretive, it was a public beach, however it was *my* beach, always had been.

I could still feel the soft pressure of his lips on mine as I turned out the light for sleep. My resistance against him was dangerously compromised. Every time I caught him laughing with Aunt Caroline or offering to help me out I softened. He had to be good. He had to be.

* * *

Next on my never-ending list of tasks to improve the inn was to clean out the boathouse. We only had the one small boat, so it didn't actually count as a true *boathouse*. It was basically a storage shed by the water. My parents had used it to host events sometimes back when it was only a *little* messy. Now it was a disaster.

I'd woken up early to conquer the task, knowing it was going to get warm later in the day. I pushed open the heavy barn-style doors to let in some air. A gust of wind sent a wave of dust spiraling. I covered my face

Geez. The whole place was *packed* with stuff. A lot of our belongings when we moved into the inn were initially packed away in the attic. Then the attic had become part of the third story apartment and anything we weren't using got moved to the boathouse. After my parents died even more boxes and memories landed here. *All of their stuff.* Maybe that was why it had taken me so many years to work on it. The task was a painful one.

I hadn't touched anything in a decade. There was simply too much to go through in one day. If I could at least move some of it into the loft to get it out of the way, I could clean the space and take some photos for the new website. As much as I hated it, Berk had been correct about the website. I wasn't a particularly tech-savvy person, however everything was made easy now. I only had to pick a domain name, *The Ruby Island Inn*, choose a nice looking preset, and suddenly there was a website with a contact page. I'd have to get someone to help me figure out how people could book a room that way, but...baby steps.

First, I needed to move all this stuff. I hesitated to call it junk, however with a decade of space between it and me I could see that most of it was probably going to be sentimental. That's why it was out here and not inside being used. I passed a mountain of plastic storage bins, stacked three high. This was going to be a *long* day.

I tried moving some of the boxes into the loft without looking through them, however after a few trips curiosity got the better of me.

Then I wasn't so much *moving* them as I was *sorting* through them. Some items had been donated only months after it happened: clothes, shoes, and bedding. While others were thrown out, like with toothbrushes and hair ties. Aunt Caroline and I had probably kept a lot more than we should have with the promise that we would go through all of it regularly. Only, it was *too damn hard*. Ten years later, I was sorting through stacks of pens and blank notecards. Why keep anything my parents wouldn't have even known were gone?

I started a trash pile, filling a metal trash can to the brim with miscellaneous nothings. This was so much slower than I'd been hoping. An hour later I'd only gone through three boxes, keeping the majority of two of them.

"Will?" Berk called from outside.

"*In here.*"

He reached the open barn doors and stared in, his eyes bouncing across the space. "Wow, that's a lot of stuff."

I sighed and placed my hands on my hips, already tired. "Yeah, it is."

He took a couple steps inside. He was dressed in a pale suit with matching trousers and his blue boat shoes. "Are you cleaning it out?

I moved a box with my hip, pushing it to the side. "I was hoping to use this space for events or something. That way we can host parties and wedding receptions."

He turned to catch my gaze. "And how is that going?"

I shrugged. "Slowly."

"Do you want some help?" he offered.

I shook my head. "I can't ask that of you. You're probably busy."

He smiled and pulled his brows together. "You didn't ask me, I offered? Plus, I don't have anything to do until this afternoon. *I'm all yours.*"

"Are you sure?" I gestured at the tower of boxes. "It's...a lot."

He slipped off his suit jacket and flexed his biceps for me, posing like a Mr. Olympia winner. "I *think* I can handle it."

I chuckled. "Okay, your choice, tough guy." I directed him to the corner stacked full of items I knew I didn't have to look over: old chairs, stools, and musty cushions. Some of what was stored here had been ruined by the weather. The boathouse was contained, although it wasn't exactly a storage locker since it sat on stilts over the water. Luckily, most of the sentimental stuff had been kept safe in plastic bins.

Another hour later and we were both panting and covered in dust. We carried a heavy hope chest full of my mother's books up to the loft— which was no easy feat.

"*Man.* Your family has a lot of books," Berk said through a heavy breath. He'd rolled his sleeves to his elbow and unbuttoned the top two buttons on his white dress shirt.

This was the third trip of boxes containing old books. Both my parents had read like crazy, my mother most of all. She read anything she could get her hands on: romance, fantasy, non-fiction, cookbooks, and even encyclopedias.

I grinned at the idea. "Yeah, it's a wonder that the inn doesn't have its own library at this point."

Berk shrugged. "Could be a good idea if you can find the space."

Would I want strangers touching my mother's books? She'd probably say yes, that they're just books. But they weren't *just* books, they were *her* books. "Maybe."

We ambled downstairs and surveyed what we'd accomplished so far. There was a wide space in the middle of the room completely empty of boxes. The wooden floors were stained and dirty, in need of a good spit shine, although still in usable shape.

"Thanks for this," I said, finding Berk's gaze beside me. "I know there's still a lot more to go, but getting this big chunk out of the way took me a decade."

"*A decade*, huh?"

Berk had been asking me small questions all morning: what was my mother's favorite book, *Wuthering Heights*: why did my dad own so many ties, *he was a collector*: how come nobody had thought to keep my dad's model pirate ship somewhere inside the inn, *I don't know, but we should*.

It was easy talking with him. Usually I'd only talk about my parents with Aunt Caroline or sometimes Rory—people who knew them. Berk

150

hadn't known them at all and still he seemed curious. It made my heart tight in a way that it hadn't been in a very long time—reviving their memory with somebody new and telling old stories I hadn't thought of in years.

Berk moved to the center of the room. "A couple more hours and you'll have yourself a regular dance hall." He threw his hands in the air and performed what I imagined was an old white guy dance-off. "Dance with me!"

I put my hands out in defense. "I *don't* dance."

He pouted. "Ah, come on. Nobody is going to judge you. Nobody except me." He grinned.

He was so cute; whatever he wanted me to do, I couldn't resist. "Fine." I walked into the circle of cleared space and started rocking back and forth, imagining some kind of annoying wedding playlist in the background, like best hits of the nineties or something. When Rory and Maria had gotten married a couple years ago, Maria and I fought him on almost all the songs—Rory had trash taste in music.

"There you go." Berk moved closer to me, bobbing his head and rocking his hips.

I chuckled at the sight. "I think we're dancing in two different clubs." He looked like he was about ready to mosh and I was two-stepping to a leisurely, sultry ballad.

He wrapped his hands around my neck and lowered his energy. "Is slow more your style? I can do slow."

He was close enough that our chests brushed together as we swayed back and forth in a lazy arc. My chest did a little annoying fluttering thing. "I uh..."

"He looked up at me with his obsidian eyes, wide with anticipation. "*Yes?*"

"I should probably get back to work," I said, my voice low. He was making me want things I shouldn't want and distracting me from my goals. It was painful, but I *slowly* detached from him and turned to find another box.

He didn't seem offended—as far as I could tell. "Okay, back to work it is. Although, you know what they say, *all work and no play made Jack try to kill his wife with an ax.*"

I laughed through my nose and lifted another storage bin. "I don't have an ax laying around—promise." I carried the bin to the loft and moved it to the side with all the others. I wasn't sure what this loft had been used for back in the day, although it was mostly covered in old equipment: there was an old canoe, camping gear, an old army cot that was decades older than me—probably from a real war, and a bunch of other random crap like volleyball nets and outdoor games we'd never played.

Berk came up behind me and lowered a box next to mine; a wave of dust unleashed onto us. I laughed as Berk cringed and I went to wipe off some of the dust from his chin, however I missed and accidentally caught his lip—his soft, plush lip.

"*Oh, what the hell.*"

We clashed together, immediately forgetting about all the dust. My mouth found his and I tugged at his bottom lip with my teeth. He groaned into my mouth. *Oh*, he liked that, *huh*? I did it again and got the same reaction out of him, it was intoxicating. I backed away to catch my breath for a second, then pointed behind him at the old army cot. "You. Me. That cot. Now," I got out, like I was some kind of deranged caveman.

Berk nodded eagerly and in a tangle of limbs we crashed onto the cot. It squeaked with our combined weight—it definitely wasn't made to hold two people, much less fifty years later. That didn't stop us. I tugged at his dusty dress shirt and he ripped at my flannel. Clothes were coming off faster than a strip tease in Atlantic City. He tugged at my hair to bring me closer and I let out a sharp breath of pleasure.

I kissed his jaw and asked in a low voice near his ear, "Mind if I fuck up your pretty hair?"

"*Fuck no.*"

I'd been longing to do it since I'd first met him—thread my fingers through his dark, textured locks. I found his lips again and kissed them

153

until they were red and puffy. One thing led to another and suddenly pants were optional. Through my lusty haze I remembered that we were actually two people, not one. I broke away. "Is all of this...okay?" I asked, practically begging to hear the right answer.

He frowned. "Of course. Don't be tepid on my account." He pulled me back down, his hands exploring *everywhere*.

I was not tepid. I released something that I'd apparently been holding in all week, possibly longer.

* * *

"Will?" a voice called.

I opened my eyes and wiped my face with the heel of my hand. *Did we...fall asleep?*

"Will, are you in here?" the voice called again—such a familiar tone, not Aunt Caroline, not Maria. *Oh crap.*

My eyes darted around, searching for my clothes. I jerked to a sitting position so violently Berk woke up immediately. "Wha—"

"My ex is here," I stage whispered. There was the shirt. I pulled it on, realized it was backwards, and then twisted it around.

I don't think Berk truly understood what was happening, though he had no problem panic-dressing alongside me. After maybe thirty or so seconds we were basically dressed, although clearly rumpled. We could blame it on all the heavy lifting.

I walked to the railing of the loft and leaned over. There she was, in a pretty sundress and sandals. "Alicia?"

She raised her head in surprise. "Oh, you *are* here."

"Um, yeah, just tidying the space." No need to elaborate.

"I can see that. I didn't even know the boathouse *had* a floor."

I laughed lamely, leaning against the railing in an attempt to look casual.

Berk was standing by out of sight, his hands in his trouser pockets and his cheeks a dull pink.

"Um, so, what's up?" I asked. "I didn't know you were in town."

She frowned, placing a hand on her hip. "Rory didn't tell you?"

I barked out a laugh. "It must have slipped his mind. You know how flighty he is."

Berk tried to get my attention and I subtly waved my hand in his direction.

"*Um?*" She frowned, pinching her brows together.

Alicia probably thought I was crazy. It had been long enough that if Berk showed his face now it would be *even more* awkward.

"I have to go," he mouthed. "I'm late for a meeting."

Oh, he *did* say he had something to do later. When was later? I checked my phone for the time. Wow, a few hours had passed.

"Give me one second, Alicia." I raised a finger and turned around with a deep sigh.

Why? I should have dragged Berk to the railing as soon as he was dressed. Why did I imagine hiding him in the loft from my ex was going to work out for me? "Let's go down, I guess," I told him. The damage couldn't be avoided.

Berk smirked, and I hit him in the shoulder.

We walked down the rickety stairs from the loft and Alicia dropped her jaw when she realized that there were two of us. I was trying my damnedest not to blush. It wasn't that I was *embarrassed* exactly, but I'd had enough of people rushing in on me when I was at my most vulnerable.

"Uh, Alicia, this is Berk. He's staying at the inn this week, and he was helping me move some boxes around upstairs." That was *technically* all true.

"Hi?" Alicia waved slowly, her brow raised in suspicion.

"Yes, I was, and now I'm off—I'm late for an important meeting. We lost track of time, I guess. Anyway, nice to meet you." He gave her a measured smile and ran off. He turned back just as he was leaving, and waved.

I returned the gesture, pretending this was all *very normal* behavior.

Why was Alicia here in the first place? Did Aunt Caroline tell her where I was? *Must have.*

"*So.*" I dragged out the word, placing my hands in my front pockets. "What are you doing on the island? Back for a visit?" If we just ignored what had happened maybe this would all go smoothly. *Well*, as smoothly as it could when you were forced to talk to the ex that messed you up for the first time in a decade.

She cocked her head to the side and narrowed her eyes slightly, as if she was trying to look inside my brain and parse out what was going on. "Yeah, something like that."

"Cool."

She grabbed the cord of her purse with a tight fist. "Do you have a minute to spare?"

Was *she* nervous?

"Uh, yeah, I suppose. Let's go inside, it's all dirty out here." I followed her out of the boathouse and closed the barn doors to keep it clean and dry. We walked to the house in silence; the whole time I was trying to figure out what she wanted and what I was supposed to say. When we slipped inside, Aunt Caroline was sitting behind the front desk.

"Oh good, you found him," she said with a warm smile, lines creasing around her eyes.

So she *had* directed Alicia to the boathouse. I supposed I couldn't be mad at her for that. In all the craziness with the new resort development and Berk occupying all my time, I hadn't remembered to tell her that Alicia was in town and that if she came to the inn to tell her I was out, or dead, even.

Alicia grinned. "Yep, working up quite a sweat with one of your lodgers—Berk, was it?"

Thanks for that Alicia. Why did you have to say that?

Aunt Caroline cocked her head and found my eyes, her smile brightening. She looked like she wanted to laugh at the whole thing, however she contained herself. "Oh yes, Berk is *very* helpful. He's been a delight to have around the inn this past week."

I pointed off to the right. "We're going to go talk in the sitting room." No need to keep this conversation going any longer than necessary. It would only get more awkward.

"All right, dear. Make sure to offer your guest a drink."

"Yes, Aunt Caroline, thank you." Why was she treating me like I was still a teenager? I supposed it *had* been that long since Alicia was last in this house.

As I ushered her into the sitting room I asked gracefully, "Do you want anything to drink? Water? Lemonade? Tea?"

She smiled warmly and sat down in one of the navy upholstered chairs. "I'm okay, thank you."

I sat down on the sofa—which wasn't the closest spot I could have chosen, there being a coffee table separating us. I hoped she didn't notice the distance.

"You seem to have really taken to being an innkeeper. Everything looks great. It feels almost untouched."

"Thanks."

The air was thick with tension. I didn't know what to do with my hands so I shoved them under my legs as subtly as I could.

"And you're happy?" she asked.

The question threw me for a loop. Was I happy? What did happiness look like? I was content. I was fine. But...was I *happy*?

I must have been taking too long to answer because Alicia then added, "You don't have to answer that, It's kind of a nosy question."

"No, it's fine." It wasn't. "I was trying to think how best to answer. Happiness isn't as simple as people always make it seem, right?"

She shrugged. "I guess that depends on the person. Or whether you're trying to give a genuine or placating answer."

"Are *you* happy?" I asked, though I didn't add, *away from me and this island?*

She pulled her red lips into a smile. "Yeah, I am. I work at a law firm in Boston now. I'm due to make junior partner this year, and I...have a boyfriend whom I love."

It seemed like everything had gone great for her since she'd left. "That's great." I smiled tightly and hoped she didn't notice.

"You know..." she paused, fiddling with her nails, chipping them like she had when we were kids, "...sometimes I wonder what my life would look like if I had stayed on Ruby Island; if my parents had stayed." She looked up to catch my gaze.

"*And?* Does it terrify you?"

She laughed through her nose. "No, of course not. I just think sometimes about how as people, we're terrible at predicting the future. We think we're great at it because we can look back in hindsight and alter our predictions, however in reality we have no idea what's coming. Even if we plan ahead. I didn't know exactly what I was going to find when I left Ruby Island, although I'm still glad that I did."

So...she didn't regret anything, *cool*. "I'm happy for you. It sounds like everything worked out."

She grinned. "Yeah. Of course it was hard, harder than I ever thought it would be when I was daydreaming about my future. It was worth it, though."

Why was she telling me all this? Was she *trying* to make me feel terrible? Stabbing me in the gut with all her happiness and niceties. I grinned. "You probably have places to be, don't you? You must have a lot of people you want to catch up with." I stood. "I won't hold you up."

She lowered her brows and stuttered to speak. "Uh, okay."

"Glad we could talk." I wasn't.

"Maybe we could talk again later? she asked, searching my face.

"Sure." That was a no. Sit there and get emotionally pummeled by the girl who'd already broken my heart? When I was down and out with two dead parents and a legacy to take care of? Not likely.

"Okay." She stood there for a second, staring at me. What was she looking for? "I guess I'll see you around. I'll be on the island for a few more days before I go back home to the city."

"Have fun *reminiscing*." It might have been a harsh thing to say, although she didn't seem to take it poorly.

"Bye." She waved and made her way through the arch, past the lobby, and out the front door.

My whole body sagged with relief. I clutched my chest, my heart hammering against my ribs. After taking a second to breathe, I walked out into the lobby where Aunt Caroline studied me.

"That went well?" she asked, though she must have known from my body language that it *had not*.

"Sure."

There was a long pause where I was stuck standing in the middle of the lobby. What was I supposed to do now? My hands grasped at material, holding onto my jeans with a vise-like grip.

"Did Berk leave?" Aunt Caroline asked.

"Uh, he had a meeting or something," I said absentmindedly.

She tapped her fingers against the counter. "Oh?"

I shook my head after realizing what I'd said. I turned towards the front desk. "Uh...I meant a lunch date, meeting, same thing."

Aunt Caroline burst into laughter, the sound echoing across the open space.

"What?" What was so funny?

"Your face, Willy. Did you think I couldn't figure out who Berk was? I've been running this inn for over twenty years. I know how to read people."

I let out an exasperated breath. "You've known this whole time?" How could she have led me on for so long?

She shrugged.

"You didn't say anything."

"Was I supposed to? I guess this is partially my own fault. I pushed the idea that he was only a photographer mostly for the fun of it. It's not often I get a chance to play around."

"Does...he know?" I asked slowly, putting two and two together for the first time all week.

She breathed in deeply and let it out. "As of yesterday, yes. I was going to keep it going for longer, though it seems to be creating more tension that I expected."

I scoffed. "But don't you realize who he is? He works for that development group. They want to build a resort here that would destroy local businesses."

She smiled warmly and batted her hand through the air. "Calm down, Willy. You don't think that developers have tried to buy up Ruby Island in the past?"

I frowned. "They have?"

"Many times, and it never goes anywhere. Berk is simply doing his job like everyone else. It's all going to be fine."

Hearing Aunt Caroline's casual attitude about the whole thing both calmed me and intensified my anxiety. This didn't seem like a *little thing* to me.

"So you and Berk were working in the boathouse?" Aunt Caroline asked, barely containing an outburst of emotion.

"Yes." I tried not to blush. "He was pretty helpful."

"I *bet* he was."

"*Aunt Caroline.*"

She shrugged innocently. "*What?*"

I sighed. "I'm going upstairs, call if you need anything."

She beamed. "Okay, dear."

I turned and stomped up the stairs. Sleeping with Berk had probably been one of my worse ideas. Sleeping with a lodger? And one that was trying to destroy Ruby Island, at that?

Was it going to be awkward when he came back? I guessed I'd have to wait and find out.

ELEVEN

Berk

Will's ex? Everyone had an ex—of course Will would have one. I just hadn't expected them to be a *girl,* and also so beautiful. What was she doing poking around where she didn't belong? And why did I care so much? *Ugh.*

I quickly put on my suit jacket, grabbed my bag with all my papers and my laptop, and hurried out the door again to make it to my meeting with the mayor on time. I *could not* afford to be late, especially with everything riding on this project. If I fucked this, I was going to get fired and my parents would carry the ultimate shame of having a loser son.

I was already sweaty on my way into town and rumpled from the loft. I was pretty sure I had some hay or something stuck in my hair product that I couldn't for the life of me pull out again—it was trapped in amber. Thank God this town was so sedate and laid back, otherwise Mayor Lancaster might have been fuming when I finally arrived at the coffee shop. *Only a few minutes late.* Better than I'd expected, however I shouldn't have been late at all. The island was so small, everything was less than a fifteen-minute walk away.

I smiled sheepishly and tried to tame down my locks with my hand. "Hello, sorry for being late, Mayor Lancaster." I pulled an excuse out of thin air. "I was helping Caroline down at the Ruby Inn. You know Caroline, right? She broke her ankle and has a hard time getting around."

Did it make me a terrible person to use someone else's injury to my advantage? *Probably.* Did it matter right now? *No.*

He smiled, his eyebrows pulling down in sympathy. "I did hear about that—awful thing. That's so great of you for helping her out. And don't worry about it, you're the only thing on my schedule today."

"I am?" I found that hard to believe. Were there no big fish contests to judge or sailboat races to observe? *Whatever* they did for fun out here.

"Well, this project will change the course of Ruby Island. I've been putting a lot of thought into it."

I steadied my features. "As you should. You're so right, Mr. Mayor. This is an important decision, one that *will* impact the island's residents —in a positive way, of course."

He pulled his lips into a nervous smile and rubbed his hands together. "Yes."

"So, I've been doing everything on my end. How has it been going on your side? I heard from Mr. Schwimmer that you've been in contact with Sandy Brook. Any questions so far?"

He folded his hands together on the table between us. "Yes, they sent me some extra sketches, plans, and some financial documents. It was interesting to read, to see how this project would pan out over five to ten years. Those are the details that are extra important to me. The longevity of the island."

"I wholeheartedly agree, Mr. Mayor. It's all part of the big picture, and you have to make *big decisions* to alter *the big picture*."

"Yes, I see that." He took a sip from his Americano. "So...what are our next steps?" he asked.

I launched in on my preplanned attack. "The first thing we'd do after signing the contracts would be to get someone out here to do an updated land survey. We need to make sure the lot we're looking at is the best spot for the resort. All kinds of testing has to be done to ensure we comply with local codes and by-laws. Then after that we would look at improving the image of the island. I've already been working on a marketing package that I can show you."

His face brightened. "Oh yes, that would be wonderful."

I grabbed my laptop from my bag and searched for the presentation I'd spent the last few days working on. "Here we go." I clicked on the file and a picture of the Ruby Inn filled the screen. "Oh, oops. Wrong file." That was the secret project I'd been putting together for Caroline and Will. *Damn, I need to label things better.*

"The Ruby Inn is quite beautiful, isn't it?" Mayor Lancaster said with a smile. "It's been one of the island's most prominent landmarks for decades."

"Yes, it's great. And as I've been explaining to the owners, this new resort deal will only bring in more tourists to fill their rooms. It's a win-win, really."

He clasped his hands together on the table. "Amazing."

I opened the *correct* file and showed him how I planned to rebrand the island. I'd designed a mock-up for a new website with a new logo— the island as it was didn't have either. I wasn't much of an artist so I'd hired someone online to make the design. The logo depicted a red rose hanging over an anchor. It worked with the red white and blue color scheme that the island seemed to love so much already.

He leaned in closer to the screen. "Oh, that's great. Does this new resort have a name yet?" he asked.

That wasn't really in my pay grade, however from looking at other projects we'd worked on, it usually ran along the same lines. "There's nothing final as of yet, however I was imagining something like, Seaview: a Hyacinth Resort and Suites." Hyacinth was the name of a preexisting resort chain down the Massachusetts' coastline that had been developed by Sandy Brook.

"*Seaview.* I like it. Sweet and simple."

"And what a beautiful view it is. Why not highlight that?" This meeting was going great. I tried not to tap my leg under the table; my usual veneer of confidence was rumpled along with my hair.

His features firmed, his eyebrows lowering. "Now I suppose comes the hard part."

"The hard part?" I asked, wondering what he was going to throw at me next.

"Now I have to bring it to the people."

I waved my hand through the air. "That's not the hard part, that's the easy part. Residents of Ruby Island trust you to make decisions for their town; they trust you to know what's best. You just have to lean into that."

He smiled wide, lines creasing around his eyes. "Yes, I suppose you're correct about that. I'm planning a town hall meeting tomorrow to get some feedback from the community. It would be great for you to be there and maybe show your presentation. Visuals make a huge difference."

I spread out my hands and grinned. "Of course."

"Then if everything goes as planned, contracts can be signed and we can get this show on the road."

"Amazing." It wouldn't exactly be a *quick* show. What I didn't tell Mayor Lancaster was that there was usually a two to three year dip in the economy while the resort was being built. It was factored into the stats, although it wasn't exactly *highlighted*. Progress took time. A lull wouldn't kill the island, and after the resort was finished and more people flocked here, it wouldn't matter. They weren't exactly thriving now, anyway.

After the meeting ended I began the slow walk back to the inn. I took my time since I wasn't rushing anymore. The sun beat down on me, the sweat pooling in all the wrong places.

When I got back, Caroline was behind the front desk, which was a surprise. Someone was standing beside the front counter, a suitcase sitting on the floor. *A customer?* They hadn't had a single call in the entire week I'd been staying here. Seeing a customer—or lodger, as they liked to call them—made my heart do a little happy dance. Where was Will? I was sure he would be celebrating too.

I slipped past the front desk, looking back to catch Caroline's gaze before climbing the stairs. I went into no-man's-land, climbing the stairs to the third floor. Will's bedroom door was ajar. "*Will?*" I knocked on the door and pushed it in.

Will was laying on the bed with his hands behind his head, wearing only a pair of blue boxer shorts. He must have taken a shower to wash off all the dust and grime—which I desperately needed.

He looked up, his eyes widening. "Oh, *Berk*." His face was pale and he looked like he'd just woken from a nap.

"That's me." I froze at the threshold, not wanting to invade his personal space uninvited.

He rubbed his eyes with the heel of his hand and sat up in bed, rumpling his dark blue sheets. "Come on in." He patted the empty space beside him.

I laughed through my nose. "But I'm all dirty."

He rolled his eyes. "I'll *wash* the sheets. Come over here."

"Okay, *bossy*." I stepped inside the room and slipped off my shoes before crawling onto the bed. "You know I don't like being bossed around, right?"

He smirked. "Isn't that in your job description?"

I sighed. "Touché"

A stretch of silence filled the room. I'd been holding in questions for the last hour. It was all I could think about during my meeting with the mayor. "So, what happened with that girl?" I asked, trying my best to sound casual, staring into the dark sheets. "Your ex?"

He shuffled and crossed his arms over his chest. "Um, it was fine. She just wanted to catch up."

"Oh, okay."

I couldn't say I'd ever *caught up* with any of my ex's before. Though, I supposed they had probably dated a while, that changed things. He hadn't actually told me that, however the subtext was there—the tension.

"Did you hear what's happening downstairs?" I said, to change the subject. If he didn't want to get into it, I certainly wasn't going to force him.

"Downstairs?"

I grinned, finding his eyes. "Your aunt was checking in a customer."

He cocked his head. "*Are you serious?*"

"Yeah.

A smile spread on his lips and he drew me in, wrapping his muscular arm around my shoulder. I savored the moment. He was out of whatever funk I'd found him in, even if only temporarily.

"Maybe it was the website I designed that did it," I suggested. I'd been meaning to tell him about it and had never quite found the right opportunity.

He pulled away and looked me square in the face, searching my eyes. "You designed a website for the inn?"

"Yeah, I hope that's okay," I said slowly. "I put everything in your name, so I can transfer all the information to you when you get a chance."

"Uh...I already made a website for the inn."

My face warmed. "*You did?*"

"Yeah, yesterday."

Was he mad? "Oh, well..."

He pinched his brows together and motioned his hand towards me. "Let me see yours."

"Okay." I grabbed my laptop from my leather messenger bag and opened it on my knee. I logged into the website and showed him the home page, scrolling through its features.

A cute little line formed between his brows. "*Damn.*"

"What?" I asked. *Does he hate it?*

He groaned. "It's *a lot* better than mine."

I laughed with relief. "Sorry?" Usually I wouldn't care so much about what people thought, however Will was different. Why was he different?

"No, this is great." He smiled. "I know this is kind of your thing. I'm stubborn I guess, always believing I can do something myself."

The design for the inn's website mirrored my package for the island itself, lots of red and white with accents of navy blue. Some of the work still needed to be done, like filling out the *about us* page with more history on the inn and setting up bookings through their new email address.

"So you like it?" I asked, making sure he wasn't placating me.

He grinned. "I love it." He leaned in close to my face and hovered there, looking into my eyes for a second and kissing me slowly on the corner of my lips. "Thanks."

Something in my insides flipped, causing my chest to squeeze in on itself. "You're welcome."

If only I got that kind of thanks from all my attractive clients.

I set down the laptop and kissed him back, pulling us down into the covers. "Just *how* thankful are you?" I asked, my voice low. Was he up for round two?

He smirked, a fire in his eyes. "*This thankful.* He pinned me against the mattress and held my wrists above my head, immobilizing me.

"*Oh, I see.* Can you expand on that?"

* * *

Many hours passed and we called it a night. It was silly, but I was sneaking out of his room with my shoes in my hands—trying to be as quiet as possible. Which wasn't actually all that quiet with the squeaky old stairs straining underneath my weight. When I reached the second floor landing I almost bumped into the woman who had been checking in earlier. "Oh, hi."

She smiled politely and then glanced down at the pair of shoes in my hand.

I rushed to explain. "Uh, they were *muddy*, and I didn't want to ruin these beautiful original floors." I didn't *need* to give her an excuse, however it rolled easily off my tongue. She gave me a weird look as I slipped into my own suite. Now that I didn't have the whole place to myself I'd have to be a little more careful. Though, it *was* kind of fun, messing around.

I dropped my shoes when I got inside and removed all my soiled clothes. Man, they'd experienced *way* too much adventure for one day.

I took a quick shower, which I still hadn't done yet—though it hadn't seemed to bother Will all that much—and redressed in some comfy clothes. I checked my email and found another positive message from Mr. Schwimmer which *almost* made me smile.

The town hall tomorrow would be the final push I needed to get the project completed. I was *so* close to freedom. Though in all honesty, it hadn't been nearly as bad as I'd been expecting. Well, I hadn't been *expecting* much at all. Certainly not Will, or the kind and wonderful Caroline. This town was growing on me, and I needed to pump the brakes. I'd be gone in a few days.

Will had been so immovable, so headstrong when we first met. I'd wanted to win him over and possibly knock him down a peg. I supposed I'd done that. The big challenge that had occupied all of my down time was over.

What if I didn't want it to be over? The big oaf was actually kinda great. It had turned out that he was all bark and no bite—at least only when I *wanted* him to, that was.

My phone started ringing and I rushed to answer it—Ada again. Of course it was, *I had no friends*. I answered and flopped down on the bed to relieve my back. "What's up, sis?"

"Hi, *abi*." She paused. "I'm really sorry," she whispered.

"Um, for what?" I didn't get a chance to hear her reply because the voice suddenly changed.

"Berk?"

It was my mother. Ada was going to *pay* for this.

"Hi, *anne*." I brightened my tone, hoping to make up for the fact that I had been ignoring my parents' calls for the last two weeks.

"Don't *anne* me, Berk. I've been calling and calling, but does my son answer? No, he doesn't. He doesn't respect his parents. He can't pick up the phone when they call him. Too busy, he says."

"Ma, I *have* been busy. Didn't you get my text?"

She laughed, and not in a humorous way. "That *one* little text with a picture of the ocean? That was supposed to summarize what has been going on in your life?"

"Uh—"

"The answer is *no*, Berk Kaplan. No, I demand that you explain in detail everything that has happened this week."

How much detail did she want? Surely I could skip the liaisons with Will. "Fine, Ma, I'm sorry." I told her about Mr. Schwimmer's request and about the island. I didn't exactly stress how crucial this job was to my future employment—there was no reason to scare her. The whole thing took about twenty minutes. She wouldn't stop pestering me for answers, poking and prodding. The whole time I was cursing Ada for tricking me into this familial bonding session.

"When are you coming home?" she asked finally.

I rubbed my temples. "Uh, in a few days if everything wraps up nicely."

"*Hmm*, good. My friend Emine is in town. You remember Emine, right? Anyway, she brought her daughter with her; she's looking at colleges in Boston."

"Colleges?" Not only could I read through the lines and see what my mother was pushing for, she was pushing a *college-aged* kid at me. "You want me to *meet* someone younger than Ada? Ma, that's gross."

She pshawed. "Men have been doing it for centuries, what's the problem?"

I sighed. "You know what the problem is, Ma. Why do you keep insisting I meet all your friend's daughters?"

The line went quiet for a second. "You never know, Berk. There might be one that you're compatible with."

I tried to control my blood pressure, taking in deep breaths. "Ma, that's not how it works."

"Why not?" she whined. "I want grandchildren, and Ada is too busy with university to meet someone right now. When will I have my grandchildren if you only go out to your *clubs*? *Hmm?*"

How was I even supposed to answer that question? What if I *never* wanted kids? I couldn't exactly tell *her* that. It would crush her heart. She seemed to have this idea that if I only met the perfect girl, or if the circumstances were *just right*, I'd be able to give her what she wanted.

"I'm not even thirty yet, Ma. Let me get a dog or something first, a houseplant, even."

She laughed. "You kill all your plants, Ada told me so."

"Exactly, so why do you want me to try and raise a baby?"

"You only have to do the easy part. A good wife will do the rest."

I let out a long breath. "That's so sexist, Ma. Didn't your generation fight for equal rights for women? Don't you want Ada to succeed in university without a baby on her hip?"

She let out an exasperated sigh. "Yes, however you're the *eldest*, Berk. If you only go to clubs, and your sister is always working, when am I going to get my grandchildren?"

Never? Did it matter? Was the Kaplan line *so* special that it demanded to be continued?

"When one of us is ready. And not to burst your bubble, Ma, but it's probably not going to be me. And definitely not if you keep pushing these college-aged girls at me like I'm a cash cow or something."

"If you only met her—"

"*No*, Ma. Nothing is going to change the way that I was made. If I decide to have kids one day in the future, you'll be the *first* to know. *I promise.*"

She clucked her tongue. "Fine, be that way, just know that it makes your mother cry."

"*Ma.*"

"No, you've been incredibly clear. I'll give you back to your sister now." There was silence over the line and then a scuffling sound.

"I am *so* sorry," Ada said quietly, probably trying to get out of Ma's earshot.

"You're *not* forgiven."

Ada rushed on, "She demanded that I call you and she took the phone as soon as you answered. What was I supposed to do?"

"*Anything!*" I cried out. "Claim your phone was dead or smash it against the ground if you had to."

Ada scoffed. "*Berk*, you are *so* dramatic."

"This *family* is dramatic," I corrected. "Didn't you hear Ma? I'm basically destroying our lineage by being gay, because I don't want to have a baby with a barely legal coed."

She sucked her teeth. "Yeah, that didn't go very well."

"*No shit.*"

I'd been avoiding my parents for a reason. I guessed I should be grateful that for whatever explanation my father was out of the house. If he had been home he would have been first on the call.

"Um, so how's it going?" she asked sheepishly, knowing she was in the dog house.

I sighed as loud as humanly possible. "Fine I guess, all things considered."

"What about that guy you like? Anything on that front?"

My chest did a little wobble and I forced it to still. "We might have *come together*, as The Beatles would say."

She laughed through her nose. "*Ew*, I *so* did not need to know that."

I barked out a laugh. "I didn't mean it like *that*, it's part of the song!"

"Yeah, I know the song. Anyway, that's great for you. I guess that little island isn't as boring as you thought it would be? Before, you acted like it was going to be torture."

My voice dropped to a whisper. "Yeah, I suppose so."

"*Hmm*."

"I should probably go," I said. "I have to finish a presentation for tomorrow afternoon. I have to give a speech at this town hall meeting."

"Town hall meeting, huh? Sounds *super* fun."

I laughed. "Yeah, I'm sure all the old white people will have a lot to say. Or whoever goes to these things."

She sobered from laughing and cleared her throat. "Well, have fun. And I'm sorry again."

I rolled my eyes even though she couldn't see it. "It's fine, sis. Just try to avoid doing it in the future. What's the point in being the favorite youngest child if you can't use it to your advantage?"

She giggled. "Okay, I'll practice pouting or something."

"Goodnight."

"Bye, *abi*."

I ended the call and starfished out on the bed. How could Ma want me to have kids? I couldn't even take care of *myself* correctly. I'd screw up a kid so fast. I was benefiting society by *not* having a baby. I'd be a terrible father.

Though a small sliver in the back of my brain was wondering what a baby with Will's and my genetics would look like, I knew it was stupid and impossible. In a few days I would be gone, and my God I really needed to start acting like it. My mother's nagging only confirmed what I had always known. I couldn't handle a relationship. Always fighting, always bickering and controlling each other.

No way. I was single for good reason.

TWELVE

Will

I knocked on Berk's door the next morning with a silver breakfast tray resting on my raised knee to keep it steady. I'd laid out everything: toast, butter, jams, coffee, oatmeal, fruit, eggs, and fried potatoes. It was the full deal.

When he didn't answer I slowly pushed open the unlocked door. I wasn't used to walking into a lodger's room without permission, but this was *Berk's* room. And he wasn't really a lodger anymore...was he? I didn't know what he was. What *we* were.

I found him curled up asleep in the bed, his mouth gaping open. *Sexy.*

I set the breakfast tray on the corner of the desk—avoiding any of the papers that were laid out—and crouched down by the side of the bed. I ran a hand through his unstyled dark locks and leaned down to kiss the corner of his lips. "*Good morning,*" I whispered.

He cracked open one eye and grinned. "What are you doing here?" he mumbled.

"I brought you breakfast. I hope that's okay." I knew what time he usually got up in the morning, so it wasn't *too* early.

He rubbed his eyes and pushed himself up against the headboard. He'd slept shirtless and wore silky, gray pajama bottoms. "You brought me breakfast in bed?" he asked with surprise in his voice.

"Uh, yeah." I rubbed the back of my neck and stared at the sheets.

His face broke out in a grin. "Do you offer this service to *all* your customers?"

I laughed through my nose and leaned in. "No, only the *really cute* ones."

He patted the space on the bed beside him. "*Promise?*"

"Promise." I joined him underneath the covers and wrapped myself around his frame. Where his bare arm touched mine was warm to the touch.

"Are you going to the town hall meeting today?" he asked out of the blue.

Did he actually want to talk about this? I thought we were kind of ignoring the subject now that we'd gotten...closer. "Yeah, Rory is going to pick all of us up in his truck."

He paused, then turned his head back to me. "I'm presenting."

I nodded. "I figured you would be." This was Berk's last chance to win over the island, and *damn* was he charming.

We laid in bed for a while, not saying much of anything. The angle of the sun coming in through the blinds was about to hit my face, so I forced myself to stand and grab the breakfast tray. "Your meal awaits you, sir." I placed the tray over Berk's lap and pulled the cloche off with a flourish.

He smiled brightly and examined the spread. "Whoa. Did you actually think I could eat all of this?"

I shrugged and sat beside him, bending the mattress down with our combined weight. "Maybe I'm trying to fatten you up." Berk was pretty skinny, although he obviously spent some time in the gym judging by his muscled arms and chest.

He chuckled. "*Many* have tried, *many* have failed. My aunts force feed me every holiday and it does nothing."

"*Holidays.* Is your family religious?" I asked. He'd told me about his sister and briefly about his parents, although we'd skipped over the big topics.

He cringed, pinching his features together.

"Sore subject?" Should I not have brought it up?

"No, it's just *complicated*. I'd say my family is culturally Muslim, but not that religious. A lot of Turkish customs and holidays align with Islam, though my family doesn't really practice."

"Are *you* religious?" I asked.

He barked out a laugh. "*No*, I'm not. Far from it." He turned to catch my gaze. "Are you? The Irish are usually pretty Catholic, I thought."

I shook my head. "I guess you could call me agnostic. My aunt is Catholic. My parents were Catholic adjacent. I'm open to there being a god or something bigger than myself, however I'm also not holding my breath, if you know what I mean."

He nodded. "*Gotcha.*"

We spent the rest of the morning picking at the breakfast tray and spending time together. It was nice just *being* with someone, doing nothing at all and lazing under the sheets. This room was a bubble where we didn't have to worry about our inevitable separation or the fact that we were fighting on different sides of a life-changing decision.

I was technically supposed to be working downstairs, preparing for the day. We *finally* had another lodger besides Berk. Though, if a lodger needed something Aunt Caroline was at the front desk. She'd been feeling a bit better as the week went on and she'd started doing some small things around the inn on her crutches, like paperwork or fluffing the pillows. Nothing too tiring.

When it came time for the town hall meeting we all went as one, seeing as we were all going to the same place. Berk was wearing his tight blue suit and the shiny leather loafers he'd been wearing when I met him. With his little messenger bag over his hip he looked like the perfect city boy. If the evening hadn't been filling me with anxiety I'd be strangely thrilled by his corporate look. Berk getting all dressed up made me want to take it all off again.

Rory's truck wasn't meant for so many people, so *I* was sitting in the bed of the truck with Barnabas while everyone else sat up front. He didn't seem to mind the company; he wagged his tail and barked at me for scratches.

The small parking lot beside the recreation center was filled, so we parked over in the tall beach grass along with many others. It seemed like *everyone* had come to see this presentation.

Knowing what Aunt Caroline had told me, I wondered how many times they'd done this exact dance over the years. Would this be the first time it stuck? Due to my little event a few nights ago I'd gotten acquainted, or reacquainted, with many of the local business owners in the area. I hoped that we could all stick together on this thing and—sorry Berk—crush the idea before it got out of hand.

The midafternoon sun was high in the sky, beating down on my back. The recreation center was luckily one of the only buildings on the island with air conditioning. I was grateful for it then.

We filed inside with the others trailing in, Berk ahead of the pack. We were a little early, however it seemed like everybody else had thought of the same idea.

The recreation center was a multi-use building. Sometimes it was the high school basketball court and other times it was used as a stage area for the local theater troupe. Currently it was in town hall mode—metal folding chairs were set out in rows and an old wooden podium sat at the front of the room for the Mayor and Berk to present and answer questions. Ruby Island was small, so the town counsel was *also* small. It consisted of Mayor Lancaster, Mrs. Dirk—the choir teacher, and Samuel Evans—the guy who owned and ran the marina. *Not a terribly intimidating group of people.*

We found ourselves a place to sit with Barnabas laying down at my feet. The room was filled with familiar faces—some were business owners, while some were merely residents, either year round or part time. This concerned all of us. Maria and Rory sat together on the other side of Aunt Caroline. Maria caught my gaze and smiled, no doubt trying to be reassuring.

Mayor Lancaster was already standing at the front of the rectangular room, dressed in a blue seersucker suit. It almost made me laugh. Had Berk and the mayor color coordinated? He greeted people as they filled in and shook some hands. Mayor Lancaster had managed to win his seat every election cycle for the last fifteen years. I remembered voting for him when I was only a teenager.

He tapped the microphone that was sitting atop the podium and smiled brightly. "Good afternoon everyone. I'm so glad that you all could make it today. I know that many of you have busy schedules, so we want to keep this as brief as possible. Please hold your questions until the end and we will answer them in the order that they were received. I have something I want to say first and then I'll pass off the microphone to someone you've all probably seen around town, Berk Kaplan. He's here as a representative from Sandy Brook, the Boston land development firm."

He put on his glasses and pulled out a stack of cards from his suit jacket pocket. "It should come as no surprise to you when I say that the economy of Ruby Island is down. Covid hit the tourism industry hard all over Cape Cod—us most of all. Limited access to the island in combination with a changing of the guard have resulted in a few summers of poor tourism. Most islands in the area have since bounced back, while others like Ruby Island have not."

Berk was waiting patiently off to the side, his laptop bag over his shoulder.

The mayor flipped to the next card. "I know that many of you are wary of bringing outside development to the island. You see them as an intruder trying to change our town. However we *must* change. Change is a necessary part of business and in life. Sandy Brook has proposed a new resort development that could bring in much needed revenue and tourism back to the island. Here to speak on that more, Berk Kaplan, everybody."

The crowd clapped, though it was the quiet and polite kind.

Berk took over Mayor Lancaster's spot at the podium and smiled wide, showing off his white teeth. He had such a great smile and his dark eyes shone even in the harsh overhead lighting.

"Hello everyone. As Mayor Lancaster has said, my name is Berk Kaplan. I'm here on behalf of the Sandy Brook development group." He placed his laptop on the podium and pressed a button on the fob in his hands. A projector mounted on the ceiling flicked on, casting his computer screen against the blank white wall behind him. "I've created a short presentation on what the project could look like and what it could do financially for the island. I've also created a strong marketing package for Ruby Island as a whole to drum up more tourism. You can't bring people in if they don't know who you are, can you?"

Berk worked through his presentation. I'd already seen most of what he was showing the crowd, though some details shone through—the new logo and the new website. He was certainly talented, even if his talents were being used for the wrong reasons.

It was hard to gauge how the crowd was reacting. We'd sat somewhere in the middle of the room and everyone seemed entranced by Berk's captivating personality. The screen switched to the next slide, showing the area that they were planning to build on through many artist's renderings of the new resort. It was massive, bigger even than what I'd imagined. Five stories of white plaster and gray cedar siding. They were trying their best to blend into the style of Ruby Island, but failing miserably. It would easily become the tallest building in town, looming over the landscape.

"And here are some of our projections on how this could affect the local economy." He flashed a few reports across the screen. Charts and graphs that looked impressive, though probably didn't mean all that much. Bars of red, green, and blue that proved...what, exactly?

At the end of the twenty minute presentation I was curious what the final reaction would be. Surely nobody was actually buying his crap —his beautiful, but nonetheless still dirty, crap.

Everyone began to clap, and some even stood. I turned to Aunt Caroline and she seemed as surprised as me, her mouth gaping. Was everyone truly so desperate that they could be hoodwinked this easily? I had the urge to say something. I *needed* to say something.

The Q&A portion of the night began with both Mayor Lancaster and Berk sitting down behind a folding table to the left of the podium. The first few questions asked how the new resort could affect residents' property values.

"The new resort would be subsidized by the state as a way to bring revenue back to the island, so it would hardly affect local property taxes. Maybe a slight increase, if anything at all. Nothing we haven't dealt with before," Mayor Lancaster answered.

Interesting. It almost seemed too good to be true.

A couple people asked how the resort could affect the culture and history of the island. Ruby Island had been more or less the same for the last fifty or sixty years, what would building a massive modern building do to its surroundings? As hard as they'd tried, the design of the mock-ups were a poor imitation at best.

Berk cleared his throat. "We're committed to matching the style of the island as you could tell by the sketches in the presentation. And also, I should be clear that we're only in the very beginning stages of the process. If the people of the island feel like the first concept doesn't match their expectations, then please *speak up*. Most of the changes should be made now while everything is still a hypothetical."

Berk was such a great speaker. He seemed to have an answer for everything that was *perfectly* reasonable. If it didn't piss me off so much it would make me admire him more.

Questions dwindled as the hour went on. Everyone was missing the most *obvious* question and I raised my hand to be given the microphone. The community needed to hear this.

"Yes, Will Kirkpatrick," Mayor Lancaster said.

I stood and avoided looking at Berk. His handsome face wasn't going to stop me from saying what I needed to say. "Yes, hi, I had a question. It hasn't seemed to come up yet. How exactly are businesses going to be impacted in the, I don't know, two or three years it will take for this resort to actually be built?"

Mayor Lancaster had the gall to smile. "How do you mean, son?"

I arched an eyebrow. "I *mean*, that for probably three years that side of the island will be an active construction site. People come to Ruby Island because we have a cozy, small town vibe that relaxes them. You know what's not relaxing? A *jackhammer* or an *excavator*." Several people in the crowd made a noise of agreement. "Surely I can't be the only one concerned about that? How will this help the economy during *that* time?"

Mayor Lancaster balked. "Well uh—"

"Great question, Mr. Kirkpatrick." Berk grinned like he was getting his headshot taken. "I hear you, that is a real concern. And how Sandy

Brook would respond to that is—progress takes time. The project would be an investment into the island's future. The numbers are there. We already know this from compiling regional data at other Hyacinth resorts. I understand that two or three years might *seem* like a long time on paper, however you wouldn't question how long it takes to repair a road, or construct a new school gym. Should we not work on projects like those because they take a long time to build?"

God, he's a trickster. "That's not really a fair comparison, now is it? Both those examples are public works that benefit everyone in the community. A resort on the island might bring in some attention a few years down the line, though it's not guaranteed."

He smiled tightly, his hands laced together on the table in front of him. "The numbers have shown across multiple data sets that building a Hyacinth resort boosted the economy in that area."

My heart beat sped up and I pressed my fisted hand into my side to still it. "That doesn't mean it still couldn't fail, or tank the economy in the meantime."

"Nothing is guaranteed, Will." He stood and looked out at the audience. "And that goes for all of you. It's not about *will* this development bring in guaranteed income to the island, it's about risk and reward. It's only my job to *ask* the question, it's yours to *answer* it. Is it worth the risk to save Ruby Island's economy, whose projected numbers are only falling? Something has to change, right?"

More murmurs of agreement. God, this crowd was so wishy-washy. Where was the conviction?

Berk found my eyes again before dropping down into his seat. It was almost like a great courtroom drama; I was the prosecutor and he was the defense, going head-to-head. If I didn't want to kiss him so bad I'd want to punch his innocent little face.

After a couple more pitiful questions the town hall meeting was over. There would be a quick vote the day after tomorrow to decide if the town should accept the deal with Sandy Brook and build the damn resort.

When everyone had finished packing up and we were all ready to leave, Berk rejoined us by the truck. Rory had been quiet the last twenty minutes and Maria only smiled when I looked at her. We were all in a bit of shock. Only Aunt Caroline seemed unfazed.

"I'm going to walk back," I said to the group.

Berk pinched his brows together. "Oh, *come on*. Don't be like that. I thought we were being civil?"

I forced out a laugh. "I'm not *being* like anything. It's a nice evening for a walk. Is that a crime?" The afternoon sun was dipping closer to the water, casting a golden wave across the grassy hillside.

Berk narrowed his eyes and then conceded. "Okay, if you say so. Meet you there, *Willy*."

I cringed hearing the nickname come out of Berk's mouth. I turned to Aunt Caroline. "Look at what you've taught him."

She smiled warmly and squeezed my shoulder. "All in a day's work." Rory helped her into the cab of the truck and I waved them off as they drove down the dusty dirt road.

Alone, I started walking. I needed a breather. It was so hard to separate in my mind the Berk who was so kind and caring—who did things like build us a website, or help me cook—from the treacherous snake-oil-selling salesman who wanted to poison the local drinking water.

There was no way that someone that nice and amazing actually bought any of his own horse shit. Why was he doing this? I understood that it was his job and that I shouldn't hold it against him personally, because it *wasn't* personal. *But God dammit it feels personal.* Telling people that life was about risk and reward? *Sometimes* you *have* to play it safe because you risk losing *everything*. Did he not get that? This wasn't a casino, it was a town.

What would happen if we lost the inn? If the bank foreclosed it? My entire family's legacy, over a hundred years, just what, gone forever? And not only was it our business, but it was our home. The home that I'd been born in, the home that I'd grown up in, had my first kiss in, and broken my first bone in. Was I willing to risk something like that, just because a guy with beautiful eyes said that I should?

I tried to imagine what my parents would tell me to do. They were always great at giving advice, and if one didn't know, the other *always* did. And if all else failed, Aunt Caroline was a pretty good listener. *They* would fight back. *They* would fight for their legacy. I know they would.

I walked up the hill towards the inn and stopped right as I caught the top of it above the bend in the road. The light was at the perfect angle to illuminate the porch. There was the porch swing that my grandfather had built for me and Rory to play on while the lodgers relaxed with a book and a glass of scotch inside.

My head was so jumbled with conflicting feelings. I couldn't keep acting like everything would turn out okay like Aunt Caroline wanted me to. I had to take action and get my neighbors to stand beside me and other local business owners to keep the island safe.

I marched up the front steps filled with a resolve and a fire I hadn't felt since that first day I'd learned who Berk was. He might have filled an emptiness that I'd been carrying for a while, however we couldn't keep going like this. I had to give him a piece of my mind, to tell him what I *really* thought about risk and reward.

I opened the front door and stepped inside. "Aunt Caroline?" I called.

"In the sitting room, dear."

I turned and passed through the archway, then I stopped in my tracks. Berk was standing on a chair with a couple nails wedged in his mouth, trying to hang a painting that had been sitting in the boathouse loft for maybe two decades. He turned and caught my eye. "Hi," he said around the mouthful of metal.

"A little more to the left, Berk," Aunt Caroline directed.

Berk precariously moved the frame to the left and waited for her approval.

"Yes, I think so. What do you say, Willy? Does that look straight?"

I was dumbfounded, staring at the two of them performing such a normal domestic task. "Uh, yeah. I guess so."

"Good. Nail it there, then."

Berk lowered the painting and replaced it with a heavy duty nail, hammering it into the wallpapered plaster.

He straightened it until it was placed *just so*. "There."

"Thank you, Berk." Aunt Caroline squeezed his arm. "You're such a big help around here. One of the best lodgers we've ever had." She turned to me. "Isn't he, Willy?"

My lips pulled into an unbidden smile, all the anger draining out of me as fast as it had arrived. "Yeah, he's pretty great."

The grin that he gave Aunt Caroline made my knees buckle and my chest tighten. He couldn't *truly* be bad. The sweet talking had to be the lie. *Not this.* It wasn't possible to fake this level of generosity and kindness. It just wasn't.

THIRTEEN

Berk

Last night's town hall meeting had gone better than I could have hoped. Of course Will's little question at the end *could* have derailed everything, though I had handled it well enough. Everyone had seemed to buy what I was selling. And it was *all true*, so it wasn't like I was manipulating them. Business *was* about risk and reward. Sometimes you took big risks and they didn't work out. It wasn't my job to mitigate that for them. My job was to get this damn resort built so I didn't get fired and lose my apartment, my parents' respect, and my self-worth. Not that I had much to begin with, *ha ha.*

I had thought for a moment after the event that Will was mad at me or something—he'd had that cute little crease between his brows. However, when he came back from his sunset walk he seemed totally back to normal, so maybe I'd only imagined it. That night he'd made us some corn chowder—which was delicious—and we got to show Caroline all the new features of the website that I'd designed. She'd been exceedingly impressed and gracious. "I'm not too sure about computers and all that, although it looks wonderful. I'm sure it will help draw in new customers."

"We're going to need it," Will had said. "Now more than ever."

Despite Will's concerns, I was genuinely confident in the island's ability to bounce back. It had all the romanticized trappings of a touristy getaway that people were looking for. It just needed a little bit of a spit shine, that was all, a fresh coat of paint.

The vote was tomorrow, my last day on the island as far as I'd planned. As soon as I got that green light, my job was finished. I'd convinced the island that Sandy Brook had their best interests at heart. Which wasn't exactly true in a personal way, though when everybody got what they wanted, why did the fine print matter?

That morning I'd spent a slow, relaxing hour with Will, cuddling in his bed. We'd been careful to not wake Caroline. Will was a little paranoid about it actually, which made me wonder if he'd done this before. Which intrigued me. How did someone go about having a one-night stand on a small island? The dating pool was more like a dating puddle.

Later in the afternoon Will had said he was going to go help his cousin Rory with something at their shop. I think it involved putting furniture together. Maria was due to have her baby in the next week and so she was barred from doing any kind of manual labor herself.

That was why I was alone with Caroline in the sitting room. She was reading something—she was always reading—and I was messing around on my laptop, writing a final report for Mr. Schwimmer highlighting any future problems I could anticipate. He was also sending out someone to survey the land and all the boring parts of a development project. There were so many rules about building things now. It was funny to imagine that when Will's family first built The Ruby Inn at the turn of the century there probably hadn't been *any* rules at all. I wondered how structurally sound it was and then realized the idea was silly. It had been standing for over a hundred years with no complaints.

"So," Caroline started, looking up from her book. "That was a pretty impassioned speech from you last night."

I pulled my lips into a smile. "I don't know if *impassioned* is the right word. I was merely trying to get some points across."

"And so you did. You know this isn't the first time that a development group has wanted to buy part of the island?"

I shrugged. "I kinda figured that. It's actually pretty impressive that the island has never brought in any big players over the many decades."

She grinned, setting down her book. "We're a tough group of people, Berk. What interests me most is that last night was the closest I've seen to an agreement."

That perked my ears. I closed my laptop. "You think people are going to vote in favor of the resort?"

She cocked her head. "I can't read people's minds of course, though it does seem likely."

"I-I know maybe it's a little unprofessional of me, but I gotta ask. What is *your* opinion? How are you voting?"

"*Berk*." She clucked her tongue. "I've lived on this island my entire life. I've been around for quite some time. I have to hand it to you, you're great at what you do, however I will *not* be voting in favor of the resort."

My chest fell, yet I couldn't say that I was surprised. "Okay, thanks for letting me know."

It's not that I'd truly thought I'd convinced her, she was just so kind to me. She'd known who I was the entire time and while Will had thrown a little bit of a fit, she'd acted like I was only a normal lodger, or even *better* than that.

"I expect that you'll be leaving after the vote?" she asked, even though she already knew the answer. My booking at the inn would end the same day.

"Yes, back to the city I go." I tried my best to smile, however it didn't reach my eyes. How could I have known I'd be so reluctant to leave when I first arrived on the island with puke all over my shirt and trousers? How could I have known that I would meet such amazing people like Will and Caroline?

Will. I was going to miss him. I wasn't used to that feeling. Usually one-night stands were fun, and then they were over. I'd never missed anyone or exchanged numbers to call back. I grinned at the idea. I didn't even have Will's number. I'd never needed it sleeping only one floor below him.

"I'm going to go say goodbye to Rory and Maria and maybe drum up some more votes along the way," I said, rising from the sofa. Maybe it was an excuse to spend more of my precious remaining hours with Will, maybe it wasn't.

"All right, if you say so, dear. Tell them I said hello."

"Will do." I grabbed my jacket, though it wasn't particularly cold outside. We'd been having a taste of some early summer weather the last few days.

I followed the road into town, having become familiar with its curves and divots. Seabirds circled above the rocks to my right as I passed the trail through the tall grasses that led to Will's secret beach. I was even going to miss that stupid death trap he called stairs. The memory of holding his hand, a comforting safety on our descent.

Ruby island was more than beautiful, it was charming, and that wasn't something you could easily buy. It was cultivated by the people who lived there over decades. They could turn it around—with or without the resort. Though my life depended on them picking the latter option.

The dirt road ended and cobblestone began. The sun shone through the strings of dormant hanging glass lights, and colorful banners were hung across the street from building to building. I was going to miss this place when I left. Maybe I'd come back one day. It truly was an amazing summer getaway.

Rory and Maria's shop was near the end of Main Street by the corner closest to the marina. I passed a couple restaurants, a cafe, the donut shop—Supernova Sweets. *The donut shop?* I slowed my pace to a crawl, peering in through the large window. Will was sitting down across from the same brunette girl who had found us in the barn the other day. The ex. What was he doing talking to his ex? In his favorite donut shop, no less? It was hard to read their facial expressions from so far away, although it was *definitely* Will, that much I was sure about. I wanted to get closer and see if I could hear what they were saying, however I stopped myself, because that would be *crazy*. What was I? The jealous boyfriend? We weren't even dating. We were...hanging out, and by tomorrow it would be over. It didn't even matter. So, why did the thought make my pulse jump?

Were they getting back together or something? He never said what she was actually doing on Ruby Island. Was that her goal? To steal him away?

God, so stupid. I passed the shop, forcing myself to look ahead as if wearing blinders. That wasn't what I came down here to do. I came down here to say goodbye to Rory and Maria since I probably wouldn't see them again before I left. Or at least that was my *new* objective. Maybe I'd buy one of her postcards for my sister or a gift for my parents who were still pissed at me. They'd called again this morning and I'd ignored it. No babies for them.

I reached The Merry Marauders and went inside, setting off the little copper bell at the top of the door. Maria was sitting behind the front counter reading a magazine. "Wow." The store was small yet packed with memorabilia and trinkets. Swords were hung on the wall along with an old sea diver's helmet, a replica of a shark's head, a myriad of flags, and lots more that I couldn't process in the time it took Maria to notice me.

"Oh, hi Berk. How's it going?" she greeted.

"Fine, it's fine." I forced a smile, trying to move past what I'd seen in the donut shop and failing. I rushed over to a spinning display rack of postcards and sorted through them.

"Looking for something in particular?" she asked, rising from her chair.

"Oh, *not really*. Something for my sister Ada, and something for my parents, maybe."

"What do your parents like?" she asked.

I laughed through my nose. "Nothing. They're not easily impressed, not by me anyway." *Wow, that sounds whiny.* "Uh—"

She smiled. "Don't worry, I understand the type. Do you think my parents were excited when I told them I'd met someone and I was going to move to this little island to run a gift shop?"

I narrowed my eyes. "*No?*" I guessed.

She laughed. "That's an understatement. My dad couldn't understand why I would want to live this life and take photographs."

"Did they ever come around?"

She shrugged. "I suppose. Once they saw how happy I was living here—happy with Rory—they backed off. It took a while, though."

"*Hmm.*" I turned the display rack and grabbed a postcard with a gray and blue hummingbird sipping from a flower.

"For your sister?" she asked.

I nodded. "Yeah, she loves birds. I always imagined she was going to be a zookeeper or something—or whatever kind of person works with birds, but then somehow she ended up in law school."

"*Relatable.* I have more cards with birds in the back; they don't sell as well as the ones of the island. Let me go check."

"Okay."

She shuffled to the back of the store and reached above her for a cardboard box.

"*Whoa*." I rushed over and lifted the box before she could grab it.

She narrowed her eyes and sighed. "This might be my first child, however I'm not a fragile porcelain doll. I wish everyone would stop acting like I'm going to break or something.

I smiled sheepishly. "Sorry, but if you hurt yourself while I was standing by doing nothing, not only would Rory kill me, Will would probably kill me too."

She rolled her eyes as I set the box down on the edge of the counter. She removed the lid and began shuffling through the cards.

"Can I ask you something?" I was trying to hold myself back, because frankly it was none of my business, however I couldn't seem to get it out of my head.

She concentrated on the cards. "Uh, sure."

"Do you know anything about this ex that's visiting the island?"

She looked up. "You mean Will's ex?" She smirked with a twinkle in her eyes. "Why do you want to know?"

I shrugged and stared at the counter. "I...saw them together earlier and I was curious, that's all."

"*Uh-huh.*"

I frowned and pinched my brows together. "Do you know something or not?"

"Um, I mean, I wasn't around when they dated. They were high school sweethearts."

Gross, how could I compete with that?

"And why did they break up?" I asked.

Maria continued to look through the cards, pulling a couple out and placing them on the counter. "From what Rory has told me, it seems like she wanted to go off to college and Will had to stay behind to take care of the inn."

"And...do you know why she's back?"

She shrugged and placed the stack of cards in front of me to look at. "I'm not positive. Like I said, I don't really know her like that."

"But they were in love...before?" I was such a loser for asking. Who was *I* to be jealous? We didn't owe each other anything.

"Yeah, I think she was the one that got away, if you know what I mean. Rory said that Will was super broken up about her when she left."

"*The one that got away*, huh?"

She put her hands up and widened her eyes. "Again, I don't know her. I wasn't around back then. Plus, Rory likes to exaggerate old stories with me."

Something told me he wasn't exaggerating about this one.

I searched through the postcards and picked out a couple Ada would like. I pulled out some cash from my wallet and paid. "Thanks for helping me. I wanted to say goodbye to you and Rory since I probably won't see you again before I leave."

She put the money in the cash register. "You're leaving after the vote tomorrow?"

I smiled and nodded. "Yep, might as well. My job here is done either way."

She closed the register and handed me my change and receipt. "Oh, well Rory is helping Magnus down by the Marina. He was having some seal problems."

"*Seal problems?*"

She grinned.

"Never mind, I don't want to know what that means." I lifted the cards. "Thanks again. *Bye.*"

"It was nice to meet you, Berk. Good luck tomorrow."

I was sure she would be voting against the resort along with Caroline and the whole family, though it was still nice of her to say. I waved as I left the store with my postcards. Nothing for my parents, however I could always give them the *I love Ruby Island* shirt that I'd bought on my first day. The idea made me smile. Dad would hate it, plus it would be two sizes too small for his large frame.

I turned towards the water and sat down on the stone retaining wall. Now that I was out of Maria's sight I could contemplate what she'd told me. This ex was *the love of Will's life.* If they were getting back together I was happy for them. That's the way that it should be, honestly. Who was I to get in the middle of true love? Between two long lost high school sweethearts? The day after tomorrow I'd be gone and I was glad that Will had someone to fill my place. What we had was only a bit of fun—that's all it had started as anyway. A way to pass the time on this little island. It filled a need, and that need had come to an end.

We didn't formally start anything, and so there was no need to formally end anything. Will had moved on. So would I.

I tucked the postcards into my jacket pocket and walked along the street, passing the bar that I'd gotten cozy in last week. It was still early—midday, really. But as the saying goes, it's always loser time somewhere.

I entered the mostly empty bar and sat down for a drink. I ordered a vodka soda and pulled out my phone to text Ada. I needed a good distraction. Which was silly, because there was nothing for me to need distracting from. My own stupid brain getting carried away?

B: What are you up to?

She sent me a picture of her notebooks spread out on her bed.

A: Studying.

B: Anymore Mr. Hotstuff?

A: No :(Turns out Mr. Hotstuff is more into studying with my friend Mark than me, if you know what I mean.

I chuckled.

B: Oh, all too well. What do you think *I* did in college?

A: Lol, I know. Which is why I'm mad that I didn't see the signs. How could I have not seen the signs?

B: Don't worry, I'm sure there are plenty of other Mr. Hotstuff nerds who want to get freaky with you.

A: Berk!

B: What :)

A: I'll let that slide. You're glad that Ma doesn't go through my texts anymore.

B: I should hope not, you're 23.

A: Remind *her* that.

B: It's never worked before.

A: What are you up to?

I sent a picture of my drink and tried to make it look classy.

A: Celebrating?

I took another sip, wincing as it went down.

B: Something like that.

A: Don't drink too much. You make me worry sometimes.

B: I won't. :) Besides, this island is too small to even drunk drive. I'll be fine.

A: Okay, love you, abi.

B: Love you too. See you the day after tomorrow

I downed the rest of the drink and ordered another. Might as well stay a while. I didn't know how long Will's little date was going to last and I didn't want to catch him on the way home. Better to avoid him entirely.

* * *

Drinking may not have been a wise decision. I glanced over at the three, no, four empty glasses atop the bar and groaned. *Why did I do that?* I paid my tab and shuffled out of the bar onto Main Street. The sun was starting to go down in the distance. I hadn't realized I'd killed *so much* time. Unless Will had been on the best reunion date of his life, he was probably home by now. *Good.*

I started down the street and reached up to tap one of the now lit string lights that hung across the path. I'd forgotten how pretty they could be at night. The last time I'd been out at night I had been *way* more drunk. I couldn't even remember walking home, only what had happened afterward. When Will had taken care of me.

I *wasn't* going to throw up this time—I knew that much. I traced my way along the dirt road until it curved back up the hill to the inn. The porch lights were on; I could see them in the distance. As I got closer I noticed someone was sitting on the porch swing, their profile cast in a warm orange glow. He turned as I reached the front gate. *Will.*

"Hi," I said, making sure I didn't slur any of my syllables. I avoided his eyes as I walked up the steps to the front door, however a wall of muscle blocked my path. "Hey, what gives?"

Will had his arms crossed over his broad chest. "Where were you? You've been gone all day."

I frowned. "I don't see why that's any of your business."

What right did he have to be monitoring my movements? Just because we'd slept together? Should every one of my one-night stands get access to my location tracking on my phone?

He leaned in and sniffed. *What is he doing?*

" You smell like alcohol."

I scoffed. "Give the boy a prize, that would be *the alcohol.*"

He raised his eyebrow. "Is this a habit of yours? Getting drunk and stumbling home?"

A flare of anger lit my chest. "So what if it is? What I do with my time is *my* business. Why are you being so controlling?" I tried to scoot past him to the door, only he moved with me.

"I'm not trying to be controlling, however I was concerned when you didn't come home."

"Okay, well, I'm home now. You can stop being concerned. *Move.*"

He relaxed his features and moved enough for me to open the door.

"Berk, I'm sorry." He sighed. "I'm truly not trying to sound like a dad or something. I just wanted to know where you were."

I beelined for the stairs. "And yet you don't even have my number to call me to find out." I turned after taking the first step. "Because we're *not* dating, Will. We hardly know each other, and this just proves it."

He laughed. "Because I don't have your phone number? And I never said that we were dating. I said that I cared about you enough to wonder where you were all day. Is that a crime?"

This was getting us nowhere and the effects of the alcohol were starting to catch up to me. I closed my eyes and let out a deep breath. "Will, can we not argue?"

He took a step closer. "I wasn't trying to argue."

I smirked at that. "*Right*. No arguing from Will Kirkpatrick."

He took another step. "No way, not from me. I'm a pretty easy going guy." Another step. "Isn't that what you like about me?" Another step. He was standing directly in front of me now.

My lips pulled into a smile against my wishes. "Among other things."

He arched an eyebrow. "Oh, really? Pray tell, what are these *other things*?"

I internally kicked myself for allowing his charms to tempt me, then I got over it. It was hard to say who leaned forward first, either way, we were kissing. He pushed me up against the stairwell, his hands finding all my sensitive places.

"Upstairs?" he asked, breathless.

I nodded, too eager. "Upstairs."

My clumsy drunk ass and Will's long limbs made a lot of noise as we scrambled up the steps to his room. We'd probably awoken Caroline and the new lodger. Either that, or they were left wondering how a pack of elephants had somehow squeezed past the stairs.

We made it to Will's room and he practically tossed me onto his bed —none too gently—shutting the door behind him. I tore off my shoes and shirt, and then he took care of the rest, throwing everything onto the floor.

I pulled away from his kiss and found his eyes.

He grinned, his cheeks flushed. "What?"

"You know I'm leaving tomorrow, right?" Even in my drunken haze I knew he should know if he didn't already.

His expression didn't change, although he leaned in closer, bracing his heavy body against mine. "Then let's make it count," he whispered next to my ear.

I grinned against his cheek. "You got it."

FOURTEEN

Will

A heavy weight pressed against my chest. I opened one bleary eye to look around my room. The sun was coming in through the cracks in the drapes, running lines against Berk's back. His head was pressed against my ribs, the rest of his body sprawled in a tangle on top of my own.

His hair was a mess, his lips were red and puffy from last night, and his skin was warm. I couldn't move with him on top of me and there was no part of me that wanted to. My brain was doing stupid things instead, like committing his features to memory, etching the contours inside my hippocampus. His strong nose, his long dark lashes, and the freckle on his shoulder—an island trapped in an ocean of latte-colored skin.

He murmured something as he shifted, his arm dropping over my waist and his feet bumping into my leg. The dark navy sheets were barely keeping us decent.

Today was the day we'd vote. The vote to determine the future of Ruby Island. Aunt Caroline hadn't seemed worried, even after that disaster of a town hall meeting where *this* beautiful trickster convinced half the town that it was a good idea.

Today was also the day that Berk was leaving, leaving the island like everyone else.

I tried to push the hazy thoughts aside and focus on the present. The exact minute we were living in, the two of us in this bed—the same bed I'd had since I was a teenager. It was funny, looking at us now. I'd hated him so much when I'd figured out his lie. And slowly, without even realizing it, I'd softened. He still annoyed *the shit* out of me, especially when he was going on about trickle-down economics, however that was now merely a low buzz in the background. His smile was too distracting, his eyes too bright.

He shifted again, this time opening an eye. "Are you watching me sleep?" he mumbled, pinching his brows over his sleepy eyes.

I grinned, holding back a laugh. "No, I was watching you kick me in the shin. I probably have a bruise now."

He rolled his eyes. "You'll get over it."

Will I get over it? When he's...gone?

"I demand restitution," I said in an authoritative voice.

He smirked and pulled himself up a little bit, his warmth leaving me. Goosebumps rose on my skin. "What kind of restitution?"

I pointed to my lips, trying to keep a straight face. "It's only fair."

He grinned, his bedhead only making him more adorable. "Okay, I'll pay the tax." He leaned forward, trapped me into the covers, and kissed me.

"Oh." I cringed. "Maybe you should brush your teeth before you pay the tax."

He barked out a laugh and hit my shoulder. "*Shut the fuck up!* Maybe *you* should brush *your* teeth."

I braced his hips and flipped him over so that I was on top of him. "I was only joking. I don't care if you taste like death." I leaned in to kiss along his jaw.

It was late in the morning, however the more time we killed, the less time there would be when we finally separated. Once we left, it was over —the fantasy.

He punched my abs, trying to push my weight off, although I probably had fifty pounds over him. "I don't kiss *liars*."

I chuckled. "Luckily I don't have that problem." I leaned forward and deepened the kiss. He stopped flailing and submitted, wrapping his arms around my neck and bringing me down on top of him.

* * *

We went down for breakfast—more like lunch—right before the vote was supposed to happen down at the mayor's office. Everyone who owned or rented property on the island was eligible to vote. So that meant Berk couldn't vote for himself even if he wanted to.

Caroline had ordered lobster rolls from Sal's and we ate, sitting around the dining room table. The full length windows filled the entire room with bright sunlight and the pale blue walls were covered in beadboard. I also noticed a few new paintings had been hung. Well, not *new*, newly old—paintings Berk must have snuck out of the loft from the boathouse when they'd been hanging new paintings the other night.

Lunch was quiet. It wasn't exactly *tense*, though we all knew what was about to happen and what it meant. Aunt Caroline smiled as she took a bite of her coleslaw. She was always the optimist. I wished I could be more like her, that I could believe in the best even when the worst was on the horizon.

When we finished eating I grabbed my coat and got ready to go. Berk decided to stay.

"You don't want to be there when people are voting?" I asked.

He shrugged. "I figure that people have already made up their minds by the time they get to vote. What's the point in standing by and watching? You can tell me when you get back."

Ruby Island was a small town, it wouldn't take long to count the paper ballots. "Okay, if that's what you want."

He pulled on a smile, though his expression was hard to read. "It is."

"Okay then, we'll see you in a bit."

When it came time, Rory and Maria picked us up in their truck and we rode into town. A line of people ran out the front doors of the mayor's office. I recognized their faces as neighbors and fellow business owners. I'd made some calls and sent some emails the day before to try and rally as many votes as possible, but there were unfortunately still some wild cards left on the table.

I helped Aunt Caroline out of the truck and we wandered over. The energy was tense waiting in line. Rory had wanted Maria to stay home since she was so close to having her baby, but she'd refused. "Today is an important day, I need to use my vote." She was affected as much as anybody else.

It didn't take long for us to make it inside. We were handed paper ballots and shown to a booth to vote in—a table with a cardboard shield surrounding it. It wasn't as formal as something like an election, just enough to make sure our votes were private.

I dropped mine in the box at the front of the room and walked out. Everyone joined me when they'd done the same. It was only a couple hundred ballots, after all. We crowded outside the front steps, blocking the middle of the dusty road. I was sweating under the morning sun, so I took off my coat and shook out my arms. Maria caught my eye and gave me a smile, and I tried to return it, though I wasn't feeling particularly reassuring.

Maybe twenty minutes had gone by when Mayor Lancaster popped his head out the door. He slipped onto the front steps and gathered us around with a picture-perfect grin. "The results are in." He plucked a small slip of paper from his suit jacket pocket someone had likely written the tally on. He paused dramatically, holding the paper in his hands.

I wanted to strangle the man. *Just tell us already!*

"With a slight majority, there were one hundred and twenty-six votes in favor of the resort, to one hundred and thirteen votes against."

"No way," I whispered. The people had voted to build the resort. I hadn't imagined it was possible. The past few years of poor tourism must have had business owners feeling desperate for a change. If only they realized what a terrible choice they'd made.

A light sprinkling of applause went across the crowd. Mayor Lancaster beamed, showing off his bleach-white teeth. "You've all made a wise decision for the future of Ruby Island. I'll be in touch with the people at Sandy Brook soon. I'm sure they'll be able to start construction this summer if possible."

Rory tried to smile and failed while Maria squeezed my arm.

I thought that I'd be angry if this happened, but I wasn't. I wasn't mad. I was numb. It was so silly, and yet I wished that Berk was here, holding me. Then I remembered that this was all *his* doing. Even *still* I wasn't angry. I'd moved past anger to resolute—there was nothing I could do. The votes had been cast, the resort would be built, and Berk was leaving tonight...leaving me.

Aunt Caroline smiled warmly as I helped her back into the truck. "Don't worry, Willy. Everything will work out the way it's supposed to."

I didn't reply. What I wanted to say was, *since when*? When had anything ever worked out the way it was supposed to? Where did she get her unlimited optimism from? After everything we'd gone through?

Rory drove us home and I helped Aunt Caroline inside. Rory and Maria said good night, plastering on fake smiles. We were all on edge, however there was nothing to do now.

Past the front door a suitcase and a duffle bag was sitting beside the front counter on the floor. *Right.* Berk was leaving. Maybe that was why he had wanted to stay behind. He'd wanted to pack so that he'd be all ready to go when we returned. Why was he leaving tonight instead of tomorrow? He couldn't stand to stay here another minute after hearing the results of the vote?

I helped Aunt Caroline into a chair and mumbled something about having a project to work on. She smiled and said, "All right, dear." No doubt sensing my mood.

I headed out to the boathouse. We'd never finished cleaning it, and there was still so much stuff waiting in there. I had just enough daylight left to get a couple hours of work in, so I flung open the barn doors and got busy—moving boxes to the loft, sorting through what I knew was random crap, and setting aside family history and important papers.

It was slow going by myself, however I wanted to be alone right then. There was so much to think about and a headache was already forming behind my eyes. The island was changing. That was a fact. I'd lived here all my life and I'd seen it change in small ways—new businesses come and go, but never something as impactful as this. Aunt Caroline had been so calm when the results were read. My resolve melted as I carried each box up the flight of stairs and stacked it with the others, my emotions yo-yoing. I was so *sick* of this. Sick of all this *stuff*, physically and metaphorically. Another box, another table, another container. Why did we have so much stuff? My parents were dead. They didn't care about any of this. We'd been storing it for decades, all this nothing, and now the inn might be shut down.

What would happen if the inn was forced to close? Would we move to the mainland? What would happen to the inn? Would they bulldoze it? Would they throw away everything in this boathouse? *Dammit.* I dropped another box on the floor of the loft and took a breather, leaning against the wooden railing and looking over the space.

"Will?" Berk called from outside.

I didn't answer, though I wasn't truly hiding either.

He walked around the corner into the boathouse and spotted me standing above. "Hey, I was wondering where you went."

"You found me," I said dryly.

He took a few steps closer, craning his neck to face me. "Yeah, Caroline told me what happened, that Sandy Brook won."

"You mean *you* won," I said.

He frowned. "I just work there, Will. I'm not responsible for this project."

I scoffed. "*Not responsible?*"

I walked down from the loft so that I could speak face-to-face. He'd changed his clothes since lunch—into sweats and a t-shirt. He was probably getting ready for the long journey back home. "How exactly are you *not* responsible for this project?"

He lowered his brow and shook his head. "I—"

I stepped closer. "You're quite literally the spearhead of this project. Without your contribution it would have never passed the vote today."

He took a step back. "Are you trying to pass blame on me? All I did was give a presentation and answer some questions. I'm not the boogeyman, Will."

I sighed. This conversation was already more than I wanted to deal with. "I understand that you work *for* Sandy Brook, that you're just the little guy. It may not have been your decision to take this assignment, however it's certainly your fault that it went so well."

He laughed, but there was no humor in it. "That almost sounded like a compliment there. Are you saying that I'm *too good* at my job?"

I struggled to find words. "A little bit, yeah." I wanted to strangle him and kiss him at the same time. I couldn't kiss him, he was leaving me. His project here was done.

He closed his eyes for a second and let out a breath before opening them again. "I told you that this was my last chance, right?"

"Yeah, you did." I remembered the conversation, though it felt like it was a million years ago.

He barked out a tense laugh. "I'm on my *last* strike. If I didn't knock this project out of the park I was going to be fired and probably blackballed from the development industry. My parents would never talk to me again out of shame."

"Are you saying that makes it okay? Because you were desperate?"

He cringed. "I'm saying I did what I had to do."

I held up my hands to push him away when he tried to move in closer. "Just let me ask you one thing, before you go. I have to know."

He crossed his arms over his chest. "What?"

"Do you genuinely feel like this resort will be good for Ruby Island? No bullshit like in your speech at the town hall meeting. What do *you* personally think?"

He sputtered, trying to find his words. "I-I think that based on the numbers, this type of resort has helped a lot of communities that rely on tourism for their economy."

"You actually believe that?" I searched his features for tells.

He shrugged. "Yeah, I do. I know it will be hard while the resort is being built. It's true what you said about people not wanting to relax next to a construction zone, though it will hopefully pan out in the future."

"*Hopefully?*"

"It's like I said, Will. There are no guarantees. I can't promise anything, and if you remember, I never once promised anything during that meeting either. You can call me whatever you like, however you can't call me a liar."

I shook my head. My heart was thumping out of my chest. How could he believe his own crap? "You might not have lied, although you definitely spun some truths to fit your narrative."

He waved his hand through the air, his eyes widening. "Do you want me to say that I'm not happy that I won? *I am.* I have a job to go back to now. I'm not a failure."

I blew out a sharp breath. "Did you even stop to think about anybody but yourself?" My temper began to flare. *How can he not see it?* "The inn is already mortgaged to hell; one missed payment and we're going to have our doors shut. My family legacy—gone in a heartbeat."

He paused, staring at my face. What was he looking for?

"I'm sorry about that, I truly am. But...what do you want me to do about it?"

"*Nothing!* Nothing at all." I lifted another box, shifting the pile and causing a cloud of dust to bloom. "Nothing *can* be done, so it is what it is."

"And that's it?" he asked behind me.

I set the box down and turned. "That's it. You said it yourself, *you won.* Your job is finished, and you're leaving tonight. What more is there to say?"

He stood there like a statue, his eyes glazed over. I wanted him to say *something*, to tell me he was wrong about the whole thing, to tell me that he'd stay and fix it with me.

"I guess this is goodbye, then."

My heart dropped. I tried to keep my face impassive. There was *no way* that I would let him know that he'd gotten to me. "I guess so."

He stuck out his hand, waiting for a shake. I would have laughed if it wasn't so damn sad. *Am I really just a business deal to him?*

I thought about leaving him hanging, however I decided to take the high road, to show him that he couldn't get to me. I dropped the box I was about to lift and walked over to him, grabbing his hand in a firm shake. He tried to hold on for longer, but I pulled away quickly. Goodbye, Berk."

He stood there for an extra second. "Goodbye, Will."

I turned once again to the boxes and by the time I'd grabbed one and hauled it to the stairs, he was gone. Berk was gone and he was never coming back.

FIFTEEN

Berk

I left the boathouse and stomped through the grass as I climbed the hill back to the house. Will had stared at me so expectantly like he wanted me to somehow fix this mess he blamed me for creating. *What does he want me to do about it?* Sandy Brook had already won. The resort was going to be built and I got to keep my job. If anything, on this trip I'd realized how *great* I was at my job. I took an island of people that were struggling and transformed them into a group that saw reason.

I couldn't apologize for being talented. It sucked that the inn was in such hot water—I hadn't realized that. Maybe that explained why Will had been so angry the last two weeks. Caroline on the other hand, was a ball of sunshine no matter what you threw at her. I wondered how she truly felt about the vote being passed. When I'd come down the stairs earlier and asked her who'd won, she'd replied with a smile, not fazed at all, like she knew something that nobody else did.

I slipped inside the front door and raced to the stairs.

"Was he out there?" Caroline called from the sitting room.

I backtracked and pulled my features into a smile. "Uh, yeah. He's moving some more boxes and clearing that space out. He'll probably be there for a few more hours. It looked like a lot of work still had to be done."

She nodded. "I see. Are you going to see him before you leave?" She glanced over at the hanging wall clock. "It's getting late. Aren't you leaving soon?"

I forced a grin. "We said our goodbyes just now. He seemed busy, though."

She frowned and pressed her lips together. "That boy is *always* busy, that's not an excuse to avoid a proper goodbye."

"It's okay. It is what it is." He couldn't even stand to be around me long enough to shake my hand. We were done.

"Okay, dear." Her eyes searched mine, analyzing me. "Come say goodbye before you go."

I smiled warmly. "I will, I promise." I turned towards the stairs to my room. I'd already packed my things and left them by the front counter so that I could grab them on my way out. I still had almost an hour to kill before Magnus said he could take me back to the mainland to make my late-night train ride on time.

I sat on the edge of the bed and pulled out my phone. I'd only told Ada as little about Will as possible, wanting to keep him to myself, but now I *needed* her perspective. I obviously couldn't stay on the island. He was pissed at me *again*. I was public enemy number one. Plus, I didn't need someone judging my choices and telling me what I should be doing all the time. He'd made it pretty clear we were over. It had to be. And I knew that. That was always the plan. He'd been a fun island fling to pass the time, and now we were going our separate ways.

I found Ada's contact and called her. The line rang a few times until she answered. "I'm at home with Ma and Dad," she said quickly.

"Oh."

Before I had a chance to say anything else—or hang up even—Ma took over the phone. "Berk? I tried calling you yesterday and you didn't answer. When are you coming home."

I blew out a breath and collapsed onto the bed for probably the last time. "Tonight, Ma."

"Oh, good. You can come over for lunch tomorrow after mosque." Despite not being terribly religious my parents still went to mosque so that they could socialize with the other Turkish families.

"I'll probably be tired after my journey home," I argued, even though I knew it was futile.

"Nonsense, you can rest here, with us. I'll feed you; I'm sure you've barely eaten over on that island."

I sighed away from the phone and then brought it back to my face. "Okay, Ma."

"Your father wants to talk to you."

"*Ma.*" I *so* didn't want to talk to him.

"Berk?" he said, his low voice gruff.

"Hey, Dad."

"Mr. Schwimmer called me a little while ago. He says you did a satisfactory job on this resort development deal. That's good."

"Thanks, Dad." He hadn't actually complimented me, although it passed as one in his book.

"*Hmm.* Why do you never answer your mother's calls, huh?"

Ah, back to the nagging and criticizing. That's what I was used to.

"I was busy, Dad."

"*All month?*" he asked, incredulously.

I switched the phone to my other hand. "I have to go and pack, actually. I'm supposed to be leaving for the ferry soon," I said, even though I had *already* packed.

"*Hmm.* That's fine. We'll talk more tomorrow. Are you coming to mosque?"

"No, Dad. I'll see you after."

"Fine, travel safe."

"Thanks, bye."

He ended the call before I could ask to talk with Ada. They took any invitation to barge in and take over.

She sent me a text a few seconds later.

A: Talk tomorrow?

B: Yeah, okay. See you then.

* * *

I puttered around my room until it was time to leave. The sun was setting outside, shades of gold and pink on the horizon.

I went downstairs and found Caroline in the same spot, still reading her book. "Hey, Caroline. I'm about to go."

She set her book down and found my face. "You know, you really are one of the best lodgers we've ever had at The Ruby Inn."

I put my hands in my trouser pockets. "Stop, you'll make me blush."

She rose from her seat, leaning against the chair's armrests to push herself up. "I mean it, truly." She pulled me in for a hug—not the polite kind you get from your teacher or an old hookup buddy, a *real* hug.

I laughed. "You've got a firm grip for a lady who's down and out."

She smirked. "I have a broken ankle, not broken arms, Berk."

"I know." I bit back a laugh. "You're more than capable of doing anything. Over the past week I've seen that."

She placed her hands on my shoulders and looked me in the eyes. "I hope your stay at the inn was satisfactory," she said, falling into hostess mode.

"It was." I grinned. "I loved every second of it. Once I figure out how to set up reviews on your new website, I'll leave a raving one."

"That would be lovely." She stepped back and looked me over, making me feel self-conscious. "I'm going to miss you, Berk. I've loved having you stay here. And I know Will has too."

I pulled my lips into an awkward, lopsided smile, rocking my weight back and forth. Was I supposed to respond to that? "I guess I better get going. Magnus won't wait forever."

She smiled, though the usual twinkle in her eyes was dull. "No, he won't. That man is as stubborn as an ox."

I stepped away to grab my bags and then rolled the suitcase towards the door. "Goodbye, Caroline. Thanks for everything."

She waved, her eyes glassy. "Goodbye, Berk. Have a safe trip home."

I gave her one final smile and slipped out the front door and down the steps. The air was still warm from the sunny afternoon, though there was a light breeze hitting my shoulder as I passed the gate to the road.

I had taken maybe ten steps before someone called my name. "Berk, wait!"

I turned. Will was running up the side yard in my direction. He must have been working hard the last hour, his gray shirt was stained with sweat and his blond curls were damp around his forehead.

His impassioned run made my heart pick up a fraction. What did he want? We'd already said our goodbyes.

He reached me, slowing to a crawl as he joined me on the dusty road. "Don't go," he said through a breath, his voice low and strained.

"*What?*"

"Don't go, don't leave. Stay."

I would have laughed if I couldn't tell how deathly serious he was, his features etched in stone. "I-I can't. How could I stay?" What was he saying?

He shook his head. "I don't know, but do it anyway."

"I have to go back to Boston. My whole life is there—my family, my apartment, my job." The job that I had *just* saved.

"I know."

"So...what are you asking?"

He reached out his hand and then quickly dropped it to his side, thinking better of it. "Stay anyway, stay with me."

His eyes were pleading, pink at the edges. His chest was heaving from his sprint and his hands were in fists at his sides.

I don't know how to respond. "I-I just can't. I'm sorry, Will. I *have* to go."

He opened and closed his mouth, then after a long beat of dead silence he nodded. The pain carved into his features was almost enough to break me, however I *had* to go.

He turned away first, thank God. We would have been standing there all night in a stalemate if he hadn't. I walked quickly down the road in the direction of the marina.

How could he ask that of me? He wanted me to give up everything I had for him? Give up my nice apartment, seeing my family, and the job that I'd saved myself from being fired from. Still, the look in his eyes was painful. He was as stubborn as all hell. It must have taken a lot for him to even *ask* me to stay.

I reached Main Street and the bumpy cobblestone, dragging my rolling suitcase across the pebbled surface. I passed all the memories that I'd made the last two weeks: Supernova Sweets, the cafe, and The Merry Marauders. Then I walked past the retaining wall and down the cobblestone switchbacks that led to the docks. Magnus' boat was waiting in the same slip as before.

He was standing on the deck, one foot resting on the lip of the boat in an impatient stance. "There you are, son. I was waiting around for you."

I checked my watch. It was only two minutes past when I'd said I would arrive. "Sorry." This island really needed a new ferry service. Hopefully that would be the first thing Sandy Brook would change.

"Are you...okay?" he asked, his voice low and gruff.

"Yeah?" Did I look like shit? Was I wearing it on my face? I tried to steel my features as I lowered my luggage to the deck of the boat and climbed on—less clumsy than the first time I'd tried, though the bar was low.

I sat in one of the metal folding chairs and fixed my gaze out on the water. The sunset behind us was reflecting onto the dark blue ocean.

* * *

One boat ride, one ferry ride, one train ride, and one long taxi ride later, I was back in my downtown apartment. I didn't know what I'd been expecting, but nothing had changed. It was still messy, still smelled of something suspect, and the windows were still big and expensive.

I dropped my suitcase and collapsed onto my gray couch. It wasn't as soft as the one at the inn, not even close. The cheap polyester scratched my cheek as I gazed at the city lights glowing down below.

* * *

The music in the club was loud. It drowned out everything inside my head for a brief moment—the vodka was helping too. I'd primped and preened myself to death, trying to wash the island smell off of me. I doused myself in expensive cologne and styled my hair within an inch of its life. It had become a hard hat of dark wavy locks.

The club was dim with bright beams of green and pink light shooting across the space, providing barely enough visibility to not break an ankle. The dance floor was crowded since it was the weekend—a mass of oiled-up bodies pressing against each other. The baseline in the music dropped and everyone began jumping up and down like they were at a rave until the mix settled back to a familiar pop song.

This is my home. Not the apartment I hardly ever visited or heaven forbid *the office.* I'd spent more hours in this club than I could count. I passed somewhat familiar faces as I made my way onto the dance floor. Were they familiar because I'd met them before? Or familiar because everyone looked the same in a cloud of hazy lights?

I got into the beat of the music, rocking my hips and moving my feet. I wasn't a great dancer, although it didn't matter. Dancing wasn't about being good, it was about releasing whatever you'd been holding back all week and giving in to the rhythm.

Fingers grazed my arm and I spun around. A guy with deep brown skin raised his hands up in front of him. "Sorry, I didn't know you'd be so jumpy," he shouted over the *thumpa-thumpa* of the house music. He was handsome with a square jaw and full lips. His eyes were narrowed in what was probably supposed to be a sexy gaze. He learned forward next to my ear. "What's your name?" he asked over the blare of the music.

"Berk!"

He smirked, his hand trailing my arm. "Wanna go somewhere a little quieter, Berk?"

Why not? I needed a good distraction. That's why I was here, after all. He seemed nice and not murder-y, though that was yet to be confirmed. I'd had one or two freak-out experiences meeting guys at the club and I'd rather not repeat them.

I leaned in. "Sure, what did you have in mind?"

His smile grew and he grabbed my wrist to pull me through the crowd towards the back of the club. Ah, *kissing*, very inventive. The hallway next to the exit of the club was empty and almost pitch-black, except for a small neon exit sign casting us in a vampiric wash of red.

His eyes grew dark and his white teeth glowed.

Strong arms pushed me against the wall and hands traveled down my sides. His mouth found my exposed neck and jaw. I closed my eyes, leaning into the moment. However, that only made it worse. With my eyes closed I could only imagine that those lips were Will's, those strong hands were Will's.

238

Shut up brain, you traitor. This hot guy wanted to ravish me and I was thinking about *Will*. Someone I'd only known for a short two weeks. For all accounts, I barely knew him.

The hot guy's hands found the edge of my shirt and they wandered around my back and across my chest. Goosebumps appeared on my arms and not in a good way.

"Um—" I put my hand to his chest to stop him.

He pulled away, finding my eyes in the dim light. "What's up? Is this not private enough for you?"

I shook my head slightly. "No, it's not that."

He pressed in closer. "*Okay.*"

I put out my other hand. "I don't feel great."

He took a step back. "*Oh*, do you need to go stand outside?"

I nodded. "Yes, and I think it would be best if I did that...by myself."

"Oh, okay. I see what you mean." He smiled in an awkward way and it almost made me feel guilty for rejecting him.

"It's *really* not you. It's me," I explained.

He grinned and put his hands on his hips, clearly not believing me.

I laughed through my nose. "Except, I *actually* mean that. Seriously."

"*Okay.*" He took a couple steps back towards the dance floor. "Get home safe."

"Thanks." I gave him a sheepish smile and slinked out the side exit into the alley. I leaned against the cool brick and took in a deep breath—which I quickly regretted because it smelled like human piss and garbage. I had to give it to Ruby Island, at least they didn't have *that* particular problem.

I decided to walk home instead of taking a cab since the club wasn't too far from my apartment and the crisp night air was nice.

Usually I wouldn't hesitate to reciprocate someone's advances. It was easy, predictable. However tonight Will's stupid face was stuck in my brain, watching over me like a chaperone.

Why does it matter? I was never going to see Will again. *This* was my life—Boston and its dark weaving streets. Sure, there was bound to be some human defecation sometimes, and occasionally bad people, however it was generally pretty safe here.

I reached my apartment and started climbing the stairs since the stupid elevator still hadn't been fixed in the last two weeks. I entered my cold, dark apartment and didn't bother turning on any lights.

Everything I owned was so sterile and lifeless: the Ikea lamp, the non-Turkish Turkish rug that I could never show my mother or she would cry, the stacks of identical boring dishes in the cupboards, and the generic takeout in the fridge.

Everything was the same as it had always been, yet it *felt* different. I hadn't cared about the stupid rug or the stupid lamp before. It hadn't *mattered* before. My apartment was a place to come after work or bring guys over when it was convenient.

It wasn't a home. *I* wasn't home.

SIXTEEN

Will

I smiled brightly as I helped our latest lodger check out of the inn. She'd only been staying for a few days to help her great-aunt who lived close by on the island.

"Make sure to tell your friends about us," I said lamely.

"I will." She waved and then slipped out the front door, leaving the room once again in silence. It was too quiet. We needed new lodgers.

I pulled out my notebook and went over the tasks that still needed to be completed. The boathouse had been almost fully cleared of boxes and furniture, however it still needed a good sprucing up. I needed to clean the walls, oil the floorboards, and make it look inviting. Not like an old boathouse that had been used for storage for over a decade, not like an afterthought.

I could do this. I *would* do this. There was no way I was going to allow the inn to close, to let it be overshadowed by the new resort. No. It wasn't going to happen. Not on my watch. Even if some people in town *did* think the resort would fix the economy and bring in new tourists—however deluded they had become to the truth.

I left Aunt Caroline to go work on the boathouse again. It had quickly become my main emotional outlet. I could pound the floorboards with a hammer and lift heavy shit, getting out all my frustrations in the process, channeling them into hard work. I grabbed a broom and started sweeping, picking up rusted nails and pieces of glass as I found them—where they came from, I didn't know.

I'd been making a pile of objects to return to the inn all week. Possessions of my parents, like framed photographs and boxes of newspaper clippings. An idea was rattling around my brain, but it would take a lot of work. *One project at a time.*

I swept the loft too, building clouds of dust and wood particles. I passed the old army cot where Berk and I had fallen asleep. How we had both fit on the old thing was a mystery.

It was so stupid asking him to stay. Of course he would say no. What did he have to stay for? He'd performed his duties, and the project was finished. I was so dumb for imagining he might want to be with me. I was only a tool, and he'd used me because I let him.

He left the way that everyone left Ruby island.

I washed the wooden floor boards and stained them with oil until they gleamed like new. The lights still had to be fixed. I'd ask Rory if he knew how to do that. I wasn't going to electrocute myself doing something stupid—though it wouldn't be the first time. With working lights and a cheap speaker we'd have an actual dance space to rent. I needed to update the project on the new website to let people know it was going to be available.

When I finally came inside, half the day was gone. I'd inadvertently skipped lunch. Aunt Caroline had set out a sandwich and a glass of lemonade on the dining room table for me. She was sitting in the seat closest to the wall of windows reading a book. She must have already eaten. "Thanks. I guess I lost track of time." I sat down beside her.

"I imagine it's a lot slower with only one person," she said, looking over the top of the page.

I scooted my chair forwards and set the napkin in my lap. "What's that supposed to mean?"

She shrugged. "Nothing. It's just nice when you have help, that's all."

"I can do it myself," I assured her. I could do *anything* by myself.

She shook her head absentmindedly. "I didn't say that you couldn't, dear. But doing everything alone all the time is exhausting, isn't it?"

I took a bite of the sandwich and frowned. What was she trying to say? I'd asked Berk to stay and he'd flat out said no. I was by myself. Sure, it would be *nice* to have some help, to have someone around when I needed them. Rory and Maria were too busy with their own shop and the baby coming any day now, and Aunt Caroline's ankle was still broken— there were a few more weeks at least before the boot could come off.

I supposed I could ask a few of our business neighbors, though they were all busy preparing for the new tourist season—as slow as it would inevitably be. Who else was there? I wanted to laugh, however I restrained myself. There was no point in causing Aunt Caroline to think I'd had a nervous breakdown from stress.

I ate my sandwich in silence, and Aunt Caroline didn't say anything else, just read her book, which frustrated me a little bit. She was pushy sometimes, and I knew she meant well, though what exactly did she want me to do?

I took my dishes to the kitchen and went back out to the front desk. It was empty and quiet.

I stayed there the rest of the day, doodling in the margins of my notebook, feeling sorry for myself. Alicia had left. Berk had left. Was I someone who was easily leave-able? Why did it feel like nobody ever wanted me enough to stay?

As long as I was throwing a pity party for two I could use some snacks. I ran back to the kitchen and grabbed some chips and a beer. When I returned the front door was cracked open.

"Alicia?"

She was standing in front of the counter, a wary expression on her face with her eyebrows drawn together.

I couldn't exactly blame her. When she'd accosted me the other day at Supernova Sweets I hadn't known what to do. I should have left immediately when she said that she felt bad about how we left things and that she wanted to talk. *Yeah*, that didn't exactly go as she'd probably planned. She'd only just started what I could tell was going to be a deep conversation before I shut it down and explained that I needed to return to the inn, that Aunt Caroline needed me. It was kind of a cop-out, I knew that, even at the time. It was *so* hard to talk to her. What if she told me something I didn't want to hear?

"Hi." She waved and then leaned her arms against the tall counter.

"What are you doing here?" I asked. I thought she would have left by now.

"I know you don't want to talk to me." She shook her head and smiled self-consciously. "But, maybe we should anyway. I'm leaving in the morning and I don't know if or when I'll ever be back."

"*Okay.*" I stepped closer, but kept the counter between us. What did she want to say that she hadn't already?

"Do you want to go sit outside maybe?"

I shifted my weight and crossed my arms. "Not really."

"Please?" she asked, her eyes wide and hopeful.

I sighed—unable to make a woman sad—and rolled my eyes. "*Okay, okay*. If you *really* think we have something to talk about."

I followed her to the door and shouted towards the sitting room. "I'll be outside, Aunt Caroline."

"Okay, dear," she shouted back.

I slipped out and closed the stained glass door behind me. I didn't want Aunt Caroline hearing any part of the conversation if it was going where I thought it was going.

Alicia sat down in one of the old wooden rocking chairs and I chose the other beside it. We weren't exactly facing each other, although that might have been better, actually. This was the *third* time we'd talked this week and I'd never let her finish what she'd wanted to say. Because I already knew what it was, and I *really* hadn't wanted to hear it before. Now that Berk was gone, maybe I *needed* to hear it.

"I know this is...hard to talk about," she started. "But I need to say this."

I shrugged. "Okay."

She tangled her fingers in her lap and played with her rings. "I'll get straight to it because there's no other way to say it. When I left after high school, I'm sorry if I hurt you. I truly am. However, it was the best thing for me to do at the time."

I scoffed, almost laughing. "That doesn't exactly sound like an apology."

She turned to find my eyes. "We were seventeen, Will. I'm sorry about the timing, I know that it sucked. Would you rather I have stuck around for you, pretending...until when?"

"You broke up with me right after my parents *died!*" I shouted, emotion getting caught in the back of my throat.

She pressed her lips together. "I know."

I let out a long breath, calming my nerves. "I just want to know one thing. Why'd you do it? Was I truly that awful?"

She dropped her jaw, gaping at me. "*What?* Did you *actually* think that's why I broke up with you?"

I shook my head in confusion. "Then what was it?"

"It had nothing to do with you, not really." She sighed. "I needed to get off of Ruby Island. I needed to leave, and I was afraid that if I stayed with you, that I'd be here forever." She grinned. "You're an amazing person, Will. I hope you know that. We were kids when we started dating. We changed—both of us. Maybe *I* changed more than you; either way it was ending. Did you know that? I knew I was going to break up with you before we graduated."

"Before my parents died?" I asked.

"*Yes.* It was never about that at all."

I let out a deep breath, my arms rigid in my lap. "I always thought that you broke up with me and left the island because you realized how much baggage I was—a burden."

She frowned, her brows knitting together. "No, that was never the problem. It was *always* about me. I wanted to go to college and see the world. And I might have been naive back then, though I know that I wouldn't be the person I am today if I hadn't left. So in that sense, I don't regret it."

I knew the answer might hurt, and yet I had to know. "Did you love me?" I held my breath waiting for her reply.

Her lips pulled into a slow smile. "Yeah, I did, once upon a time. It changed along with me, you know? But sometimes love isn't enough to keep people together. It doesn't mean that *you* weren't good enough. It just means that life was pulling us in different directions."

"Different directions?"

"Yeah, sometimes people grow along the same path, and other times they fork away from each other."

"*Hmm.*"

"You like living here, don't you?" she asked with an arched brow.

"Of course, I love Ruby Island. I've never wanted to live anywhere else."

"Seriously?" She seemed surprised. "Not even to explore what's out there?"

I shook my head. "I know what's out there and it's not *here*."

The conversation lulled for a minute. We both looked out over the crest of the island from the porch, a light breeze sweeping across my back.

"What ever happened to that guy you were seeing?" she asked, somehow knowing just where to punch.

I'd told her when I was in high school that I was bi, so it wasn't a surprise to her that I would be dating a man. "I wasn't *seeing* him, exactly."

She laughed. "Okay, then what happened to the guy you were messing around with?"

I cracked a smile, unable to hold it in. "He left. Went back to his life in Boston."

Her smile faded, reading my expression. "Oh, he did, huh?"

I shrugged in an effort to seem casual. "Tourists come and go."

"It seemed as if you really liked him." She poked and prodded. "I thought maybe you'd keep in touch or something."

I scoffed. "We only knew each other for a couple weeks. I don't even have his phone number."

She rolled her eyes. "Because that would be *so hard* to find in this day and age. You should call him."

I shook my head and ran a hand through my hair. "No, that would not be a good idea."

"Why not? Did you two end badly?"

I cringed. "Not exactly...it just wouldn't work out."

"You never know if you don't try," she said with a shrug.

"I suppose."

She rocked her chair for a beat and then stood, brushing off dust and dirt from her jeans. "I better get going. I gotta go home and pack."

I turned to find her face. "Where are you staying by the way? Didn't want to stay at the inn?"

She flushed and smiled sheepishly. "I'm staying with my aunt. I almost stayed at the inn, though I didn't want it to be awkward, always hanging around, if you didn't want to see me."

"Ah, probably a good idea." I rose from my chair to see her off. "This has been the longest two weeks of my life."

She laughed through her nose. "Keep your chin up, Will. When the rain clouds blow away they always reveal a rainbow."

I rolled my eyes, although I couldn't help but crack a grin. "Thanks. Have a safe trip back home."

She waved. "Bye. Tell your aunt I wished her well."

"Will do."

She walked down the steps, past the gate to the road, and then disappeared down the hill and around the bend.

I realized after a moment that my eyes stung, watering in the corners. "Stupid allergies," I said, though no one was around to hear or care. I hadn't cried in a long time. Maybe not since my parents died. I hadn't realized how much I'd been keeping inside wondering why Alicia had left. Now that I knew it had nothing to do with me, a weight was lifted off my chest. One that had been there for years, pushing down on my shoulders.

* * *

I was sitting at the front desk waiting for potential lodgers to walk in the door when my phone started ringing. I checked the ID—Rory.

I answered quickly. "Yeah?"

"*It's happening!*" he shouted into the phone.

"The baby?" I clarified, because with Rory you never knew exactly what you were getting yourself into.

"Yes, *dumbass*, the baby. Get over to the clinic!"

"Okay, we're on our way." I ended the call and caught Aunt Caroline standing by the archway, expectant.

I nodded. "It's time."

She grinned and clapped her hands. "What are you waiting for? Let's go."

Even with her ankle improving she couldn't walk the whole way, so I asked our neighbor down the road if we could borrow his golf cart and he agreed. It must have been a funny scene—me driving like a madman, cutting across town with Aunt Caroline hanging onto the armrest for dear life.

We got to the clinic in record time. The waiting room was empty, so we limped our way into the back, following the groaning of an incredibly pregnant woman. The medical room was small and sparse, painted white with a hospital bed dressed in cream linens. Maria was crouched over with her head between her knees, her long dark hair falling over her shoulders.

Rory whipped around when he noticed us behind him and grinned. "Her water broke thirty minutes ago."

"*Wow.*"

Dr. Brenner was standing by with his hands behind his back, monitoring the situation.

"How are you doing, Maria?" Aunt Caroline asked, waddling over to rub her back.

She flipped her hair away from her face and let out a deep breath. "So far, not too bad. I didn't even realize I was having contractions for a while. I thought I'd just eaten a bad sandwich or something. Then the water broke." Her whole body tensed, her nose screwing up and eyes shutting. She must have been having another contraction.

Dr. Brenner smiled brightly and glanced at his watch. "They're speeding up; not long now. You two better wait outside, we need some room here."

Mrs. Spalding, the nurse, came in through the doorway with a metal tray of supplies.

"Okay." I clapped Rory on the back. "We'll be waiting right outside. Let us know if you guys need anything."

"A beer?" Maria asked, her eyes shut tight.

I grinned, holding back a laugh. "Anything, but *that*."

We sat in the lobby for probably five hours. Not too bad considering. "When you were born, you took twenty-six hours," Aunt Caroline mused.

Rory poked his head out of the delivery room, leaning against the door frame with a grin. "It's a girl. Seven pounds, seven ounces."

I beamed. "That's good luck, double sevens."

We wandered back into the room once everything calmed down and Maria and Rory had spent their own moment alone together as a new trio. Maria was sitting up in the bed, covered in soft cotton blankets. She cradled the bundle of green in the crook of her arm.

"Wow, she's smaller than I thought she would be." I walked closer and peered into the wrappings. "Especially for a future star athlete."

Maria smiled, her eyes lidded from exhaustion. "Give her a few years, then we'll see."

Aunt Caroline moved past me to get a look, her eyes pink and glassy. "Oh my, she's so precious."

I turned towards the parents. "Congratulations you two. You've broken the Kirkpatrick curse."

Rory grinned. "And you know what they say, whatever you have first you'll probably have again. There will be a whole slew of Kirkpatrick girls on Ruby Island."

Maria laughed. "Calm down, babe. Let's start with the one, yeah? I can't imagine ever doing that all again."

Aunt Caroline laughed through her nose, resting her hand on the baby's covered head. "You say that now, wait a year. You'll completely forget what you made such a big fuss over and you'll be as eager as ever for the next one."

Maria turned her attention to me. "You'll remind me, won't you?"

I pulled out my phone, took a quick picture of her holding the baby, and put it in my calendar. "*There*, now on this date next year I'll get a notification. I'll remind you how amazing you were and how happy you were."

She rolled her eyes. "Thanks, Will."

* * *

We stayed at the clinic for the rest of the day. Even though their house was close by, they wanted to be extra careful. Nobody was bothered since the clinic was mostly empty—except for a Great Dane named Jerome who was getting some shots.

Maria had finally found sleep, the baby cradled beside her, and Aunt Caroline had shuffled out to go get some coffee even though I'd insisted that I'd do it for her. Rory and I were sitting next to each other in the hard metal chairs we'd grabbed from the waiting room.

"I can't believe I'm a dad," Rory said quietly.

"Yeah, you are." I laughed through my nose. "I can't believe it either."

He beamed. "You know when I first met Maria I knew that she was the one. She thinks I'm crazy when I say that, however I knew instantly— the exact moment that we met for the first time at that bagel shop."

I shifted in my chair, crossing my arms over my chest. "And you ordered a blueberry bagel plus a coffee with cream, only she mixed up your order, so then you had to go back. Then she confessed that she'd messed up your order on purpose so that you'd have to return and she could get your number," I recited, having listened to the same story at least a dozen times over the years.

He rolled his eyes. "Yes, *that* story. I knew even then."

"That's amazing." I was in awe of them. "I don't know if I've ever felt that way about someone."

Rory pinched his brow. "Never? Not even with Alicia?"

I shook my head. "No, never. Not even with her." Berk's features came to mind and I pushed them away. He was out of my life forever and even though Alicia and Aunt Caroline made it sound so easy I couldn't simply *call* him. To do what? To ask him to stay *again*? Get rejected *again*?

"Well, when you do, you've gotta hold on. Hold on for dear life and don't let them get away."

I laughed a little louder than I'd intended and I glanced over to make sure I hadn't awoken either of the girls. "Why does that make it sound like you're chasing a leprechaun or something?"

Rory grinned. "Because love is magical like that. Sometimes *it is* a chase."

"*Hmm.* I don't know about that."

"I agree with Rory." Aunt Caroline came back through the doorway with two coffees. She handed one to Rory and one to me. It was black and incredibly strong.

"Of course you would," I replied.

"This is about Berk, isn't it?" she asked, sitting in the next chair over.

"What do you mean?" I asked, evading the question.

"You *know* what I mean. Are you going to let him get away?"

I tensed my shoulders in frustration. "Who's letting him get away? I asked him if he wanted to stay and he said no."

She frowned. "*You did?* What did he say exactly?"

I sighed. "He said that he couldn't, that his life and job were in the city."

Aunt Caroline broke out in a grin.

"*What?*" I asked. "What could you possibly be smiling about?"

She jabbed a finger in my direction . "He said that he *couldn't* stay, not that he didn't *want* to stay. Those are two very different things."

I scoffed, wringing my hands in my lap. "Not really, they both lead to the same thing."

She shook her head. "Not at all. He *wanted* to stay. You should call him."

"Why does everyone keep telling me that?" I stage whispered, pulling my fingers through my hair.

Aunt Caroline arched her eyebrow. "Maybe because it's the truth."

"I can't call him, he would just say no again." I shook my head and stared at the linoleum tiled floor.

Rory nudged my shoulder. "Then do something else. *Go crazy.*"

"What if it's...not worth it?" I mumbled. "What if it all goes to shit anyway?"

Aunt Caroline took my hand and squeezed it with more strength than a woman her age should possess. "Then at least you tried. Isn't *that* worth it?

I slumped in my chair and released a long held breath. "I don't know."

She clucked her tongue. "Well you let me know when you've figured it out."

Could I try again? Could my heart take the inevitable beating?

SEVENTEEN

Berk

"Here, have another katmer." Ma placed another one of the pistachio pastries on my plate and stared at me expectantly.

"Ma, I'm full."

She scoffed. "You're too skinny, how can you be full? Look at your father." She gestured to him. "He is so big and strong. Those are your true genetics. My brothers are all tall and broad as well. You're too skinny."

I resisted the powerful urge to roll my eyes. Ada, who was across the table, smiled behind Ma's back.

I cut a slice off the katmer and shoved it in my mouth.

Ma patted my cheek. "Good boy."

Usually Ma would invite some of her friends home after mosque for tea, but today it was only the family. I chewed slowly so I didn't have to talk; Ma and Ada were carrying the conversation. Most of the time, I'd try and help her out, though after the last few days I had nothing left to give.

My whole body was itchy and tight. Something was nagging at me, and I refused to find out what it was. I'd won. I'd gotten to keep my job and my apartment. Wasn't that enough? I was happy with my life before, why wasn't I happy with it now?

I sipped the strong Turkish tea from the tulip-shaped glass and waited until Ma tired herself out.

Dad was sitting in his recliner by the TV reading the newspaper, his glasses on the end of his nose. He was a quiet man, and when he wasn't working he was usually in that damn chair. It saved me from receiving a second lecture, though, so I counted my blessings.

Ada pulled me away from the table and we escaped to her room. This was the same town house we'd lived in back when I was in high school. Except now, my room was an office/exercise studio.

Ada's bedroom was all green and brown with fluffy blankets and big stylish pillows. It was twice as nice as my dorm when I'd gone to college.

"So what's up?" she asked, sitting criss-cross on the bed.

I shrugged. "What do you mean?"

She narrowed her eyes. "I can tell you've been keeping something in this whole afternoon. You look like you're going to burst."

I sat down in the round hanging chair and slumped. "I don't know. I might have made a big mistake."

"What do you mean?" She leaned forward. "How come? You said everything went perfectly on that island job."

I put my head in my hands and rubbed my eyes with my palms. "It did, that's the problem."

He shook her head. "I don't get it."

I opened my eyes. "He...asked me to stay."

"Who?" She dropped her jaw. "That guy you were seeing from the inn? What was his name?"

"Will," I supplied.

She gasped. "He did? That's so romantic."

"Except it's not because I said *no*."

She flopped down onto her stomach so that she was stretched out in my direction. She put her chin in her hands. "How come?"

I scoffed. "What do you mean, *how come*? Do I have to count out the reasons on my fingers?" I began counting. "I just saved my job, so I can't quit. I would lose my apartment with barely any savings because I'm financially irresponsible. Ma and Dad would go ballistic on me since they're still planning for me to marry a woman. Plus, if I left I'd hardly get to see you. That's like five things." I held out my hand and wiggled my fingers.

"Something tells me you wanted to say yes, though, which must mean you really like this guy." She arched an eyebrow. "Do you love him?"

I bit back a laugh. "That's what you picked up from the long list of reasons it would be a bad idea?"

"So *do* you?" she pressed.

I ran my fingers through my hair; I hadn't bothered to style it today. "I don't know. I mean, I've only known him a couple weeks, isn't that crazy?"

She rolled her eyes again. "Don't you remember Aunt Beyza. She married her husband after only knowing him for six days. They're still married twenty years later."

I blew out an incredulous breath. "Yeah, but they're *straight*."

She frowned. "*So?* My friend Rachelle moved in with her girlfriend after only dating a month. They just got a cat together."

"Yeah, but they're *lesbians*."

She grinned. "Oh my God, you're being *so* annoying. You obviously feel something for the guy or we wouldn't even be talking about this. Do you want me to counter all your bogus reasons?" she offered.

I waved my hand and then smashed it into my chin. "By all means."

She tallied them off on her fingers, copying me. "First of all, you *hate* your job. I get that you just saved it, though maybe it's not worth saving."

"But—"

She held up her hand and widened her eyes. "I'm not done. *Hush.*"

She pushed her hair behind her shoulder. "Secondly, you *hate* your apartment, you're hardly ever there. You could totally downsize. Thirdly, Ma and Dad would *not* go ballistic. They might be overbearing, however they only want you to be happy. I truly think Ma only pushes people on you because she can tell that you're not happy in love. It's not the right method, but she tries."

"*I suppose,*" I said slowly.

She narrowed her eyes for me to be quiet and I groaned.

"And lastly, don't kid yourself, you hardly see me anyway."

I opened my mouth to protest and then shut it again.

"Besides, if you live on an island, we can visit. It looks gorgeous from the pictures you sent me. It can be my little weekend getaway."

I sighed. "Okay, even if I put *all those things* aside, I still have another problem."

Her lips pulled into a wide smile. "Always with the problems. What now?"

It was something I'd been wondering since I got on Magnus' boat back to the mainland. "When Will asked me to stay, my first thought was, how could I stay knowing I'd pushed this resort deal on the town that I don't actually believe in?"

She sucked on her teeth. "Yikes, that *is* a problem."

I threw my hands in the air. "I was trying to save my job. What else was I supposed to do? Tell my boss *no*?"

She shrugged one shoulder. "Can you fix it?"

Could I fix it? They'd already voted on whether or not to accept the deal. I was sure that Mayor Lancaster had already signed the contracts. Sandy Brook was quick at that sort of thing. *Although...*

"Maybe," I said, an idea forming in my mind.

"So fix it then." She waved her hand through the air. "The rest can be solved if you truly want to."

"But—"

She shoved her face into her comforter. "*What now?*"

"What about you?"

She arched a brow. "What *about* me?"

"Well, if I do this, if I quit my job, it'll seal the deal on me being the ultimate fuckup in this family. Then all the pressure will be on you—the grades, the family, the traditions."

She leaned over the side of the bed and grabbed my hand. "First of all, you're *not* a fuckup. And also, believe it or not, I actually *want* to become a lawyer."

"What? You do?" This was a surprise to me.

264

She nodded. "*I love it.* I want to make a difference in the world."

"I always thought you were doing it for Dad, that he was pressuring you. That's why *I* went to college, anyway.

"Nope." She shook her head. "So don't worry about me. I'll be fine. Ma can try to push me to start a family as soon as she'd like, although it won't do her any good. I'm stubborn, like her."

I cracked a grin. "Yes, you are. So you're *really* okay with this? I mean it's...crazy."

She smiled and squeezed my hand. "Sometimes life is a little crazy, *abi*. You just have to roll with it."

I tapped my foot, my knee bobbing in the air. "Will you help me explain things to Ma and Dad? I don't know how to do it by myself, and you were always better at talking to them."

"Of course I will."

I groaned.

"*What?*"Ada slapped my hand. "What could *possibly* be left, Berk."

I slung my free arm over my eyes. "What if I missed my chance? What if I don't get a redo?"

"You can't know unless you try. Besides, it sounds to me like he loves you. Not many people have the guts to ask someone to stay with them on a tiny little island after only knowing each other for two weeks. It sounds like he's as crazy about you as you are about him."

"*Maybe.*"

* * *

When I got home I sat down on the couch and pulled out my phone. It was only the afternoon. Mayor Lancaster would probably still be at the office, and I still had his number from earlier. It was easier that way than connecting through his assistant.

What the hell was I supposed to say? Hi, I convinced you of something I didn't necessarily believe in, because I wanted to keep my job, however I no longer want to keep that job so you shouldn't take the deal? *It sounds insane.* Ada made it seem so easy, however if I did this, Mr. Schwimmer might hire someone to break my legs...or worse. This deal would have been pretty profitable for them, even if it was only a small, out of the way island.

I made the call, holding my breath as it rang. When he actually answered I stumbled over my words. "Uh, hi, Mayor Lancaster."

"Mr. Kaplan?"

"Yes." I told him everything. I explained how the economy could be fixed by making some small changes themselves, and that they didn't need this resort, which could actually hurt them in the short term—at least while the resort was being built.

I'd expected him to be angry, although if anything he was dumbfounded. "Why are you telling me all this, Mr. Kaplan?"

I'd been focused on that question the whole cab ride home. Why would I want to uproot everything I'd worked so hard for? "Because I believe Ruby Island deserves a fair shot, that's the bottom line of the situation. You guys have been dealt a bad hand the last few years, but you can turn it around. You have something that a lot of places don't have—originality. Why would someone want to stay at a resort where they know exactly what they're getting? All those places are the same. People want lived-in, they want culture, and Ruby Island has all that. I think it would be a shame to ruin it."

He made an unintelligible sound. "Um, thank you, I think, Mr. Kaplan. It's a good thing the fax machine in the office wasn't working. We were supposed to sign the contracts this morning."

"*Are you serious?*" I couldn't believe it.

"Yes. Your call came in the nick of time."

Thank god for dinosaur computers and nineties fax machines.

* * *

Getting dressed the next day, I was slow and meticulous. He had to know by now, and yet Mr. Schwimmer hadn't called. The silence was more threatening than if he'd burst through my front door.

I took a cab to the office and walked slowly inside.

Harvey, the security guy, greeted me with a smile. "Hey man, look at you with your tan. Must have been a nice gig."

I laughed. "I didn't tan," I said defensively. "I was working."

He cracked a toothy grin. "Sure, sure."

I walked towards the elevators. "I'll see you in a minute."

"Why?" He knit his brows together.

I rolled my eyes and laughed. "I'll tell you when I come down."

"Okay, man."

I rode the elevator to the right floor and stepped off into the short hallway that led to the office. Everything looked exactly the same. I didn't know why I thought it would magically look different somehow. It had always been a boring gray office space with cubicles and lots of glass doors and partitions.

Jessie, my cubicle buddy, not missing a beat said, "Well look what the cat dragged in. Do you have a tan?"

I scowled at her. "No, I don't. It's called being Turkish, I'm permanently tan."

She narrowed her eyes at me. "You can still tan, idiot. Did you even wear sunscreen? Bet you're going to get skin cancer."

"Thanks, I missed you too."

She simpered and leaned over the partition. "I was counting the days until you came back, Berk."

I arched a brow. "*Really?*"

She frowned and said, "No." Then ducked her head back down.

I didn't bother setting anything on my desk. I stood around waiting by my cubicle until he noticed me—it didn't take long, only a minute or two. He opened his office door with a *bang* and marched back inside. I didn't even warrant an invitation, he'd known I was coming. I walked past the line of desks and up the stairs to the second floor walkway. I hesitated outside the open door and then said *fuck it*. *He* knew he was firing me. *I* knew he was firing me. So why did I let this jackass have so much power?

I walked inside. Mr. Schwimmer was sitting behind his desk, fingers laced together atop the wood. "Have a seat, Mr. Kaplan."

I rolled my shoulders and straightened my frame. "I'll stand. I have a feeling I won't be here very long."

He didn't feign niceties. "No. You won't be." His mouth turned down into a sneer. "You know, you're lucky I don't sue you for what you've done."

I widened my eyes in faux surprise. "*Sue me?* For *what* exactly?"

"You know what you did," he barked, pushing himself out of the chair and into a standing position. "You wrecked that deal."

I gave him a stiff, professional smile. "I don't know what you're talking about. I did my best to get the people on our side. I must have failed."

A vein popped in the side of his neck as he grappled with his words. "Y-You're fired, you damn idiot. Do you know what you've cost this company?"

I shrugged. "Deals don't work out all the time, you know that as well as anyone, Mr. Schwimmer. The market is fickle. There's no sense in crying about it."

He raised his meaty hands like he was imagining wrapping them around my neck, but then thought better of it, lowering them again. "Get the fuck out of this office and never come back. I have friends in high places, Mr. Kaplan. Don't think I won't use my influence."

I leaned forward over his desk until we were a mere few inches apart. "Go ahead if it makes you happy. I don't care."

His eyes went dark and murderous, however I backed out of the room before he could begin to form a reply. I knew that security would likely be called immediately, so I didn't even bother going back to my desk. I passed the cubical and the quizzical Jessie.

"Bye, Jessie, I never liked you, however you made working here a little more fun."

She gaped at me. "You *actually* got fired?"

I grinned. "Yep."

She raised her eyebrows and pursed her lips. "Well shit, see you never, I guess."

I waved as I walked past. "Bye."

Security *did* in fact come to meet me, luckily it was only Harvey. He arched a brow as I followed him back into the elevator. "Man, you weren't kidding. What the hell happened? Mr. Schwimmer sounded like he wanted your head on a platter."

I shrugged in an effort to stay casual. "Let's just say that I didn't meet his bottom line."

Harvey looked like he had no idea what I was talking about, although he nodded his head anyway. "*Right.*"

When we reached the lobby I shook his hand. "I'm definitely never coming back again after that meeting, so I guess this is goodbye."

He grinned. "Good luck, man."

"Thanks."

I wasn't even halfway home in the cab before I got a call from Dad. I'd told my parents about my plans to quit and find a new career. Only, I'd left out the part about leaving Mr. Schwimmer in a murderous rage. Surprisingly however, Dad was more concerned than pissed. "Are you sure you know what you're doing, Berk?"

"Nope, but I still have to try."

He paused. "I suppose a man has to form his own path, although I worry about you."

I laughed through my nose, feeling a little bit high from the altercation. "I know, don't worry. I'll be okay no matter what happens. Mr. Schwimmer's reach only goes so far, even if he believes he's the top developer in the city."

Dad sighed. "This might make things awkward at my firm when the news gets passed around. My own son, kicked out of the industry."

"You love your job, don't you?" I asked, already knowing the answer.

"Of course," he replied firmly.

"Then there is no problem, Dad. People will forget about me by next month. You'll see."

The cab stopped in front of my building, so I said goodbye and ended the call.

Once I got to the top floor I stood in the middle of my apartment and stared at all my stuff. I had a lot of work to do.

EIGHTEEN

Will

Rory and Maria took their baby home and began nesting. Aunt Caroline and I brought by cooked meals and tried to stay out of their way —this was their moment to be alone and enjoy their new family member.

On my way back from one of my many trips to their apartment, I stopped at the end of the street and caught the top of the mayor's office building in the distance. Rory and Aunt Caroline thought that I should find out Berk's number and call him. It shouldn't be *that* hard, so why did it feel like climbing a mountain? It would be an immediate embarrassment if I called and he rejected me *again*. I wasn't sure if my heart could handle that.

But the inn was lonely without his presence. I hadn't realized over the years of living with Aunt Caroline how quiet and empty the inn was. Even during the height of tourist season when most of our rooms were full, and I was cooking and serving laughing families, it was still lonely—having no one to share it all with. At the end of the long work day I still went to sleep alone.

I'd been holding so much resentment against Alicia over what I'd thought had happened that I never truly allowed myself to open up to someone in that way again. Knowing what I know now...maybe I was ready.

I turned the corner and marched with long confident strides over to the mayor's office. The faster I got there, the less time I had to chicken out.

What if they didn't even have his number? Maybe fate or the universe would decide for me. I entered the building and climbed the rounded staircase to the second floor where Marjorie was sitting behind her desk, smacking on some gum and scrolling through her phone.

"Hey, Marjorie."

She looked up from her screen and grinned. "Hi, Will. What's going on? You never come to see me and this is twice now in one month."

I laughed. "Uh, I was wondering about that guy who stayed with us at the inn. The guy from Sandy Brook, Berk?"

She lowered her phone. "What about him?"

"You don't happen to have his phone number on file or something, do you?"

She popped her gum and pushed a long strand of dark curly hair over her shoulder. "Even if I did, I'm not supposed to give out personal phone numbers through our office."

"Oh, okay." *Damn.*

She arched a perfectly manicured brow. "Did he leave something behind or..."

I hadn't even thought about that angle. "Not exactly."

"So," she shook her head, "what, then?"

I scanned her desk and found a romance book that was cracked open page side down. It was one of those eighties romance novels with a bare chested hunk clutching a blonde woman who had her skirt hiked up to her thighs.

"What if I told you I was in love with him?" I blurted out, seeing no way to avoid it.

Her eyes widened and her smile grew. "You're in love with him?"

I rubbed my hands together. "Possibly."

"And you don't have his number?" she asked in disbelief.

I laughed. "Nope, we never did that, unfortunately."

She smacked her gum again, chewing faster now. "Oh my God, that is so romantic—a missed connection trope."

"A what?"

She waved her hand through the air and closed her eyes for a second. "Nothing, it's a book thing." She woke up her computer and scrolled, looking for something. "Here it is, Berk Kaplan. I even have his address."

His address? "Why do you have his address?"

She looked up at me. "Mayor Lancaster wanted to send him some of the merchandise with the new Ruby Island logo on it that he had designed. You know, before the deal went bad."

"*Wait*, what?" I shook my head. I must have heard that wrong. "What do you mean the deal went bad?"

Marjorie lowered her voice and beckoned me to lean in closer. "Don't tell anyone else, but I overheard Mayor Lancaster on the phone yesterday with Mr. Kaplan. Mr. Kaplan was urging Mayor Lancaster not to take the deal, not to sign the contracts."

"He did?" I was shocked. He had tanked his own deal? Hadn't his job depended on it? "Are you sure?"

She nodded. "Yes, because then Mayor Lancaster was on the phone with the Vice President of Sandy Brook and when the call ended the mayor was all red in the face and flustered. He told me that if anything came in on the fax from them I should tear it up."

"So the resort deal isn't happening?" I couldn't believe what I was hearing. It was like something out of my daydreams.

"Nope. Apparently not. Mayor Lancaster will probably have to call a town meeting to explain what happened since we already voted for it. I don't know."

I stood there motionless for a few seconds, forgetting where I was. Berk had convinced Mayor Lancaster *not* to take the deal. *Why?* What changed his mind?

"So, do you want this number?" Marjorie asked, pulling me out of my reverie.

"Uh, *yes*, please. Can I have that address too?"

She grinned, her teeth white against her dark pink lipstick. "Anything for love."

I took the information and thanked her on my way out. My mind was reeling. Berk had stopped the deal at a great personal cost to himself. If I hadn't talked to Marjorie today would I ever have found out about it? Not quickly, but eventually, maybe. So...Berk hadn't done it to get my attention. He'd done it because it was the right thing to do. To save the island from investors.

When I got home I relayed the news to Aunt Caroline. For some strange reason she didn't seem all that surprised.

"Why do you have that look on your face?" I asked, collapsing into the soft cushions of the sofa.

"What look?" she asked with a raised eyebrow.

I waved my hand in her direction. "That look that says you knew this was going to happen all along."

She shrugged. "I didn't *know*, I merely hoped. Berk is a good man. I knew that he'd do the right thing."

"Well *I* didn't. What does that say about me?"

She smiled warmly, her plump cheeks dimpling. "That you're human and you've been hurt before."

"*Hmm.*" I slumped into the pillows.

"What are you going to do now? Are you finally going to call him?" she asked.

I thought over the idea, rolling it around in my head like a hard candy. "I think...I'm going to go to the city." Saying it out loud sent a shiver down my spine, my fight or flight response activating.

Aunt Caroline glanced over, her eyes wide. "To Boston?" she confirmed.

"Yeah."

"You haven't left the island since you were a kid." It wasn't a question. She knew better than anybody my fear of leaving.

"I know."

"Are you worried?"

I nodded. "A little." The last time my parents had left the island they'd come back in coffins. It was hard to get the mental picture out of my head.

She went back to her knitting. The blue wool was growing into something complicated with different stitch patterns and textures.

"Would you be okay on your own?" I asked.

She turned to me with a furrowed brow, like it was a silly question. "Of course, dear. Go bring home your man."

I rolled my eyes. "He has to say *yes* first, which isn't likely since he's already said no once before."

"Hey, don't be negative." She set down her work and looked me in the eyes. "He stopped the resort deal from going through, didn't he?"

"Yes," I agreed after a beat. He *had* done that.

She went on, "And he already basically said he would stay if he *could*."

"Not in so many words, though I suppose."

She picked up her needles and began knitting again. "So, don't worry about me, I'll be fine on my own. I'm not an invalid."

I lingered on the couch, staring at the wall for a minute, then two.

"*Yes?*" Aunt Caroline asked, drawing out the word.

"Nothing, I'm just overthinking."

She laughed. "So, stop overthinking. Go pack a bag and get out of here."

I stood up from the sofa and walked past Aunt Caroline. "Are you sure?"

She grinned, lines crinkling around her eyes. "Of course I'm sure."

"Okay." I hustled through the lobby and up the stairs to my room. I grabbed an old duffle bag and threw a couple things inside. Hopefully I wouldn't need to stay in the city, however if this was a tremendous failure I could grab a hotel room or something.

When I came back downstairs I was wearing my coat and hat, my bag over my shoulder. *Was I missing something?* I'd never been on a trip before. What was I supposed to bring? I patted down my pockets, feeling my phone, my wallet, and my keys. *I guess I have everything.* I went into the sitting room and kissed Aunt Caroline on the cheek. "I'll see you tomorrow, hopefully."

She squeezed my hand and then let me go. "See you tomorrow, Willy."

I waved goodbye and went out the door before I could convince myself to stop. I followed the road through town to the marina, passing Maria and Rory's shop. I was going to check in with them before I went, but they were busy, and if this all turned into a colossal failure they didn't need to know I'd left at all.

I found Magnus messing around on his boat down by the docks. The marina was extremely empty for May. "Hey," I greeted, walking up to his boat, The Irishman's Pride. "Can you take me to the mainland?" It was still early morning and he didn't seem particularly busy.

"The mainland?" He looked me up and down, finally noticing the duffle bag. "You want to go to the mainland?"

I stopped myself from frowning. "*Yes*, that's what I said."

"But...you never go to the mainland." He stood from his crouched position and crossed his arms. "It's always your aunt Caroline that goes."

"I know." Was he doing this on purpose?

"Well, okay then. Um, hop in, Will. I can take you there right quick."

"Thanks." I grabbed the side of the boat for leverage and climbed onto the deck.

I sat in one of the folding chairs and secured my bag beneath me. Magnus started the engine and we rolled out over the waves. The sun was shining bright and the water was a shocking shade of blue. I gripped the sides of the chair as we got further and further away from Ruby Island. It became a mass in the distance and then merely a dot on the horizon. My home, just a dot in the middle of the blue expanse.

"You all right there, Will?" Magnus asked, his face not giving anything away.

"I'm fine." I clutched my chest and listened for my heart. It was banging against my ribs like a bird trying to escape a cage. I took in large gulps of sea air and let it out slowly, calming my nerves. I was off of Ruby Island. I'd done it.

The mainland appeared in the near distance. For some reason I'd expected it to look different, and yet it looked a lot like Ruby Island with its green grasses, rocky beaches, wild flowers, and driftwood. Magnus pulled alongside the dock and tied off the boat.

"Are you sure you know where you're going?" he asked with a raised eyebrow, the most expression I'd ever seen on his face before.

I shook my head. "No, but I'll figure it out. Thanks, Magnus."

I paid him even though he didn't want to accept the cash and wandered the docks until I found an information booth. The man directed me to where I could get a ticket for the main ferry that went across the bay. I remembered from what Berk had told us that he'd taken the ferry when he got off the train. Since I didn't own a car I thought it would be a good idea to copy his journey.

I got a ticket and took the ferry from one small touristy town to another. Then from the ferry I walked the three blocks to a small train station where I bought yet another ticket into Boston. The trip was a few hours long, so I'd be getting into the city in the early afternoon.

I'd never been on a train. I'd only ever seen them in movies where they were getting robbed by bandits on horses. The constant rocking of the ferry hadn't done much to calm my nerves, but the train had my body buzzing with a gentle hum as it ran along the tracks. It raced through cities, towns, and fields of empty dead grass until we came upon Boston.

It was so much bigger than I'd imagined with towering glass and metal buildings. It made Ruby Island look like a speck in comparison. The train station was large and beautiful with slick marble floors and tall archways. I made my way to the street and grabbed a taxi. I gave the driver Berk's address.

The whole ride I was going over what I wanted to say. Would he be mad that I'd showed up unannounced? Would he turn me away from the door? How was I going to convince him to come back with me? There were so many questions left unanswered. I was hoping that seeing each other would be enough, at least for the moment. That he had experienced the same spark that I had. That there was something there to be rekindled.

The taxi driver dropped me off in front of one of the many glass high-rises that lined the street. Berk lived *here*? The structure towered hundreds of feet above me. I checked the address that I'd written down just to confirm. *Yep*, this was the place.

Unfortunately, when I tried the front door it was locked. It was one of those buildings you needed a code to enter. I searched the digital callbox for a name, found Berk's on the list, and tried calling up to his apartment. It rang for a while and then nothing happened. *Is he not home?* I got desperate enough to try and call his neighbors and see if *they* would let me in. The first one had no idea who I was talking about, *nice neighbor*, and the second wouldn't let me in. She said something before she hung up about there being a lot of men coming and going from Berk's apartment. But I wasn't just *some* guy. Was I?

"Damn it." I got frustrated and started asking anybody on the list who would answer if they would let me in. Eventually one of them caved and the door buzzed. "*Thank you.*"

The elevator had a sign taped over it saying it was broken, so I took the stairs. Buildings this tall had no right to have broken elevators. My heart was pounding in my chest and my lungs were heaving when I finally reached the top floor.

It didn't take me long to locate the correct apartment since it was directly across from the stairs. I stood in front of his door and hesitated with my knuckles poised against the wood. What if he didn't want to see me? What if he was avoiding me? I blew out a deep breath and steeled myself.

Then I knocked. No answer. I knocked again and waited for several minutes. Still no answer. Maybe he actually *wasn't* home. I'd wait. He had to come back eventually, right? I sat down on the floor across from his apartment and made myself comfortable.

As it turned out, I didn't have to wait long. A tall guy with deep brown skin spotted me sitting on the ground and walked over with an arched brow—he was dressed in a dress shirt and trousers. "Hello, I'm the manager here, are you...waiting for someone?"

I gestured at the door, flustered that I'd been *caught*. I probably looked so silly. "Uh, yeah, I'm waiting for Berk Kaplan to get back."

He shook his head. "Berk Kaplan doesn't live here anymore. He moved out yesterday, actually."

"*What?*" I gaped for a second and then pulled myself together. "He *moved out?*"

"Yep."

I pulled myself up off of the floor. "Do you know where he went?"

He shook his head. "No idea. Although he broke his lease in the middle of the month and paid a fat fee, so it must have been pretty important, wherever he went."

He left. Berk had left the city. He was probably long gone by now. "Thanks."

The manager nodded and left down the long hallway.

I pulled out my phone and hovered my finger over Berk's freshly made contact. What would be the point in calling him if he was already gone? He'd said if he ever got fired from his job he would be barred from the land development industry. That had to mean he'd left Boston. And If he'd moved to a far away metropolis, he wasn't going to be enticed back for a little island in the middle of nowhere.

Dammit. I thought about calling Aunt Caroline, only I didn't know what I'd say. I'd failed. Berk had already moved on without me. I'd been worried that I would have to stay overnight in the city, but suddenly the draw of home called to me. Why would I want to stay in this big empty city when I knew that Berk wasn't here? *I might as well just turn around and go back home.*

So that's what I did. I grabbed a cab back to the train station and got on the first train north of the city.

I'd never been more dumbfounded. Why had I thought that this plan would work? Simply showing up and expecting miracles to be performed. Life didn't work like that. Life was complex and often difficult in ways that couldn't be easily understood. Why did I think that I would be the one in a million? The lucky one?

The first time on the train I'd been interested in the trip—I'd admired the landscape and was calmed by the motion. Now, going back, I was not. I avoided the window and stuck to my own micro bubble, crossing my arms over my chest. This was something to be endured until I was home. Back to what I knew.

When the train stopped at my station I disembarked and made my way through the small town in the direction of the ferry. I *barely* made it. The cars had already parked along the belly of the boat and everyone had boarded. They were starting to close the gates just as I got to the ticket booth.

I raced to make it in time and stopped at the top of the ramp to catch my breath. All the other passengers had gone to the top deck of the boat to watch the view of the water. I filled my lungs with air, and with my duffle slung over my shoulder, I made my way to the top level to find a seat.

The afternoon was melting into sunset, the horizon an orange glow against the darkening blue water. I collapsed into a chair and set down my bag. About a dozen people were around me, mostly tourists with their suitcases and beach bags.

I was glad that I was back on the water, anything to get me away from the mainland. The city wasn't sinister or cursed like I'd assumed as a teenager. What it was, was disappointing. *It's only a place.* I had so desperately wanted everything to work out. I supposed that I should have been counting my blessings and been content that at least the resort deal had been squashed and everyone was healthy—Maria and the baby were good, and Aunt Caroline was on her way to freedom of mobility again. All in all, things could be worse.

Then why was I still thinking about him? His dark tousled hair, his warm skin, his long muscled limbs, and the way his laugh made his eyes and nose scrunch up. The way his eyes glimmered in the early morning light after just waking up. His kindness towards Aunt Caroline—and really everyone he came into contact with. I was going to miss so many things about him. It was hard to imagine never seeing him again.

I let out a deep breath as I gazed across the ferry. A man stood at the front of the boat with his hands on the railing—he fit Berk's description perfectly. My brain was performing mental gymnastics; I was even seeing him in other people now. What did that say about me? Would I start seeing him in my dreams too? In faces around town? In every silky black shirt and spice filled cologne?

I turned away. It was silly that I was staring at a total stranger. However something had caught my eye. What was it? I searched over his body once more. He was wearing boat shoes, a pair of dark chinos, and a black polo. He had a suitcase by his side, rolling slightly with the motion of the waves. His dark hair was parted to one side, shiny with product, even in the low golden light. He turned his head slightly to look at the watch on his wrist, showing off his profile—a strong nose and round chin.

I rose from my seat before I could realize what I was doing and walked over to him.

My brain was playing cruel tricks on me. What were the odds? In all the world?

"Berk?" I asked quietly. *He won't turn if it isn't him. He won't turn.*

He turned, a look of surprise on his face. "*Will?*"

NINETEEN

Berk

"Berk?"

The voice was so quiet I almost missed it. How many people on this tiny ferry could be named Berk? It was common in Turkey, not in the states.

I turned slowly, my heartbeat picking up with anticipation. "Will?"

He was standing there, gobsmacked, his jaw slack and his eyes wide in surprise.

"Wha—"

"What are you doing here?" he asked, stealing the question from my lips.

I didn't know what to do with my hands so I shoved them deep into my front trouser pockets. "I...I left Boston. I quit my job."

He nodded quickly. "I know."

"*You know?* How do you know?"

"I was just there."

I let in a sharp breath. "At my apartment?" Will had come to the city...to see me?

He took a step closer, his hand inadvertently skimming the side of my arm. "Yeah, and the manager told me that you left. I assumed he meant you moved to another big city like Philly or New York or something. I never imagined you'd be...here."

I was so taken aback that I struggled to form words. This was happening. He was here in front of me on this ferry. "Where else would I be?" I said. "I was coming back."

"To Ruby Island?" he confirmed, his features twisting in surprise, much like my own.

"Yeah, if..." I looked up then, catching his stormy blue eyes, "the offer still stands. I held my breath, waiting for his reply.

He straightened his shoulders and a smile formed on his lips. "Of course the offer still stands. I was coming to get you in Boston. Coming to convince you to return with me."

"You were?" When I'd said no the first time, I never imagined that I'd get a second chance, that Will would try again.

He took a step closer until we were practically touching. Our chests only a couple inches apart. "Great minds think alike I guess."

We stood there for a few painful seconds, staring into each other's eyes, before I made the first move, grabbed a fistful of his coat and pulled him towards me into a kiss.

He was stunned *until he wasn't*, snaking his arms around my waist and deepening the kiss. Everybody on the ferry probably thought we were crazy. From their perspective two random strangers were making out in front of a crowd of people. Will pulled away first, finding my eyes. "So, we're okay?"

I nodded, my lips pulling into a grin. "We have a lot to talk about, though."

He laughed through his nose. "No kidding." He put his arm around my shoulders and we walked over to the line of seats. One must have been his because a bag was sitting underneath. I sat down beside him.

"So...I'm kinda homeless now," I blurted out.

He smiled like it was the funniest thing he'd ever heard. "No, you're not. You can stay at the inn. Even if you want your own space, we can do that."

"Are you sure?" I asked. " Going from knowing each other for two weeks to moving in together seems fast."

He shrugged. "There are no rules here. It's whatever we're comfortable with."

Was I comfortable moving in with Will? Living at the inn? Strangely, the answer was *yes*. "Well, I didn't come all this way to be apart from you."

He held out his hand and laced his fingers with mine. "I missed you so much," he said. "I can't believe you're here."

I beamed. "I can't believe it either. And I missed you too. I'm kind of in shock right now."

He pulled me in closer until we were pressed together. "So, what exactly do you want to do once you're living on the island?" he asked with a raised brow. "I don't want to make the assumption that you'll help with the inn."

"I *do* want to help the inn," I stressed. "I have a lot of ideas bouncing around my head. Some of them are for the inn, and some of them are for the island itself. I would hate for all my hard work the past two weeks to be for nothing. Ruby Island could turn a huge profit if certain things changed."

He grinned and squeezed my hand. "Okay, so you want to work for...the island? Mayor Lancaster?"

I shrugged. "If he'd be up for that after everything I put him through. He'd seemed pretty shocked when I called to tell him not to take the deal."

"Why *did* you do that?" Will asked, looking into my eyes intently.

I shrugged. "Isn't it obvious?"

He shook his head.

"I had a lot of time to think on my way back to Boston—if I were to live on Ruby Island what would I have voted for? If I hadn't worked for Sandy Brook I would have voted *no*. There are other ways to improve the economy. Better ways."

Will's eyes were wide and his mouth turned up into a toothy grin. "Wow, so we somehow turned you into a townie, an islander."

I laughed. "Looks like it. You're stuck with me now that you've ruined me."

He squeezed my hand. "So what's our first step, now that we're in this together?"

"Well...*my* first step is making it to the island without throwing up."

Will cracked a grin and patted my stomach with his free hand. "Don't worry, you'll be okay. We can get some seasickness pills."

I laughed. "What do you think I'm on right now?"

He shook his head and rolled his eyes. "Okay, then what's our *second* step?"

"For us or for the inn?" I clarified.

"Either."

"Well, I'm going to have a stern conversation with this ferry company and lobby them to bring back the route to Ruby Island. It's criminal that they never replaced the line because of Covid."

He shrugged. "I'm sure Mayor Lancaster has tried."

"Yes, however they've never met *me* before. Some say I can be *very* persuasive."

He smiled, laughing through his nose. "That you can. And then after that?

"We get someone to paint the outside of the inn. The chipped look is no good," I said matter of factly.

"Really?" He raised his eyebrows. " I thought it added a certain charm to the place."

"It makes it look haunted, is what it does."

He clutched his chest with a pained expression on his face, then relented. "Okay, fine. You're the expert."

"We're *both* the expert."

We sat around talking about our plans for the inn, our plans for the town, and our plans for our future the rest of the ferry ride. He told me that Maria had her baby and the joy and excitement it had brought them. It turned out that Caroline knew I was coming—I was hoping to surprise her, so I was imagining ways that I still could.

When we docked at the small town outside of Ruby Island Will bought me more seasickness pills and an ice cream. Two things that should probably never go together, however I was so happy to be there, to be with him, I didn't question the poor decision.

I'd been dragging along my stupid-heavy suitcase, but like the gentleman that Will was, he took over for me. After about an hour of waiting around on the docks Magnus finally came to pick us up. He seemed surprised. Will clearly hadn't told him his grand plan to steal me away from the city.

"Come back again, son?" he asked, his bushy white brows furrowed over his dark eyes.

"I've come back for good, actually."

Magnus grinned and tipped his hat as Will placed the luggage on the boat and then helped me over the side. The ride wasn't nearly as bad as any time before, though that might have been because of the excellent company.

Once Magnus docked the boat and dropped us off, Will and I walked hand in hand through the middle of town. There weren't many people around, though it was still exhilarating being seen together for the first time by strangers and soon to be neighbors. I glanced over at Will and he gave me a self-conscious smile, his cheeks tingeing a shade darker. *This must be a new experience for him too.*

We took our time, walking at a leisurely pace around the bend and along the long dirt road to the inn. "That's another thing we're going to change," I said. "We need a freakin' taxi service."

He grinned and looked at me with one eye closed from the late afternoon sun. "Noted."

When we crested the hill and I caught the house in the distance I was shocked to find tears welling at the corners of my eyes. I hadn't realized how much I'd missed it and how much I'd loved staying here. Now It seemed like I'd be staying here permanently.

We climbed the stairs, though I stayed outside at the threshold with my suitcase. Will Went in, leaving the door cracked open so I could still hear.

"Will?" Caroline said. "You're back already?"

"Yeah." He wasn't a great actor, although it appeared like his downtrodden expression was enough to convince her.

"No luck, huh?" The hurt in her voice was *almost* enough to make me abandon my plan.

"He'd already left," Will told her.

"He left?" she asked in shock. "What do you mean *left?*"

"*Surprise!*" I rushed in through the open doorway and caught the expression on Caroline's face. It went from taken aback to playfully annoyed, her brows furrowing. "You shouldn't do that to an old woman, Berk, you'll stop my heart."

I blew out a quick breath and grinned. "Caroline, you're not old. We all know if you didn't have that boot on you'd be pummeling me right about now."

She raised her arms into a boxing stance. "I still might. Get over here."

Knowing she was playing, I walked over and was embraced in a tight hug that smelled of lilacs and wool. "You came back."

"I did. Funny story too."

I retrieved my suitcase from the porch and we all moved to the sitting room to talk. Will and I told her all about our timely meeting on the ferry.

"I wasn't sure it was him at first," Will said. "It was too crazy to be real. What are the chances that we'd be on the same ferry at the exact same time?"

I beamed. "You can thank my sister Ada for that. I promised that I'd go meet her friends at this dorm party before I left, and so I wasn't able to catch the morning train."

"Wow, actually?" Will grinned and looped his arm around my back, pulling me in closer on the sofa. "I'd been wondering about that—how I could travel to Boston and back and still meet you on the same ferry."

Caroline smiled, lines creasing around her mouth. "Wonderful."

I chuckled. "It's like one of those math problems in high school, if train A is going sixty MPH and train B is going forty MPH..."

Will barked out a laugh. "Yeah, I didn't do well in math. At least not that kind."

We sat around talking for hours, the sun long past gone. We told her what our plans were for the future, basically everything we'd discussed on the ferry ride over. I asked if it was okay if I worked at the inn. It *was* partly hers after all.

She smiled warmly, her hand finding mine. "Of course you can, dear. In fact, I *insist* on it."

* * *

When it finally came time to go to sleep we both helped Caroline up the stairs. She said goodnight and gave me a final hug before retreating to her room.

I peered across the hall at Will's open doorway. *Should I go back down to my old room or...* What were the rules now that all the pretense was gone?

Will answered that question for me. He wrapped his strong arms around my frame and carried me bridal style into his room, taking me by surprise. "Oh my God, I was not ready for that." My heart jumped in my chest as he dropped me onto the soft bed.

He closed the door behind him and stared down at me in the low light with a devilish grin on his face. "You're not going anywhere."

"*Oh?*" I was both thrilled and scared. I'd never truly dated anyone. What if it ruined our chemistry? Changed what we had?

He moved slowly to the bed and leaned his weight over me, his arms on either side of my head. "Nope." He dipped his chin and kissed me, soft and gentle at first, then deepened the kiss. Every touch made me forget what I'd been so worried about. Of course we worked. Of course I wanted this.

He pulled at my clothing and I couldn't get it off fast enough. It had only been a couple days and I'd missed him so much. Missed his smile, missed his touch. I raked my fingers across the smooth expanse of his back.

He flipped us over so that I was on top, straddling his waist. "I really missed you."

He smiled wickedly. "I really missed you too."

The night was far from over.

TWENTY

Will

"Oh my God, she's so cute." Berk leaned over the new baby in Maria's arms and peered past the wrappings.

"Have you decided on a name yet? I asked, curious as the rest of them. We'd gone over to Rory and Maria's apartment the next morning to tell them of Berk's arrival and neither had seemed that surprised. I supposed everyone had seen something that I'd missed.

Rory sat down on the sofa beside his wife and put an arm around her shoulders. *"Maybe."*

Aunt Caroline batted his arm with her hand. "Don't tease an old woman, it's not nice."

Maria's lips pulled into a wide, proud smile. "Her name is...Nora Rosalía Kirkpatrick."

Aunt Caroline teared up and dabbed under her eyes with her sleeve. "That's beautiful."

Berk cooed at the baby. "Hi little Nora."

Nora was still in the quietly staring-at-nothing phase of her infancy, however I couldn't stop imagining all the memories we'd make in the future. There was for sure a tire swing—possibly a treehouse—in her future.

"I have gifts," Aunt Caroline announced, shuffling through her large bag for two hand-wrapped packages.

"Gifts?" Rory asked with a raised eyebrow. "You already gave us a ton of stuff, Aunt Caroline."

She shook her head. "Nonsense. One is for the new baby in our lives, one is for the new Berk in our lives."

Berk looked up from the baby in surprise. "Something for me?" He knit his eyebrows together in confusion.

"Yes, but baby first," Aunt Caroline said. "She's more important to the parents."

Maria laughed. "Rory, you open it. My hands are a little occupied."

He grinned and took the small package. He untied the string and unwrapped the paper revealing a small purple hat—small enough to fit on the tiny baby's head.

"Aw. Thank you, Caroline," Maria said, watching as Rory tried it on Nora. It fit perfectly.

Berk grinned. "It brings out her eyes." Blue of course.

"Now you." Aunt Caroline handed him the second—slightly bigger —package."

He took it apprehensively, lifting it up and down to test its weight. "It's light."

"Just open it already," I said, rolling my eyes.

He made slow work of unwrapping the paper—teasing us—before pulling out a blue knit hat. It was textured with cables and patterns I didn't know the name of.

"Wait, is that what you've been working on the last few weeks?" he asked.

Aunt Caroline nodded.

Berk grinned and pulled the hat on over his messy hair.

"I knew from that day you wore Will's Aran sweater that you were going to come back to us. Something compelled me to make you a hat in the Kirkpatrick patterns. Now, I know why."

He beamed. "Thank you. I can't believe you made this for me. It must have taken a lot of work. I don't even know how to begin to thank you."

She waved her hand. "You're a part of the Kirkpatrick clan now. It's official."

Berk met my gaze and beamed. Yes, he was.

* * *

Berk was standing behind the front desk while I poured us some coffee from the steaming pot in the corner. It had been a few more days and Berk was settling in nicely. Our routine was idyllic: wake up, drink coffee, stay in bed way too long, work on improving the inn and getting the word out there, cook meals together, go to bed in the same bed, and repeat.

"*Will!*"

I took the mug of steaming coffee and brought it over to his side. "What?"

"Read that."

Berk had an email open on the ancient computer and I read it aloud. "I was looking around at all the different islands trying desperately to plan my vacation and just saw your website for The Ruby Inn. I was wondering if I could book a couple rooms, but I don't see anywhere on the website to do that. Can I confirm over the phone?"

I smiled and turned to Berk's ecstatic features. "The website worked."

"The website worked!" he shouted. "We have customers."

"*Lodgers,*" I reminded him.

He rolled his eyes. "Yes, lodgers. She said she would call and book some rooms later today."

I wrapped my arms around his waist and pulled him in closer to me. "What would we ever do without you?"

He smirked. "Good thing you're never going to have to find out."

After weeks of feeling dread over the future of the island, things were finally starting to turn around, on all fronts.

"I'm so happy that you came back," I said, searching his eyes.

Berk wrapped his arms around my neck. "I'm happy you accepted me back."

I lowered my voice. "You know, as much as I love Aunt Caroline, it was lonely working here, trying to get everything going again. I'm *so* glad to have a partner to help lighten the load."

"And I'm so glad *to be* a partner. Don't sell yourself short, Will. Most of the great ideas for the inn were your own. I merely helped them along."

"We're *both* geniuses. There. Does that make you happy?"

He reached up to kiss me. "Sure does."

Epilogue

Berk—Three Months Later

"Do you want me to start serving the wine?" I asked Will, who was currently stirring a big pot of crab boil. The kitchen was a huge mess with abandoned projects strewn everywhere.

"Sure, all the bottles should be in the fridge. If we run out we have more in the pantry," he called over his shoulder, not taking his eyes off the task at hand.

"Okay." I gave him a quick kiss and rummaged around for the bottles in the fridge. I placed a few of the champagne bottles in a large bucket full of ice and managed to carry most of them out in one go. I shuffled through the swinging hidden door with my armful and almost bumped straight into Ada.

"There you are," she said, eying the bottles. "Here, give me a couple." She lighted my load, grabbing a few of the remaining bottles from my grasp.

"Thanks." She followed me out the front door and down the lawn to the boathouse where the event was almost finished being set up.

"Ma and Dad are gushing about the room. They love it," Ada said as we walked.

"That's great. I'm glad." They'd been apprehensive about coming to Ruby Island, however I convinced them that if I was going to be living here with Will for the foreseeable future they should get over themselves and come visit us. Okay, I hadn't said it *quite* like that, plus Ada had been a huge help in convincing them. It was the end of the summer and her fall classes would be starting soon; she'd told them that she needed a quick reprieve from the city and why didn't they all go along? It was genius. She'd always had our parents wrapped around her little finger, even as a kid.

"Where are these going?" she asked as we reached the open barn doors outside the boathouse.

Tables were set up on one side for refreshments, dressed in white tablecloths and covered with little wooden baskets and decorations.

"Over here." I set my armful of bottles down at the end of the table and Ada did the same.

She turned and scanned the space. "Wow. It's hard to imagine this place was ever used for storage. You guys cleaned it up really nice."

"I do have the muscles to prove it," I said, flexing my biceps for her through my pale dress shirt.

She rolled her eyes and walked past me. "I'm sure you do."

Ada helped me carry more supplies and covered trays of food down to the boathouse while a few people started to wander down the hill towards the event. The Ruby Inn was fully booked for a change and everyone who was staying as lodgers had been invited as well.

After getting designated the director of tourism for the island I'd called and given the ferry company a piece of my mind. After wearing them down they promised to reinstate the line that went to Ruby Island as long as the numbers kept improving over the summer. Well...we smashed their goals out of the park and soon the island's economy was at an all time high. Suddenly, Ruby Island was the hidden treasure that everyone in Massachusetts wanted to see.

The inn couldn't even handle all the business we were getting, so a slew of rental homes began to pop up along the west side of the island. Will had told me that the west side of the island had been pretty empty for years, houses abandoned by their owners. Some had also begun renting out apartments over their business in the heart of town. Ruby Island was bustling.

The next thing I did as the director of tourism and co-manager of the inn was hire a freakin' taxi driver. It wasn't hard. I found a young, eager high school graduate, and we set him up with a pretty decent car. The deal was that if he became the taxi driver for the island he could keep the car after the summer tourism season was over. He was *very* motivated and was on call day and night. There would be no more walking through the grass. Though I *did* convince Will and Caroline to invest in a golf cart like their neighbors. Lodgers liked to use it to get into town and back, although some still preferred to walk, funny as it was. They liked the slow style of living on the island, it harkened back to a different time.

Caroline stood in the middle of the lobby wearing a pretty yellow dress that brought out the blue in her eyes. She'd finally gotten the boot taken off her foot and was starting to walk around without the annoying crutches she'd been complaining about for the last couple months. "You look gorgeous," I told her.

She smiled and patted my cheek. "Thanks, Berk." She turned to my sister. "And thank you for helping us set things up. I can finally walk again, however hiking down a hill carrying trays of food would probably be my undoing."

Ada grinned. "It's no problem, I'm used to picking up the slack for my brother."

"*Hey!*"

She laughed. "I'm only kidding. You're very hard working, *abi*... when you want to be."

"Thank you." I nodded and searched the room. "Now, where's Will? Is he still cooking? People are starting to arrive."

Will had met my parents last night when they had come in, although it had been late and we hadn't had much of a chance to talk. I was hoping that the inn was leaving a good first impression on my parents. They weren't easily won over, but once they were, they were loyal forever.

"He said he still needed to change," Caroline said.

"Seriously?" I asked. "Again?" I smiled at my sister. "If you can keep Caroline here company I'll go see what all the fuss is about." We didn't want Caroline seeing the surprise in the boathouse before it was time, so she needed a chaperone.

"Gladly." Ada looped her arm with Caroline's and they headed in the direction of the sitting room where a few people were already milling about waiting for the main attraction.

I marched up the stairs to the top floor and found Will's room— our room—cracked open. He was standing in front of his full length mirror, adjusting his collar.

"You look great."

He startled at my presence, though once he realized it was me he smiled, showing off his straight white teeth. "You think so?" His eyebrows knit together, a line creasing in the middle of his forehead.

"There's no reason to be nervous." I took a few steps closer and smoothed out the shirt across his chest.

"Why not? Tonight is a big deal. I'm officially meeting your family, I'm unveiling the new boathouse space, and over fifty people are coming from all over the island. Rory's dad even showed up for this, and he hasn't been back to the island in years."

I shook my head and smiled. "But besides that, there's no reason to be nervous." I grabbed his hand and brought it to my chest. "Because we're doing it together."

The corner of his lips quirked up until he couldn't stop himself from grinning. "You're sure I look okay? I've never been into this whole *dressing up* thing."

"You look hot," I assured him, which made him blush.

"Not exactly what I was going for."

I shrugged. "You can't help it, I'm afraid. Sorry, babe." I gave him a quick kiss on the cheek. "Now let's go get this party started. People are starting to arrive and the host is missing."

"Right."

I followed him out the door and then stopped as he descended the stairs. His broad shoulders and muscled back filled out his suit nicely. Everything fit perfectly, showing off his hard-earned figure.

We joined Ada, Caroline, and my parents—who had beat us downstairs. They were dressed in a matching shade of dark blue, my mother in a dress that touched the floor, and my father in a suit with loafers. They must have been talking with Caroline while they waited for us. Everyone was smiling.

I wrapped my hand around Will's back and pushed us forward into the fold. "Ma, Dad, I know you didn't really get a chance to say hi last night; this is Will, my boyfriend."

The room was dead silent for a couple seconds and worst case scenarios began running through my mind, however Dad stuck out his hand for a shake and Ma went in for a hug. It was better than I'd been hoping for, given everything in my life. "Nice to meet you," Ma said. "Berk has told us so much about you."

"It's great that you guys were able to be here this summer for the boathouse reveal." Will grabbed my hand and laced our fingers. "Your son has been working super hard to help me pull it all together."

Dad cleared his throat. "You have a beautiful inn, the view is very nice."

Caroline beamed, standing behind them.

"Thank you," Will said. "Shall we go down? I think more people have arrived now."

"Yes," Ada said. I looped an arm around Caroline's, and Will did the same around her other side. We maneuvered slowly down the grassy slope, because even though Caroline had the boot off, it didn't mean she'd started running marathons in her spare time. We reached the edge of the boathouse and stopped.

"Ready?" Will asked.

Caroline nodded, sure as ever. "Of course I'm ready."

We entered the space, which was already filled with a couple dozen people, with more entering behind us. I picked Maria and Rory out of the crowd; Maria was holding little baby Nora in a swaddle on her chest.

"Oh my goodness." Caroline exclaimed, looking around the space. "I can't believe the transformation." She hadn't been able to see any of our progress because of her ankle, and we'd wanted to keep that way. She wandered over to the far left wall—the gallery wall.

Will and I had collected dozens of pictures and newspaper clippings from his family's archives. We framed everything and arranged them on the wall for a sort of historical gallery. Will even had a small family tree made that showed the Kirkpatrick lineage over the last few generations, tracing them back to Ireland.

"This is amazing." Caroline stood in front of the wall and her fingers grazed a framed picture of Will's parents. They were young and holding a toddler version of Will, who was rambunctious and wild as ever, barely in frame.

Will hugged her shoulders from behind. "Even though we cleared out all the boxes and the dust from this space, we wanted to save the memories and display them so that the people who stayed here would know its history and how it came to be." He pointed at a picture of an old man—his great-great grandfather who built the inn—posing with a long bowing saw in his hands. "How it was built by hand."

Caroline turned, a tear escaping her eye, and hugged us both.

"I guess she liked it," I whispered over her shoulder to Will.

He beamed, though I could tell he was trying not to cry himself, his eyes turning glassy.

Caroline let go and pulled herself together, dabbing at the corner of her eyes with an embroidered handkerchief. "That was so nice of you both. It feels wonderful to know that they won't be forgotten. That they will live on in other people's memories."

Even my parents seemed impressed. They were super big on family, so this probably showed them what kind of person Will was. He was doing great so far.

"Refreshments?" I asked.

Caroline let out a small laugh and our group followed us to the food and wine bar. We'd hired someone to serve for us so that we'd be able to have fun at the party instead of standing behind the counter all night. Everyone got wine and finger food and we mingled.

I could tell that my extroverted parents were happy about the crowd size—they had this light in their eyes I recognized from all the large family gatherings we'd attended together. So many people had come. Some from the island, some from the inn, and even some from the mainland, like Rory's dad.

We made our way around the room and said hi to Maria, Rory, and Nora. "Someone is awake," I said, smiling at little baby Nora.

Maria let out a long breath through a grin. "For now anyway. We'll probably have to leave early; little babies are so demanding."

I nodded and gave Maria a hug. "Totally understandable. Great that you could be here at all."

Rory clapped Will's back. "Everybody loves the gallery wall. My dad just about cried when he saw it and you know that man doesn't cry."

Will smiled, a hint of a blush tingeing his ears. "Thanks, man."

I was so proud of him. It was hard for Will to take compliments, although he deserved every last one. He'd worked damn hard to make tonight perfect.

We circled the space and Will greeted anybody who'd slipped past him earlier, some of them were local business owners from our new business association we hosted once a month. Ada stayed at my side, rolling around her glass of white wine with her wrist. "You really lucked out this time, Berk. Will isn't like any of your old boyfriends."

I grinned, finding him again in the crowd. "Yeah, you can say that again."

"He's handsome, kind, successful, and he doesn't let you pull any of your usual crap."

"I know, right?" I shook my head in disbelief. "I don't know how I got so blessed."

She cocked her head to the side. "His butt is cute too."

"*Ada.*"

She giggled. "*Sorry,* it's true." She calmed herself down. "You've really made a life here. I'm impressed by you."

"Thanks." I turned away, trying to hide my glistening eyes. "What do you suppose Ma and Dad are thinking?"

She looked across the crowd to find them. "They're happy for you. Come on, you know if Ma hated Will she'd let you know immediately. She's not known for her subtlety. And Dad has already eaten a whole plate of food."

"This is true. So...I guess it's all okay?"

She clinked her wineglass against mine. "I think so."

* * *

The night wore on. Once the sun began to set, the real wonder of the boathouse came to life. The golden glow of string-lights and soft music made the room somehow feel cozy and lively all at the same time.

We were eating a seafood dish that Will had cooked and sipping on our wine. There was only room for a few tables so Will and I had opted to stand and let the others have a seat—mainly Caroline who couldn't be on her ankle for more than an hour at a time.

My parents seemed to be getting along with Will and Caroline, and they also couldn't help but talk to everyone that they met along the way. Ma smiled when she caught my gaze, then went back to talking with an older woman about something that made her laugh.

When I focused my attention back to the table again, Caroline was musing.

"I remember when your parents used to host parties here back in the day. It was so nice, the lights hanging across the space, the music. You've captured it perfectly, Willy."

Will flushed, tugging at his collar. "Thanks, Aunt Caroline. I'm glad to hear that."

He was starting to get all glassy eyed, so I pulled him away. "Ready to dance?" I asked, setting down my near empty wineglass. People were mostly still eating and talking, though there *was* a space available in the middle of the floor and the music *was* playing.

He shook his head. "I told you, I'm a *terrible* dancer."

I shrugged. "So is my sister and that's never stopped *her* before."

Ada frowned, overhearing us a few feet away. "*Hey!*"

Will gave me a toothy grin and accepted my outstretched hand. "Okay, but *you* lead."

I smirked. "I was planning on it."

He rolled his eyes and walked with me to the middle of the floor. Someone must have realized we wanted to dance because suddenly the music got louder. It was hard picking a playlist for this party, because as it turned out, Will and I had *very* different tastes in music. He liked...country music. And I liked house or electronic music. We decided neither was appropriate for this event, so chose a light jazzy mix—perfect for a slow dance.

I wrapped my arms around his waist and he wrapped his around my neck. It was feeling almost like a middle school dance for the first few seconds, but then we both relaxed. A few couples began to dance next to us, so we weren't all alone.

"Hey, you're not too bad at this whole *swaying* thing," I said.

"*Ha, ha,* thanks." Maybe it was the warmth of all the bodies in the room or the effects of the alcohol, either way Will was positively pink, his ears and cheeks flushed.

The warm August breeze blew through the space, raising goosebumps on my arms. We'd been planning this party for months, and

317

now that everything was finally happening we could finally take a breath and relax.

We weren't so much *dancing* as we were moving in a slow circle, though it was nice, being surrounded by friends and family, everyone happy. I rested my chin on his shoulder."You don't have any regrets do you?" I asked.

"What do you mean?" His voice was so close to my ear I could feel his warm breath.

"I don't know. Anything. Do you regret staying on the island your whole life? Do you regret letting me take over with all my big ideas? Do you regret inviting me into your world?" I hadn't meant to say it, but the worries slipped from my brain in my relaxed state.

He pulled away and found my eyes. "Of course I don't. Don't imagine for one second that I regret meeting you. I don't know what I would do without you. And as far as leaving the island, no, I don't regret that either. What's out there that I don't have right here?" He pulled me in tighter, wrapping his strong arms around my back.

"Are you sure?" I wasn't usually one to be insecure or question my feelings, but meeting Will had been such a big moment in my life, it forced me to think about what I would do if I didn't have him anymore.

"Yes, I'm sure." He smiled, his mouth pressed against my unshaven cheek. "If anything, I should be asking *you* those questions. You're the one from the city. Do you miss it? Do you regret moving here?"

I knew my answer immediately. "You know, I thought I might miss it. I thought I would miss going to expensive nightclubs or miss the noise of the city, but I really don't. It's like you said, everything I need is right here." I placed a hand on his heart. "And I'm not going anywhere."

He grinned and leaned down for a kiss; his lips were wine stained and sweet. "I'm glad to hear it."

Author's Note

Thank you so much for reading Rough Waters! I'm a self published author; I don't have the backing of a huge publishing company to help me out. So if you could please leave a star rating and a review, it would mean the world to me. Thanks a million xoxo, Austin Moon.

Acknowledgments

I love these types of stories—where someone from the city gets trapped in a small town against their will and over the course of the story learns to love small town living as well as the hot guy next door. This book is dedicated to all the stories that inspired Rough Waters.

When I was a teenager I was fascinated by the hustle and bustle of the city and wanted to live in one. However, over the years that fascination has faded and I've grown in love with small town living. I'm perfectly happy talking walks by the river or bike rides by the beach.

Thank you to my friends and family for the endless support and for alway encouraging me to keep going. Where would I be without you? And a special thank you to my mum for always being my first reader. Love you Mum.

I'm furiously working on the next book in my little hermit's den, so look out for that in the coming months! Let's just say it involves murder, lots of shenanigans, and a heavy dose of romance.

What's harder than cycling hundreds of miles down the west coast? Doing it with the annoyingly hot guy who hates your guts.

Cal is excited to go on a two-week cycling trip with his best friends. He doesn't want, he *needs* the relaxation in order to kill his artist's block—he has a new show coming up and he's nowhere near finished.

However, things get complicated when one of his best friends brings her standoffish brother Nate along for the ride without telling him. Which would be fine if the guy wasn't a total pretentious jerk. Nate made sure to let Cal know that even though they are both gay they are *not* the same.

Sharing a tent with this guy every night is torture...until it isn't. Turns out getting the prick to smile does something to Cal he can't explain. Nate might just be exactly what Cal is looking for, whether he knows it yet or not.

Only 856 more miles to go. Can Cal and Nate make it to their destination without killing each other first?

About The Author

Austin Moon writes swoon-worthy queer romances and twisty mysteries. When they're not obsessing over their latest novel, they can be found crocheting, illustrating books, and cycling around their rainy little town in the PNW. Sip on a matcha latte and curl up with a good book during a thunderstorm for them, why don't you?

Amazon author page: Austin Moon
Goodreads: Austin moon
Instagram: @Austinmoonbooks
YouTube : @ryanwrites
Tiktok: @Austinmoonbooks